AFTER THE GOLD

ERIN MCRAE AND RACHELINE MALTESE

AVIAN30
NEW YORK, NEW YORK
2018

Avian30
New York, New York
After the Gold by Erin McRae and Racheline Maltese
Copyright 2018
ISBN: 978-1-946192-11-0

www.Avian30.com

First Avian30 Printing: July 2018
Printed in the USA

THE ROMANCE OF FINALLY, HOPEFULLY, WINNING IT ALL

Athletics Monthly Special Expanded Olympics Edition

Eight years ago at the Winter Olympics in Annecy, France, Katie Nowacki and Brendan Reid were the United States' best hope at a figure skating medal. But amidst a short-lived romantic relationship, they lost spectacularly and split their partnership not long after returning home.

Four years ago, skating with other partners at the Winter Games in Stockholm, they fared even worse. This time when they returned home, they got back together – but only on the ice.

Now the Olympics are in Harbin, China. And it's time for them to win.

PART I

1

The Most Recent Winter Olympics

Harbin, China

Katie listened as the scores for the previous pair were announced in English, French, and Mandarin. She did the math in her head. There was absolutely room for them to win.

She tried not to look at Brendan; this wasn't about another team's scores. Keeping her eyes on her own work was essential if she was going to get through this without being hit with a wave of anxiety. There were all sorts of Olympic medals that could be won on math, but pair figure skating wasn't one of them.

Their names boomed over the loudspeakers, and Brendan took her hand as they took to the ice.

Smile at the crowd, she told herself. *Smile at the judges, at the walls, at the ice if you have to, just fucking smile!*

She plastered a grin on her face as they made a lap around the rink. Katie found these moments unendurable. They were hard for anyone of course, but the difference between reasonable and unreasonable nerves wasn't always clear to her. This time was worse than ever.

Because this was it. Twenty years of a singular dream were down to these four and a half minutes. Brendan would turn thirty next year; she'd follow soon thereafter. They were getting too old for this, if they weren't already.

Katie looked up towards the booth that held the announcers and wondered what they were saying about her and Brendan. Probably nothing kind. Probably way too much about their messy history. *Inconsistent. Dramatic. A reality TV soap opera waiting to happen.* She smiled at them anyway and mocked them in her head.

Brendan tugged her hand sharply. A check on her nerves, maybe. On her distraction, certainly.

But the announcers fascinated her. In a few months she might be one of them. Once she and Brendan retired from competition – and they would after this – it would be one of the few obvious career choices available to her. But she wasn't sure she wanted to be a part of that.

She'd watched enough replays of her own competitions to know how rude the commentary often was in hopes of keeping viewers interested enough to buy more cars, cereal, and makeup. She and Brendan would probably get endorsement deals for all those things if they won; the cereal especially. She wasn't sure how she felt about it, but this was not the moment to examine her relationship with capitalism.

"With me?" Brendan whispered to her as they skated to center ice.

"Always," she replied. The exchange was both ritual and habit for them.

They took their starting positions and waited for the music to begin. Katie willed herself to shut out her anxiety, the judges, the audience, everything but her awareness of Brendan's body so close to hers. She shut her eyes and listened to the sound of the deep breaths he was taking to calm his own nerves, and matched her breathing to his.

Finally, when she thought she was going to pass out from the anticipation, the opening beats of their song played, and that was it.

Katie moved effortlessly into the first bit of choreography that let them ease from strained stillness into the meat of the program. Brendan was right there beside her, their movements a precise mirror of each other, as they went into the crossovers that led to their first side-by-side jumps. If they nailed those, if they had the audience with them…they were home free. Not because those jumps were the hardest – those came later, at seven seconds after the first minute mark – but because they set the tone. Katie reached back with her right arm and leg, dug her right toepick into the ice, and jumped.

From a triple jump a skater lands on the edge of a single blade with enough force that a thousand pounds of pressure shoots up through their body and down through the ice. Katie knew that a pair who could do that – who could endure that – in sync, on the beat, with a smile, and with their arms outstretched in victory, was a pair that had already won. Because winning was a choice. The audience could hold their breaths; the announcers could speculate, but if that first jump was perfect, if the energy was just right, the feat was always, somehow, already done.

Katie came down on the outside edge of her right skate. Brendan landed at the exact same moment as her, just as cleanly. Their eyes met, and the audience finally fell away. Everything about him – about them – was electric.

This isn't a competition, Katie thought. *This, right here, is the victory tour.*

2

The Most Recent Winter Olympics

Harbin, China

While it was happening, Brendan's only goal in a competitive skate was to exist completely in the present. He didn't want to think about the elements he had just executed or the ones that loomed ahead. He wanted to exist in perfect harmony with Katie in these moments where everything in their lives was absolutely clear. But today, the bubble in which they skated felt uniquely charged. Already Brendan could tell this was a performance that was going to live on in skating and Olympic history. They'd been good for a while. Lately, they'd been great. But in an entire life of skating, Brendan had never felt quite this certain, powerful, or free.

Two-thirds of the way through their program came the footwork pass. A lot of other pairs looked like they were taking a rest break on theirs – and with good reason. At four and a half minutes, these programs were exhausting. Without the somewhat less brutal demands of the footwork sequence, they weren't survivable. But for him and Katie, footwork and choreography were never about slowing down or easing up. They were places to raise the stakes, secure a few more points, and to sell the only story they knew how to tell on the ice: That of love and desire so powerful it could burn the world down like war.

In the four years Brendan had spent apart from Katie, skating with other women in the miserable purgatory between Annecy and Stockholm, he'd had to work to portray chemistry between himself and his partners. Where to put his hands, where to direct his gaze, and where to move his body had taken up as much mental effort as the rest of his skating put together. With Katie, he didn't have to think about any of those things at all. He never had. Their bodies simply knew each other.

They were coming up on their third and final overhead lift in the last Olympics they would ever skate in. They only needed a few strokes to pick up speed.

Katie turned in his arms and jumped.

He caught her, and then he had her above his head. Their only two points of contact were their hands, clasped tight around each other, as Brendan rotated across the ice, covering as much distance as he could while the music swelled and the audience, already caught up in the moment, roared. Brendan's face felt like it would split from smiling. They'd been perfect, and now they were only seconds from the end.

Their eyes met as he guided Katie down from the lift and back onto the ice. Her face, framed by her dark hair, was incandescent with delight.

This. This moment is joy.

Last was the pair spin. They came out of it, Katie's head on his chest, Brendan's arms around her waist, both of them heaving for breath as the final strains of the music died away.

The crowd exploded into cheers.

As they came up out of their ending positions, they

stared at each other in wonder and disbelief. They were made to do what they had just done, but they had fallen short so many times. Brendan didn't know if he had experienced destiny or a miracle. Maybe it had been both. After all, he was here with Katie. Finally.

Her eyes were wild with joy. She clasped Brendan's hands hard enough to hurt before she threw herself at him, her arms wrapped tight around his neck and her face buried in his shoulder.

Brendan folded his arms around her back and held her close. He'd never felt more whole.

"I love you." He ducked his head to whisper in her ear. Hopefully, the cameras wouldn't see. "And I'm pretty sure we just won."

3

Six Weeks After Harbin

On a Bus Somewhere Between Salt Lake City, UT and Portland, OR

This was not, exactly, how Katie ever thought her life would turn out. Oh, she had secretly expected to win gold in pair skating; she had worked too hard and faced too many setbacks not to. But the whirlwind she'd been in since…that was the confusing part.

No one had ever told her to think about what would happen after she won. In fact, lots of people had told her to avoid considering it at all; it would bring bad luck, weaken her intent, and aggravate her anxiety. And so, for twenty years, she had harbored only a single desire and a complete inability to plan for a life beyond skating.

Now, six weeks after the closing ceremonies in Harbin, she was on an International Ice Spectacular tour bus, sharing a hard, narrow bunk with Brendan. They lay side-by-side, his mobile phone suctioned to the low ceiling above them as they watched the latest episode of some makeover show, sharing a single pair of earbuds. They'd been doing this – trashy TV included – nearly their whole lives, ever since they had started skating together. She'd been nine, and Brendan had been ten.

Katie pointed at the small screen. "I like that dress, but I don't like it on her."

Brendan batted her hand away so he could see. "Yeah, but look at what the host is wearing. I'm sorry, but she doesn't get to have an opinion."

Katie laughed as she tangled her legs with his. He leaned his head against hers in response. Easy. Predictable. Safe. Their physical comfort with each other had never entirely made sense to others – especially people who didn't skate. But they had always been each other's refuge in the midst of relentless training, endless travel, and the acute pressures of the public eye. For them, physical closeness was situation normal. That, combined with the disaster of their first Olympics in Annecy and their brief, doomed attempt at dating afterwards, meant that the media constantly asked if they were a couple. It had only gotten worse since Harbin.

Katie understood why people were curious, but didn't feel like she knew how to answer the query. She and Brendan were together in ways most romantic couples never would be and which no one but them could understand. Even she didn't understand it a lot of the time. They'd spent most of their lives learning how to touch each other so that they could do things that were nearly impossible. Whether they were dating and/or screwing – which they weren't, because terrible things happened when they did – was purely incidental.

"I like this," Brendan said.

"Me too," she said after too long a pause.

The bus was uncomfortable, but being pressed so close to Brendan wasn't. His body was warm. His soft breath and steady heartbeat made Katie feel calm. She already missed competing; touring never could scratch the itch she had to push herself and Brendan relentlessly. But at least they were together. Being with Brendan twenty-four/seven because of the ice was how she functioned.

"Your dye's growing out." He touched her hair near the part, where it was a honey drab and not the rich, dark brown she favored.

"I know." Katie sighed. "I need to deal with that." The constant to-do list of keeping up public appearances was exhausting, for her so much more than for Brendan. On the days he didn't have time to shave, his fans just got more excited.

"Why haven't you?" Brendan asked. "Brushing mascara on it before every performance has to be a pain."

Katie shrugged. "Maybe I was thinking I'd let it grow out."

Brendan laughed quietly at her and fingered the strands. "You should. I always liked it. Don't know why you don't."

"If I'm thinking about growing it out, doesn't that mean I like it fine?" she said irritably. Whatever complicated feelings she had about her image, her hair, and how they were all tied up in her all-but-finished career, she didn't feel like talking about them right now. Even with Brendan.

"Maybe," he said.

"What do you mean, 'maybe?'"

He shrugged. "You're my inscrutable Katie."

She was his, wasn't she?

Katie turned her head to smile at him. In so many ways she knew his features better than she knew her own. After all, she spent the majority of every day looking at him. *I guess he's my something-or-other too.*

Brendan's face was easy. Friendly. The boy next door. Brown hair, green eyes, a smile that would assure any parent he had only the kindest heart. Which he did, but that was only one of the reasons Katie loved him. He had a fierce mind and a dogged sort of ambition; Katie loved him for that, too; perhaps more than for the qualities of his heart. If all she had wanted was a good man – or a good woman, for that matter – there were plenty at their Denver rink or at home in Wisconsin. But what she wanted was someone who didn't mind that she liked to run and who could keep up with her whenever and wherever she did.

Too bad jumping into bed together had ruined their first Olympics in Annecy, split their partnership, and sent them down a road of unsuccessful careers with other partners. Reuniting after their miserable showing in Stockholm had been Katie's idea. Four years after the fact, she could remember the visceral rush of relief at being with Brendan on the ice again. Skating had been easy at first. She'd missed her best friend and her partner in crime. It had been so good to see him first thing every morning and to go back to hanging out with each other every night.

That had lasted about a week. As ease and familiarity returned to their partnership, so did the trust between them – and the chemistry that had gotten them into trouble in the first place. For months Katie had been terrified they'd end up right back where they started, in bed with each other and broken on the ice. But after more than a few arguments – and a few awkward conversations with their coach – they'd decided to bring their connection, so impossible to deny or ignore, to the ice.

The more they acted out love in its most brutal and desperate forms, they more they were able to keep their desire compartmentalized and their energy channeled in useful directions. They shared rooms on the road. They even sometimes shared a bed – just to sleep. But they'd drawn their line, and they diligently stayed on the safe side of it all the way to Olympic gold.

But...but, Katie thought as she watched Brendan's face, mere inches from her own. Their competitive career was all but officially over. Did the old rules still apply? They were the best skaters in the world. They were in talks to do a skating tour that was all about them as headliners instead of the usual Team USA branding. No other pair had done such a thing in decades.

None of that would change if they kissed. Time would not unwind. Their medals couldn't be taken away. Maybe they didn't need to deny the totality of their connection anymore.

Slowly, Katie rubbed her face against Brendan's. If the gesture was strange, she didn't care. She'd wanted all of him for so long without being able to have him like this. The anticipation – and the suspense of whether either of them would put a stop to it – made her skin feel like it was on fire.

"What are you doing?" Brendan asked, his voice lazy and curious. Katie envied him his easygoingness. If his mind was churning as rapidly as hers – which she doubted – he wasn't showing it.

"I don't know," she admitted. "Can I keep doing it?"

"Be my guest," he said, absurdly polite for the situation they were in. But that was who Brendan was.

Katie wanted more of this, more of him. She nosed along the line of his jaw, breathing in the warm scent of his skin. He smelled like his deodorant and her shampoo; he must have run out of his own and borrowed hers this morning. Again.

When her lips pressed to the point at his throat where she could feel his pulse beat beneath the skin, his breathing hitched. He rolled towards her, and Katie mirrored him, unwilling to lose the warm press of his body against hers. Before the noise in her head could talk her out of it, she kissed him.

Brendan's lips were warm. They fit against hers as if they'd done this for years. Why hadn't they been doing this for years? She nipped his lower lip sharply. *He used to like that. Does he still?*

With a soft groan in the back of his throat Brendan opened his mouth to her. *So that's a yes.* His arm, slung loosely around her waist, tightened, but he was letting her lead. Given their shared history, that might have been a wise choice. But it wasn't what Katie wanted. On the ice, this was a man who could throw her across the rink, who ran his hands all over her body for the cheer of the crowd, who pushed and pulled in response to her relentless pursuit. Now that they were finally doing this, Katie wanted all the intensity they'd bottled up and poured out only onto the ice.

She cupped his face in her hands and pushed her fingers up into his hair, pulling at it, daring Brendan to respond in kind.

He did.

He slid his hand under the hem of her shirt, his palm warm against the small of her back, his fingernails pricking her skin. Heat unfurled from her core. Reflexively Katie shifted to wrap her leg around his waist. That was like being on the ice; Brendan being absolutely, definitely, achingly hard against her was not. He wanted her, too, and Katie needed so much more than she currently had.

Awkwardly – the space was so small – Katie helped Brendan struggle out of his T-shirt. In the dim light she could make out the strong lines of his chest, all the defined muscle that was the result of hours spent in the gym and on the ice. Katie was a world-class athlete surrounded by world-class athletes; there was no shortage of eye candy in her life. But after years of competing together she knew Brendan's body and what it could do so intimately it couldn't help but be her favorite.

Brendan tossed his shirt to the side and rolled on top of her. His knees straddled her waist; his weight was braced on his arms. Finally it was his turn to dig a hand into her hair. He kissed her until they had to break apart for breath. With his bare skin pressed to her, Katie never wanted to be anywhere else, even if there were too many people far too close to them for her to get what she really wanted.

Because if she could hear her tour mates, they could hear her. And she could definitely hear them. Shane and David were arguing about hockey again. Andrej was listening to Czech pop music without his headphones. Haruka and Yume were playing cards. And somewhere, Natalya was snoring. Katie didn't think athletes were supposed to snore. Especially really pretty Russians. But what did she know? Right now, she wasn't sure she knew anything except Brendan's body and her own.

Despite her concerns, Brendan was heedless of their lack of true privacy. He slipped a hand into her pajama bottoms and between her legs. "You're soaking wet," he murmured, pressing kisses down the line of her throat.

Katie gasped at both his touch and at his words.

"Do you think you can be quiet?" he asked.

"Obviously not," she hissed in his ear. "And I think almost everyone's awake to hear."

Brendan dropped his hand to her thigh and his forehead to her chest. "Why can't anyone on this bus sleep like normal people?"

Katie curled her fingers into his hair to hold him there. She had a million responses to that. Starting with the fact that they weren't sleeping like normal people either. Above them, his phone advanced to the next episode of the makeover show. "Do you care if they hear?" she asked.

"No." Brendan's reply was immediate. "Do you?"

Katie had spent her entire life worrying about what other people saw when they looked at her. Sometimes reasonably, sometimes not. Perhaps it was time to let that go. Or at least try. She shook her head.

As if to comment on that choice, the bus started to slow. Then it jolted. Hard.

Katie yelped.

"Well there's no need to *advertise* it," Brendan

whispered in her ear, aggrieved. He kissed her.

Whether that was to muffle any other sound she might make or for the sake of kissing her, Katie didn't know. She also didn't care. She laughed into his mouth. Brendan's body pressing down on hers was ecstasy.

After a moment, the bus started moving again, leaning into some sort of turn. The curve of it was long, the bus was fast, and the driver seemed to think he had a bobsled in his hands.

Brendan shifted onto his back as his body was pulled away from her by the force of the turn, taking Katie with him. Skating habit or desire made her go with him, but then she kept going, her body rolling over his and to the outside edge of the bunk.

She was going to fall.

She reached out to him. But just like in Annecy, her fingers slipped through his.

With a startled shriek, Katie fell out of the bunk and dropped several feet into the aisle. Curtains up and down the length of the vehicle snapped open. Everyone stared down at her, knowing exactly what she had been doing and with whom.

Brendan's head appeared last. He must have been trying to figure out an appropriate response. Not that there was one. He still wasn't wearing his shirt.

"Are you okay?" he asked sheepishly.

Katie stared up at his infuriating, genial, too-handsome face, his tousled hair, and his wry grin. She felt herself turn red. Not – despite his bare torso and kiss-bitten lips – with embarrassment, but with fury.

Physically she was fine. But in every other sense, she was a mess. Perhaps if she stayed very still, she would somehow be rendered invisible to the eyes of the other skaters. At least Leo, their tour manager, slept with earplugs.

"Seriously, Katie, are you okay?" the no-longer-snoring

Natalya asked.

"No!" Katie snapped at her, slowly sitting up from where she was splayed on the bus floor. She didn't think she was hurt. At least not physically. But every one of her fears had come true, and the risk they'd taken had ended in humiliation. As she should have known it would.

Katie pushed her hair out of her eyes and looked up at Brendan. His face was a mixture of hesitant concern and amusement.

"I am making all the worst choices!" she hollered at him, fairly or not. "Again! And they're all your fault!"

4

The Day After the Bus Incident

Portland, OR

By the time they arrived in Portland, Brendan was tired, annoyed, and more than a little off-balance. He'd spent the rest of the night bunking with Andrej and his music. Katie, who'd shared a bunk with Natalya, didn't look any more well-rested.

When they traveled for competitions and tours, he and Katie shared a room – or a bunk. Other pairs handled it differently, but for them, being within arm's reach of each other was a necessary part of their process. In fact, the only time they spent nights apart was when they were home in Denver. Even then Katie often slept on the pull-out couch in his apartment, or he crashed on the leaky air mattress in the living room of the house she shared with a rotating cast of skaters. Was it codependent? Probably. But did it work? Absolutely.

After being at odds with Katie and sharing a bunk with someone else for half the night, Brendan felt out of sorts and lost. He caught up to her as they were all grabbing their bags out of the luggage compartment under the bus before heading into the rink for practice. He tried to ignore the other skaters on the tour watching them curiously.

"Hey. You okay?"

Katie gave him a sidelong look, shook her head, and kept walking. Brendan sighed to himself and followed her into the rink. When something was bothering her, she never could just come out and talk about it; she had to worry it to death first. The cruelly interrupted events of last night were definitely bothering her. Even though she'd started them. Probably especially because she'd started them.

The routine of getting ready for practice helped center him, at least a little. *Worry about the ice. Don't worry about anything else.* He changed out of his shorts and hoodie into skate pants and a T-shirt. As he laced up his skates, he let the usual locker room chatter of his tour mates wash over him. Skating would save him. He and Katie could work this out – as they had so many other things – on the ice.

He loved Katie, desperately and completely, and had never been able to understand why she thought it was such bad luck for them to be together outside of skating. Yes, their hookup in Annecy had been followed by an embarrassingly bad free skate and a lot of ugly arguments. But they'd been kids: young, scared, and inexperienced both with relationships and with competition at that level. Given time, surely they'd have worked it out. Given time, he hoped, they could work it out again.

But until they did Brendan respected Katie, her feelings, and whatever fears and desires for space she had. If she didn't want to talk about what had happened last night – much less try for a repeat – that was fine. If she didn't want to talk about anything else either, that was also fine, but it was going to pose some difficulties for getting any work done today.

Brendan stretched out the kinks from a sleepless night

on the road as he waited for her in the hallway outside the locker rooms. Luckily they didn't have anything scheduled for this afternoon; he was going to spend every minute he could crashed on a hotel bed in blissful unconsciousness.

Except he and Katie were rooming together, and after last night, she was unlikely to want any kind of excessive proximity to him. Brendan cursed under his breath. They had a tour to get through. He needed to step back, focus on their professional partnership, and tackle the personal problems once they were both on an even keel.

Which meant he'd have to find somebody to switch rooms with. Sleep could happen after that.

With that plan solidifying in his mind, Katie emerged from the women's locker room. Brendan held out a hand to her. The gesture was one of their little rituals that pre-dated their breakup and reunion; he'd done it when they were kids, too, long before puberty and any of this drama. The way she responded would tell him a lot about how the next few hours were probably going to go.

She gripped his fingers tightly. Too tightly. She was scared. And probably angry. Likely at herself, possibly at him too. Not ideal, but he could work with it.

Brendan squeezed back, gently, trying to be reassuring. *You're fine. We'll get through this.*

Katie shook her head as if she'd sensed the thought he hadn't voiced aloud. Brendan felt his body tighten in resonance with the tension in hers. If they could put that energy into skating, they'd be brilliant, even if they needed to have a shouting match in the middle of the ice. That was something that could be fuel and, sometimes, fun. But if Katie was too upset, if she pushed too hard because she was being reactive to something…that tended to have real consequences for her physical and mental health.

Practice that afternoon was mostly focused on polishing some of the group numbers. Only when that was over did he and Katie have some time to work on their own routines. On past tours they'd performed slight variations on whatever programs they'd skated at competitions that year. But while their free skate in Harbin had been their absolute favorite, they hadn't been able to touch it since the Olympics.

Katie had stress injuries in her knee. They weren't serious, but that continuing to be the case wasn't guaranteed. On one hand, needing to take a post-Olympic break to address injuries was about as good as it got for a skater. But on the other, they now had an opportunity to shape their entire post-competitive lives, and Katie, understandably, didn't want to be sidelined.

Unfortunately, working around Katie's knee and hoping it didn't get worse meant that every time they looked at their Harbin free skate the rehearsal turned into a war. Brendan was trying to find ways to modify the program to accommodate both Katie's body and her ego, but nothing satisfied her. Eventually, Katie would heal or they'd crack the problem together, forcing the program into a new and improved shape, but for now it was not to be.

After a lot of discussion with the tour management and their coach back home, they had shifted to their free skate from their first year back together after Stockholm. Their Harbin program had been huge, bold, daring. Even overconfident. And sexy enough Brendan had been slightly embarrassed to have his grandmother watch videos of them performing it.

But the post-Stockholm program was softer and at least somewhat more conventional in terms of what judges and audiences so often expected. At least for the first two minutes, before they came to the music change and all restraint shattered in desperate pursuit.

The shift took audiences by surprise, and Brendan loved that he could always somehow hear that over the music and his and Katie's ragged breath. They were four years older and so much closer than when they had first performed it together, which showed in the mood and expression of the performance. What had been genuine tentativeness then, was coy flirtation now.

The program was a massive amount of fun when Katie was with him. And a boring mess when she wasn't. Today, as Brendan had feared, she was pushing too hard and avoiding his eyes. She was always a fraction of a second ahead of him, and in response Brendan very nearly fell trying to keep up with her. She was just never where he expected her to be.

"All right," Brendan said as they came out of a spin. He kept a hand around her waist in silent entreaty that she not tear off for water in order to avoid a conversation. "Can we talk about this?"

"There's nothing to talk about." Katie tossed her head so that her ponytail swished violently.

"Okay, except, you're pissed and running away from me on the ice. We almost fell because we're rushing. I'd prefer to get through this tour without breaking anything."

"You're not going to break anything," Katie said scornfully.

"Your confidence in my ability to keep up is flattering, but I'm not the only one in this pair."

"My knee is fine, Brendan. Don't coddle me."

"I'm not coddling you. And I didn't mention your knee. I get that you're upset about last night. For the part I played in that, I am sorry."

"Yeah, you definitely tried to cool it down," Katie said.

"You kissed me first." This was not the argument Brendan wanted to be drawn into, but it was, apparently, the argument available to him.

"I'm aware of that!" Katie snapped.

Not that that'll stop us from fighting, Brendan thought, although fighting wasn't necessarily a bad thing. Yelling at each other allowed them to let off steam, mainly because it was what they did instead of screwing. Which was possibly a little messed up. But they also strapped knives to their feet and jumped very high for a living, so messed up was relative.

"I'm just saying, whatever you're angry about, please, can we deal with it before we fall all over ourselves out here?" he said.

Katie glared at him. "If you could keep up, we wouldn't be in any danger of falling."

Exasperated, Brendan let go of her waist and ran his hands through his hair. "Okay, that is really not fair. Or accurate. And the music can't keep up with you either. So cut it out. Either talk to me about what's wrong, or chill out and stop being so pissed off about everything!"

Brendan knew it was the wrong thing to say before the words left his mouth, but he couldn't stop himself. Katie threw out her hands and glided smoothly backward away from him.

"I don't know what I'm angry about, Brendan. I just know nothing is right and everything is changing. I am terrified, and you want me to shrug and get on board with how much you don't care." She turned sharply away from him. "And, by the way, asking me to be less angry is making me WAY GODDAMN ANGRIER."

✦

In the dressing room Brendan leaned his head against his locker. Then he picked it up and thunked it back against the metal. Repeatedly.

Shane patted Brendan on the shoulder as he walked past. "Hey man. How's it going?"

"Situation absolutely normal." Brendan looked sideways at Shane, not bothering to hide how tired and annoyed he was. "Thanks for asking." Complaining out loud made everything feel marginally less shitty, though.

Shane shrugged. "Don't worry. She'll come around."

"Keep dreaming," Tyler, Brendan's least favorite person on the tour, said. Brendan decided to ignore him.

"Well, she hasn't yet," he said to Shane. "And she's had twenty years. Or four years. Or ten hours. Depending how we're counting." His relationship with Katie was so long and so complex, sometimes it exhausted even him.

"You need to be clear about what you want," Shane said unhelpfully, pulling open his bag and rifling through it. A few feet away Justin, two-time men's world champion, was putting the finishing touches on his hair. They'd gotten off the ice less than ten minutes ago, and already he was showered, dressed, and perfectly styled. Brendan didn't know how he did it.

"Oh, I've been clear." Brendan straightened up and reached for his towel, scrubbing it through the sweaty mess of his own hair. He never tried to hide the torch he carried for Katie. Skaters were the most gossipy people in the world, and Brendan had no poker face, so why waste the energy?

David gave Brendan a sympathetic look from where he was sitting on a bench unlacing his skates. He and his wife Lena were a Canadian ice dancing pair from Vancouver and had taken silver in Harbin. They'd been skating together almost as long as Katie and Brendan, but their off-ice relationship was much more functional: They'd gotten married four years ago, the summer after Stockholm. Brendan and Katie had gone to their wedding. Not as dates. Technically.

"Have you talked to her?" David asked quietly.

More than I talk to any of you. That was half the problem wasn't it? The only person Brendan wanted to go to for advice about Katie was Katie, which was easier said than done.

"Sure. We talk all the time." And that was the other half of the problem. They didn't need to communicate more, they needed to communicate more relevantly.

"Actually talked. About your deal."

"We haven't had time since Harbin. Last night was the closest we've gotten, but we made out instead and now everything's a mess. And when I tried to talk about that, it turned into an argument."

"It turns into an argument every time you two talk about anything," Justin muttered.

"That's because they're not fucking," Shane pointed out helpfully.

"Thanks, both of you, so much." Brendan turned back to David and lowered his voice, not that that would stop anyone from eavesdropping. "We were fine as long as we channeled whatever feelings we had for each other into skating and ignored them everywhere else. At least, that's Katie's theory, so when we went and made out last night everything got broken, and here we are. Oops."

David's eyes widened. "Wait. Was that seriously the first time you two have been macking on each other?"

"In like eight years, yeah."

"Jesus." David blew out a breath.

"Tell me about it."

✦

Brendan looked for Katie when he was finished getting dressed but couldn't find her anywhere. Maybe she'd gone out for a run to work off some of her nervous energy. Which was fine, but Brendan would have preferred to discuss the need for a room switch before he went and did anything about it. But that apparently was not to be, and he needed to catch people before they got too settled.

Justin and Natalya were willing to help him out, and once that was settled, Brendan helped Natalya move her luggage to the room that was now Katie's and dragged his own to the one he was sharing with Justin. Logistics finally resolved, he face-planted on his bed and slept for two hours without moving. When his alarm woke him so that he could eat dinner and get to the rink in time for that evening's performance, he rolled onto his back and stared at the ceiling, letting the disorientation of travel wash over him.

Forgetting where he was, was par for the course in a life that involved so much travel. But this kind of disorientation came from the fact that the bags on the other side of the room weren't Katie's and that, tonight after the performance, they wouldn't be coming back to the same place. The decision to switch rooms was the right one, Brendan was sure, but it sucked all the same.

Despite everything, getting back to the rink for that night's performance felt like a weight lifting off his shoulders. He liked skating; he loved skating with Katie. While he missed the adrenaline rush of competing a bit, he did not at all miss the sickening, stomach-dropping nerves of stepping onto the ice and hearing their names announced. No matter how long he'd had to get used to it, that had never really gone away. But on a night like tonight, all he had to do was relax and enjoy himself. He was determined to do that regardless of whatever was happening between him and Katie.

Once he got himself changed into his costume for the first number, Brendan knocked on the door to the girl's dressing room. "It's me, can I come in?"

He was greeted, as usual, by a chorus of assent, so he pushed the door open.

Katie, seated at a makeup table along the far side of the wall, looked over her shoulder at him. Her pale, elegant arms were raised above her head, her fingers attempting to twist her hair into place. "Oh good. I was going to text you."

"Do you need a hand?" Usually the other women ignored his presence in their dressing room, but tonight, presumably thanks to the bus make-out, several pairs of eyes followed him as he went to Katie.

"God, please, I can't get it to stay."

"All right, here." Brendan put his hands over Katie's in her hair, carefully taking the braids between his own fingers.

"Do you have them?" she asked, as if he couldn't redo her braids if they came loose.

Brendan nodded. "Yeah, you can let go."

Katie slid her hands slowly out from beneath Brendan's, the gesture almost a caress. He grabbed a handful of bobby pins off her table and stuck them in his mouth before he could do something like catch her hands again and kiss the backs of them in front of everyone.

"I hate this costume," Katie grumbled once Brendan had taken over. She plucked at the short, fluttery sleeves of her dress.

"Stop moving your head," Brendan said through his mouthful of bobby pins. Katie could have figured out her own hair or gotten one of the other girls to do it, but he'd learned to help her when they were kids and her mom or her uncles couldn't come to competitions. It had become another ritual for them.

He worked in silence for a few more minutes. Katie picked up the hairbrush sitting on the counter and started turning it over in her hands. "You could have warned me about Natalya," she said, not looking at him in the mirror.

Brendan took in a breath to steady himself and made his voice calm. Casual. Neither accusatory, nor defensive. If Katie wanted to be upset about his unilateral decision to change rooms, that was more than fair, but he didn't want to have that fight minutes before they went on. "Sorry. It felt like the right thing to do. I needed a nap and I had no idea where you were."

"Stretching."

"How's your leg?" Brendan leapt at the chance to change the subject.

"Attached to my body," Katie said flatly.

No further discussion of that topic today, okay. "Excellent, now will you please stop fidgeting?"

Katie finally stilled herself. "Neon pink is not my color."

"Consider yourself lucky. Someone thought orange suits me. I look like a sunflower."

"That's 'cause you're so cheery all the time." Katie finally looked up and made a face at him in the mirror. Then she passed him the hair spray.

Brendan's heart leapt. Routine had always been their friend. It helped with the nerves that came with the sport and the anxiety that Katie battled regardless of it. If she was complaining about the admittedly hideous costumes they had to wear for the group numbers and feeling up to teasing him, things were returning to something like normal.

That hopeful feeling lasted all the way through the opening number, the girls' number, the guys' number, and a particularly fierce backstage game of *Sorry!* while other solo routines went on. But when it was time for their own program, he could feel Katie draw away from him again.

He watched her face in the dim light of the tunnel as Justin finished his routine. She'd changed out of the hated neon into the dress that their own beloved seamstress had made for her. She looked stunning in it, her dark hair and pale skin beautifully offset by the emerald green velour. But she also looked remote and untouchable, and Brendan groaned inwardly.

There was no time to talk her out of whatever nerves and insecurity the events of the last day had planted in her brain. The applause for Justin was dying down, and soon Justin himself was there, stepping off the ice as Katie and Brendan's names were announced. Brendan high-fived him reflexively and took Katie's hand. He hoped this wasn't about to be a disaster.

He knew they were doomed when their first side-by-side jumps weren't synchronized. The crowd applauded, but that almost didn't matter when he could feel how off they were. Katie was too rigid on the first lift, and Brendan was helpless to do anything for her.

He commanded himself not to hold his breath for the throw jump; it was instinct to do so, but that would screw everything up. Throws were a moment when every part of his body needed to work perfectly so that Katie wouldn't get hurt.

Katie spun through the air as he released her. When she hit the ice, her leg wobbled. It happened quickly, but Brendan felt like he was seeing it in slow motion. She tried to save her balance but couldn't. She went down on both knees, her hands trailing through the bits of ice shaved off by their and others skaters' blades before she regained her feet.

Only a few seconds passed before they fully caught up to the music again. Katie's hand was cold when he held it tightly for the death spiral. She was smiling, but her smile was brittle, pasted on for the sake of the crowds and the judges that were probably still there in her head.

As soon as they were back in the tunnel, Brendan pulled her into a hug. That's what they did when something went wrong on the ice. *Still together. Still okay. Still one.*

Katie's back rose and fell under his arms as she caught her breath. He wondered how long it would take her to remember that, after the events of the last twenty-four hours, she probably didn't want his comfort.

"Shit. Shit shit *shit*," she hissed even as she leaned into him.

"Hey." He brushed the loose part of her hair back, untangling a strand from one of her earrings. "It's okay. You're okay."

Katie didn't reply, but when she pressed her face into his shoulder he could practically feel her frown. Angry with herself, not him. Brendan ached for her. Things happened on the ice. There was no reason for her to feel more pain about it than necessary.

He touched her cheek, the soft skin by her ear. "Come on, look at me."

She raised her head. As he looked down into her eyes, all Brendan wanted to do was kiss her. If it hadn't been for recent events he would have, on her forehead, like the good friend and perfectly platonic partner he was supposed to be. But given the circumstances, he had no idea what to do.

Something in his eyes must have shifted, because she straightened up, cold and remote and made of steel. Before Brendan could say anything, Katie nodded as if deciding something in her own head.

"Extra practice tomorrow," she said. And then she was gone.

5

Way Too Early in the Morning

Portland, OR

Her alarm was set for 3:45 a.m., but Katie woke up before it went off. Somehow, the act of setting her clock always, in turn, set the clock in her head. Such had been the case since she was little, getting up while it was still the dead of night to go to skating practice or work on her family's farm. She was relieved the habit remained with her and Brendan no longer training for competition. If nothing else, it would keep Natalya from killing her for having her alarm go off so very, very early.

She found it immensely strange to room with someone who wasn't Brendan. Was this how people felt all the time on the road? Sharing space with someone they liked well enough but who wasn't – Katie didn't know how else to put it – an extension of their own body and mind? The fact that she and Brendan couldn't kiss and skate together didn't change that about them.

Enough about missing Brendan. Last night she had fallen, and now she had to fix it. She pulled on her practice clothes

– black leggings, a tank top, and a form-fitting jacket with a zipper up the front. She tugged it all the way up but knew she'd spend the whole practice slowly inching it back down as the cold of the ice gave way to the heat of the work. She pulled her hair into a high ponytail and spared the briefest of moments to brush her teeth. Makeup could wait. A shower could wait. Getting out on the ice and getting it right could not.

Katie grabbed her skate bag, slipped out of her room, jogged up three flights of stairs, and threaded her way through another hotel corridor until she was in front of Brendan's room. Damn him for having the courage and decency to take a step away from their too-close quarters.

Katie banged on the door. When no one answered, she kept banging.

Brendan finally opened the door with tousled hair, a rumpled T-shirt, and a frown. "What?" he asked. Behind him, in the bed closest to the door, Justin swore at them both and pulled a pillow over his head.

"Come on, get dressed, we're going to the rink."

"It's four in the fucking morning." Brendan scrubbed a hand over his face.

"I'm aware of that." Katie's days had started at four most of her life. She knew what the hour – and its utility – looked like better than most.

"We don't have to get up at four in the morning anymore."

Says the boy who's never lived on a farm. She shrugged as if she didn't care. That was an act, but hopefully one he would fall for. "Well, you can sleep in. I'm going."

She turned from the door, prepared for it fall shut behind her, but at the last moment, she heard Brendan's hand slap against it. "Yeah, all right, give me ten, and you're buying coffee."

Katie smiled. They may have been a disaster, but that didn't mean they weren't better together than apart.

Thirty minutes and one Dunkin Donuts stop later they were at the rink. This early, it was empty of even the most dedicated of their tour mates. Katie dropped her bags and began to work through her stretch routine, loosening ankles and knees and hips. Beside her, Brendan did the same, albeit much more slowly.

Katie considered giving him grief for that. After all, she was the one who was injured and yet here he was moving like an old man. But she didn't want to disturb their peace, hard-won with exhaustion and coffee.

In the first year that they had come back together after Stockholm, sometimes their coach had forbidden them from speaking on the ice. In the immediacy of it, Katie had felt that was a punishment for all their bickering, but it had been a trick that worked. If they couldn't speak, they had to listen – not just to their coach, but to each other's bodies and breathing and facial expressions.

She sat down on the floor, folded herself over her knees and grabbed her feet, massaging the tendons as she pointed and flexed. She was aware of Brendan watching her, but he remained silent as he focused on his arms and shoulders.

Good. He won't drop me again.

Katie lay back on the floor and kicked one leg up. She pulled it towards her, creeping into a split. By the end of the day, this would be almost easy, but for the moment, her body was reluctant. She huffed in annoyance, and Brendan, ridiculously, was instantly by her side.

"I'm fine," she said, feeling shame, somehow, at breaking the silence.

"I know. Do you want help?"

She gave a little acquiescent tilt of her head. Brendan put a hand to her thigh and another to her calf and pushed her leg back slowly, until her flexed toes touched the floor.

"All right?" he asked.

She nodded, breathing through it. She pointed her foot, and Brendan pushed again, leaning against her leg until the top of her foot hit the floor. Katie sighed in relief at the feel of him and at the stretch successfully completed without agenda, but with so much wanting.

With their warmup finished and their skates on, Katie leaned on the wall at the edge of the rink, took off her skate guards, and glided out onto the ice. Beside her, Brendan did the same.

She'd been doing this for more than two decades, but this moment had never ceased to thrill her: The rest of the world home, warm and asleep; the ice a smooth blank canvas in front of them. It was far from bliss: It was cold; adrenaline and endorphins had yet to kick in, and she could feel every bruise and blister on her feet. But Brendan would reach out – she knew, without having to look at him – their hands would meet, and suddenly everything was possible.

When their skating worked, Katie didn't have to think about what she was doing. Her mind could drift, a highly kinetic kind of meditation. But this morning, there was too much to do to let her mind wander.

They ran through the first minute or so of their Harbin routine, or at least their modified Harbin routine. The changes they were making so Katie could skate it relatively safely were far from a lock. Katie knew she wasn't making that process any easier, but after a year of developing the original program any change felt like sacrilege and defeat. No matter how long she and Brendan worked together on tours and exhibitions, they'd never skate at the level that won them gold again. Everything had been on the line at the Games. Replicating that without the pressure of competition was impossible.

Katie wanted to get as close to it as she could, though. If she couldn't have her favorite jumps, she could make other things harder. As they assessed what they could make work she did progressively harder jumps that she could land on her good knee.

The third time she landed a quad salchow throw, though, Brendan found her hand and pulled her to a stop in front of him. "I get you're pissed about falling yesterday, but now you're doing quads?"

Katie brushed a loose strand of hair out of her face with her free hand. "You throw, I spin. Don't worry about it."

Brendan frowned and gave a minute shake of his head. "This doesn't work that way."

"I can land them," Katie insisted. The warm, intimate feel of the morning was draining quickly away, leaving them where they so often ended up: On the ice and upset with each other. She knew that was inevitable, but it still felt a little like heartbreak.

"I know you can." Brendan pulled her closer and dropped his voice, not that there was anyone around to hear. "But your knee is one bad landing away from being out of commission for the rest of the tour and possibly the rest of your life."

"I wasn't landing on that leg," Katie protested.

"And you can't guarantee you won't stumble or fall and hurt yourself anyway. You want to take risks with your health, fine, whatever, it's your body. But you're my partner and it's damn irresponsible for you to take risks with my job."

Brendan was absolutely, positively, one hundred percent correct. Which only made Katie angrier. "You don't need to patronize me," she snapped, skating backwards away from him and pulling her hand out of his grasp. "I know my own limits."

Brendan followed her. "I'm not trying to be patronizing. Really. Just, Kate, you're my partner. I will always worry about you."

"And don't say you're my partner!" She spun away from Brendan, not able to look at him. He only ever called her *Kate* when he was very serious about something.

"Why? I am. And you're mine."

Brendan sounded hurt. Which only made Katie more frustrated. She loved him, more than she would ever be able to express in any kind of language. Why did she have to find a way to make that a bug and not a feature?

"On the ice. Nowhere else." Which was also neither fair nor accurate. But Brendan saying things like *partner* so easily terrified her. Nothing about what they did together was easy or simple. And she couldn't afford to give in to her desire for him again.

"Did I say otherwise?" Brendan swept around in front of her, cutting off her forward motion.

Katie's breath caught in her throat. He was magnificent when he was angry. "You implied it."

"I did not. Stop treating me like I'm your enemy. Or that this is something I did to you. I am not the bad guy. Your anxiety is real, but this is not my fault. We used to date, we've spent years being a millimeter away from fucking, and you kissed me on that damn bus first."

"That was a mistake." Katie put out a hand to Brendan's chest. She'd meant to push him away, but her fingers tightened in the fabric of his shirt instead. His heartbeat thudded against her fingertips.

Brendan closed his hand over her wrist, holding her there. "It sure didn't feel like a mistake. Other than the fact we were on a bus. I will concede that part was a bad idea."

Hah hah. Very funny. Brendan could make her laugh so easily when she didn't want to strangle him. "We do not skate well when we're together. I know this. You know this. We've been over this before, and the only thing either of us have to show for it is a four-year detour."

Brendan shook his head, his hair falling over his forehead. "One, that is superstitious crap, and also it disgusts me that you view that as wasted time."

"It was wasted! We could have been winning."

Brendan pulled her closer, so close she could make out the flecks of gold in his green eyes. "We also could have been together, but neither of those things matter anymore. Three – I think we're up to three? – if you don't want to do this at all, that's cool. I will drop it. But if you don't want to do it because you're having a freakout about the end of our competitive skating career – and I think that's exactly what you're doing – I am going to keep being right here wanting you."

The offer, or the promise, whatever it was, was far too tempting. Katie did a crossover and shifted out of his grip. "The Harbin program, two minutes in. We should make the jump an axel."

Brendan threw his hands up in the air. "Or we could change the damn topic again. The jump stays a flip," he said firmly. "Neither of us need to get hurt for the sake of your mid-life crisis."

✦

That afternoon at group practice, Katie's knee twinged. She tried to hide it, but Brendan saw her brief grimace of pain. Of course he did. At the break he grabbed her hand and, without a word, led her to the side of the rink where Dr. Meyer was sitting talking with Leo.

Dr. Meyer asked her some questions, prodded at her leg carefully, then looked at Katie over the top of her glasses.

"You know what I'm going to say, don't you." Dr. Meyer had been on the Team USA medical staff in addition to being the tour doctor for five years running. She'd had an eye on Katie's knee for as long as Katie had known her and was one of the few people Katie trusted with her injury.

"Take it easy, don't work too hard, and tell you if anything changes instead to trying to hide it?"

"Exactly. Just like I've been telling you for months."
Katie nodded.

"Except you seem to keep doing exactly the opposite,"

Dr. Meyer said, sternly unamused.

"It's complicated," Katie said, because it was. Taking it easy could radically limit her future choices as easily as pushing too hard. That it was all tangled up with Brendan and their impending official retirement only made it worse.

"Yes, and so is your Facebook status. But you don't need me to tell you what happens if you let this get too bad."

✦

Katie couldn't help pacing up and down in the hallway backstage that night before she had to put her skates on, though she knew she should be doing literally anything other than putting more strain on her leg. It ached, and that scared her, although things ached all the time in this business. She'd managed to escape serious injury during the competitive season by good luck as much as anything else. But what if that luck ran out? What could she do if she couldn't skate? Brendan would blame her for being careless. The whole solo tour they were relying on for work after this wouldn't happen. She'd be alone and out of a job. And it would be entirely her fault.

Katie realized her hands were shaking.

Incipient panic attack. Fantastic.

She rubbed her palms on her thighs and tried to focus on her breathing. It didn't work. *What if I can't stop shaking to skate? They'll say I can't handle the pressure. That we won gold but still aren't good enough....*

"Kate."

Katie whipped her head up to see Brendan standing a few feet down the hall from her. She dug her fingers into the awful neon-pink fabric of her skirt, but he wasn't fooled.

"Hey." His face softened in concern. He crossed the small space between them and closed his hands around hers. "What's wrong?"

"Nothing's wrong. I'm fine." She pulled her hands away.

Brendan let them slide out of his grasp. He always did that: gave her space when she wanted it. Because he was a gentleman, Katie thought with irritation, and from Minnesota. He was *nice*. But Katie didn't want nice. Not now when she was ruining everything and didn't deserve nice anyway.

"Bullshit," he said easily. "Is it your knee?"

"It was my knee. Now it's definitely my head."

Not wanting nice would be a lot easier if nice didn't sooner or later work. She hoped Brendan wouldn't notice the tears that were starting to sting her eyes despite all of her commands to her body to stop.

But if he noticed, he didn't comment on them. "How bad is it?"

"Not bad. I mean – really. It's fine."

Brendan's forehead creased in a frown. "Are you sure? Because we can sit this show out, you know, if you need a rest. For whatever reason."

"No!" Katie's head snapped up. "No, we can't."

"Look, if one night off is going to save you a bigger injury in the long run –"

"No!" She was sure she was audible inside the green room, which made everything worse. "No, we can't take a night off. My knee is fine. If I take a night off they'll think we can't hack a post-competitive career, and the tour will fall through, and then where will we be? I am completely freaking out."

"Hey. Hey, hey, hey, hey. Okay, there it is. It's okay." Brendan put an arm around her shoulders and gently steered her to a bench at the side of the hallway. He sat down next to her, keeping his arm around her. Katie glanced down the hallway to make sure no one was around to see, then leaned against him.

Brendan's body was warm and solid. She felt herself

relax a little just from his proximity. His hand found hers on her knee, and he laced their fingers together. This time, she let him.

"I know you're pissed." His voice was barely above a whisper. "And I know you're scared. I know your nerves are doing things without your permission right now. But you know how to take care of yourself and your knee."

"Except for this morning," Katie said, bitter with self-recrimination.

"You pushed your limits. You were always going to do that. If not today, then at some other point. It's ridiculous to think you weren't going to do that and ridiculous to be angry at yourself for it when there have been literally no dire consequences."

"Not yet, at least."

"Do you want to be stubborn or do you want me to make you feel better?"

Katie couldn't see Brendan's face, but she could hear his raised eyebrow. She smiled. She couldn't help it. "Can't I have both?"

"Sure. Turn sideways." He was laughing at her, but she couldn't bring herself to mind.

Katie shifted so that her back was to him and she was sitting cross-legged on the bench. She was expecting it, but couldn't suppress a shiver when Brendan put his hands lightly on her shoulders. His hands were deft and practiced, and his fingers sought out the knots where he knew she held her tension.

"Breathe," he reminded her softly.

Katie hadn't realized she'd been holding her breath. She filled and emptied her lungs and felt so much of the tension of the day leave her body.

"You're okay," he said. "You're going to take care of yourself, and you're not going to get hurt. We're going to get this solo tour, and we are going to kill it. Okay?"

Reassurance or platitudes would have infuriated Katie.

But in the face of Brendan's calm certainty – and the warmth of his breath on the back of her neck – she couldn't help but feel calm and certain, too. Or at least, more so than she had five minutes ago.

"Okay," she said.

◆

As they took their starting positions Katie commanded herself to relax and enjoy this. They had a finite number of performances in this tour. All she had to do was get through them. Everything that could come after was a question mark too terrifying to think about. But standing here, in a darkened arena, her arm around Brendan's neck and her head on his chest, the two of them breathing in unison as they waited for the lights to come up and the music to start…this was happiness.

The lights came up, bathing them in a vibrant purple. The first beats of the music began to play, and Katie tucked her face into Brendan's neck for the opening choreography. *So much in my life would be better if I could calm down and appreciate it.*

But that wasn't how anxiety worked.

One of the few periods of pure happiness in her life had been when she and Brendan had first started dating in Annecy. With Brendan, in bed, her brain had finally shut up. She didn't have to worry about choreography or scores or press or any of the other hundred things that whirled through her mind when she was anywhere else but wrapped up with him, their bodies entwined as surely as the rest of their beings were. And then they'd lost. Horribly. Katie hadn't known how to trust peace since.

The song shifted, and the music pulsed, slow and relentless like the soundtrack in a club. Their coach had begged them to pick any song other than this for their comeback season, but they'd insisted. Katie was still sure they'd been right. This wasn't what anyone expected two kids from the Midwest to skate to, and that had been exactly the point.

From their pair spin they moved into the throw jump. Katie made it a double, not a triple, and landed without any complaint from her knee. The audience applauded, but the concession felt like a failure.

Brendan moved beside her on the ice, sometimes ahead of her, sometimes pursuing her. Many male skaters didn't have the artistic flare Brendan did, which was one of the reasons they were the best. He had years of ballet training to thank for that, but that wasn't the only reason.

There was, in Brendan, a willingness to submit – to the demands of the sport, to the proscribed posture and technique of artistry, to his partner, to skating itself. He didn't just fill time between jumps and lifts that made him look strong and masculine. As a result, the lines of his body, the curve of his arm, the position of his fingertips, were so precise they drew Katie in along with everyone else watching him. Never mind that Brendan's costumes were simple, almost severe; no rhinestones or billowing sleeves for him. Tonight he wore a black short-sleeved shirt and pants that made no effort to pretend to be street clothes. Why should he hide the work he did on the ice? Why should he be any less feline and captivating than her? Together, they were irresistible.

This program's second overhead lift and the twist lift were terrifyingly close together. The strength Brendan needed to pick her up, hold her, throw her, and catch her, was incredible. But if they did it right, the audience wouldn't be thinking about how hard Brendan was working. They'd only be thinking about how he and Katie moved like there was nothing and no one else in the world.

Brendan caught her after the twist lift as if doing so was the most effortless thing, but as always Katie could feel the strain of the muscles in his arms and chest. He held her for the next few steps, her arms around his neck, her body curled against his. Two people, dissolving into one.

God, the sex with him had been fun. There had been a lot of it in the short time they were together. They had laughed about it then, how much they couldn't keep their hands off each other. In hindsight Katie could admit the sex hadn't been expert or mind-blowing – they'd been young and not terribly experienced – but it had been *good*, good in a way she hadn't been able to recapture with anyone else.

Guys who were skaters were too interested in their own egos. Guys who weren't skaters worked too hard to impress her, which made her nervous. They didn't really want to date her; they wanted to tell their friends they were sleeping with an Olympic athlete. And dating other women usually ended poorly for all involved. Katie liked women as driven and obsessive about their work as she was, which never left a lot of room or energy for actually having a relationship.

She and Brendan leaned into each other during the last bit of footwork, their limbs intertwining, their hands on each other, intent and wanting. Everything was about building to that final moment and making sure the tension stretched tight to the very end.

Katie leaned back and Brendan caught her, one arm around her waist, his other hand digging into her hair, too hard and also perfect. She only remembered the audience existed when thunderous applause broke out.

✦

Once the show was over, the last thing Katie wanted to do was face the bright lights, microphones, and digital recorders of the diligent sports reporters who'd come to cover the tour. Interviews felt intrusive after the intense focus of skating. But smiling for the press was as much a part of her job as landing triple flips was. If she and

Brendan wanted to tour in the future, they had to continue to be America's sweethearts. At least Brendan was suffering right along with her.

"How's life on the road?" a reporter from the local news asked.

Confusing and miserable without a competition to work towards. "Oh, you know, enjoying the chance to relax a little," she said sweetly, using her biggest TV smile. "Sometimes I feel like we're still recovering from Harbin."

"Don't let her fool you," Brendan put in. "She had us up and on the ice at four this morning."

"So you're working hard?" the reporter asked.

"We always work hard. Or, well, Katie does. I just try to keep up!" That was part of their ongoing patter, that Katie was the one who drove them hardest. Sometimes, that was true, but mostly it was a jab at the part of their audience who thought the lady in a pair was only there to look pretty.

"Does that mean you're looking ahead to another competitive season?" the reporter asked.

Brendan glanced at Katie, as if he was looking for guidance instead of giving her a cue.

"We haven't made any decisions about that yet," Katie said, smiling for the camera. Which was a flat-out lie, but they weren't going to make their retirement official until they reached Denver. "Retiring from competing would be a huge life change, and we're still working out what's going to be best for us and our partnership."

"You two famously started a relationship during your first Olympics, though of course you subsequently broke up. Is there any chance there's been another change to your relationship status after this last Olympics?"

Who writes these questions? Katie wondered. Surely someone who hated her.

But before she could say anything in response, Brendan wrapped an arm around her waist and pulled her into his side. "We're as close as we ever were," he said with a boyish grin and kissed her forehead. "No matter what we're doing, Katie and I make a great team."

She pinched the small of his back. *Behave.* But he only grinned more.

✦

"You're ridiculous," Katie said as they walked towards the locker rooms. They were holding hands, though she couldn't remember when that had started or who had taken whose hand first. Physical contact with Brendan was a lot like breathing: Almost constant, rarely conscious, always natural.

"You love me for it."

"You're also an asshole," Katie said fondly.

"Probably." Brendan gave her a teasing, sidelong smile. His thumb slid across the inside of her wrist in a gesture that he probably wasn't aware of, though it made goosebumps stand up on her arm.

She gently disentangled their hands so she wasn't tempted to do something ill-advised. Like press her lips to the hollow of his throat and taste his skin, salty with sweat. They were getting back on the horse with skating, and so long as they stuck to their established boundaries, they would stay there.

"We should do something tonight," Brendan said.

"Yeah?" Katie asked cautiously. With them returning to a fragile equilibrium, she didn't want to tempt fate.

"Yeah." Brendan echoed her. "Tonight, Portland. Tomorrow, off to…whatever the hell cow town we're going to. I want to enjoy civilization while we can."

"Excuse you?" Katie laughed, but she wasn't amused. She was shocked. And uncomfortable. And really, really disappointed.

"What? Oh. No offense to your cows of course."

"No offense to *my* cows?" Katie repeated, incredulous. She folded her arms over her chest, glad she had already let go of his hand. "What makes my cows special?"

"They're...." Brendan floundered for a moment. "I dunno, Katie. I was just saying."

"Well, just don't say things like that. It really makes you sound like an asshole. 'Civilization.'" She snorted. "You're from Minneapolis. Not New York."

"Not so special as I think?" he teased.

Katie was not in the mood for teasing. "No," she said sharply. "Not so special at all."

6

After Brendan's Unfortunate Cow Town Comment

Portland, OR

Brendan had wanted to go out with Katie and enjoy some quality time away from the ice with her. A good dinner. Maybe a movie. Things normal people did. Breathing space from their jobs would do them good. But Katie wasn't speaking to him at the moment, which he was self-aware enough to consider fair. He hadn't meant to be a dick about farms in general or cows in particular, but Katie was often sensitive about where she'd come from, and he had been thoughtless.

With his initial plan for the evening scuppered, Brendan knew he should spend his time doing something reasonable. Work out. Tend to his too-often-ignored social media. Sleep. But the disagreement with Katie had left him feeling antsy and wired, and if he stayed at the hotel he wasn't sure he could resist the temptation to go find her. Brendan always felt at loose ends without her by his side.

Which was all the more reason to get out, clear his

head, and try not to be a codependent mess for one evening.

Rounding up a crew for a night at a bar was an easy proposition. Sure, tours were hard work, but so was any job. A few drinks, a little less sleep than was a good idea – stuff like that could make or break a competition season, but on tour, fun when it could be had was fair game and eagerly sought after. A quick flurry of texts and some knocking on hotel room doors and Brendan soon had a group together: Haruka and Yume, David and Lena, Shane, Natalya, Justin, Andrej, and Tyler.

Stepping out onto a street wearing jeans, a dark blue button-down shirt, and a coat that didn't have a Team USA or Olympic logo on it was always a slightly surreal experience. So often Brendan only went outside to drive to and from the rink, the grocery store, or the airport. On tour, which added the unpleasantness of long-distance bus travel, any decent clothes he had with him were mostly reserved for media appearances. Nice clothes for a night out felt unnatural.

He covered his mouth to hide a yawn and jogged ahead a few steps to catch up with the rest of the crew. David had his arm slung easily around Lena's shoulders. Yume, Andrej and Shane were arguing about the latest superhero movie. Natalya had taken a picture of the group and was typing rapidly into her phone as she uploaded it to Twitter.

The bar they eventually found – mainly by failing to find the bar the concierge had recommended to them – was the ultimate in obnoxious hipster bars. It had wood paneling, an excess of faux oil lamps, and, inexplicably, a shuffleboard court that people were actually playing on. Brendan took a picture of the latter and reflexively texted it to Katie before he remembered that he'd meant to get some space from her. *Oops.*

She didn't reply. He couldn't blame her.

The bar was occupied only by a handful of locals,

probably because it was a weeknight. Brendan and the others staked out an entire corner, talking over each other to discuss drink choices, practice schedules, mistakes in that night's performance, and whatever TV anyone was watching. Brendan got drawn into a conversation with Shane, Natalya, and Haruka about choreography and the headache of the group numbers, which still weren't coming together.

Not having Katie by his side was a peculiar feeling. Brendan kept turning to say something to her, only to remember with a jolt that she wasn't there.

"Hey, man. Brendan. Brendan!"

Brendan snapped out of his reverie to look at Shane. "Sorry. Zoned out."

"I could tell." A smile quirked up at the corner of Shane's mouth. "Don't look now, but I think that girl over there is checking you out." He tilted his chin towards a table behind Brendan. "The one in the yellow dress."

"How do you know she's not checking you out?"

"Because her friend is checking me out," Shane said. "You should go say hi."

"*You* go say hi." Brendan could feel himself start to blush. Also Shane had terrible logic.

"My relationship rules do not cover girls in bars on tour."

Brendan could barely manage being away from Katie for a few hours. He didn't know how Shane handled being separated for weeks at a time from someone he was actually dating. "I would humiliate myself. Better let them admire from afar."

"Boys." Natalya gave a long-suffering sigh. Haruka smiled at her from behind her glass. "Katie's not here, and you want to get over her. Go talk to them."

Brendan shook his head. "I'm good. Really." He also didn't have any actual desire to get over Katie, despite what he kept telling himself, but that wasn't a conversation he wanted to get into here and now.

"Have you ever dated anyone who wasn't Katie?" Natalya asked. The question didn't sound curious so much as judgmental.

"We're not dating," Brendan snapped.

"I know that," she snapped back.

"Go on." Shane gave Brendan a friendly nudge with his shoulder. "Tell her about your Great Dating Mishaps with Women Who Looked Like Katie but Couldn't Hold Your Attention."

"They weren't that bad," Brendan protested. "I wasn't that bad!"

Shane followed up. "Are you still with any of them?"

"No," Brendan admitted.

"Have you dated anyone since you and Katie started skating together again?"

Brendan stared at his beer. "…no."

"The relationships were that bad," Shane told Natalya and Haruka.

"Okay, I don't know why I'm defending myself here, but…" Brendan sat up a little straighter in the booth. "None of this is complex. I dated a couple of girls – this was way after Katie and I broke up romantically and as partners. They were nice girls. I liked them. I even got kind of serious with one of them, but in the end she broke up with me. She said with Katie in the picture there wasn't enough room for her in my life. We weren't even skating together then! So that felt a little unfair to me."

"I bet it felt more unfair to her," Haruka said. She looked like she was enjoying herself immensely.

"They were 'nice girls?'" Natalya repeated, her tone somewhere between disbelief and scorn.

"They were! I would have been very happy had things worked out differently than they did."

Natalya took a delicate sip of her drink. "And yet you don't know why these relationships did not last."

"If you think only one of those people broke up with you because of Katie, think again," Shane put in helpfully.

"So, anyway, yeah." Brendan really, really wanted to sink through the floor and never see his friends again. "I don't know how to talk to girls. Or boys. Or really any people at all. For any reason. Just Katie."

"If you knew how to talk to Katie, you wouldn't be in this mess," Shane said.

"Harsh," Brendan protested

Haruka made an evaluative face. "He's not wrong."

"Great. Thanks." Brendan turned in his seat, looking for some sort of escape. Instead, he quickly became aware that they weren't the only ones discussing relationships.

Tyler, perched on a bar stool, was enumerating to Andrej the attributes of the various women of the touring group. The others at Brendan's table noticed, too.

"I hate when he does that," Haruka muttered into her drink.

"Hey, man, not cool," Brendan called out. He may have been bad at dating, but he was crystal clear that no woman wanted a coworker talking that way. But Tyler was either ignoring him or hadn't heard.

"Okay, but the one I would *really* want to get with, no chance," Tyler went on. "Not so long as she's got her knight in shining armor around. But if he would ever give her up, let me tell you, everyone would be fighting over her. Katie Nowacki is the hottest piece of ass on this whole tour."

Other people finding Katie attractive was fine. Katie finding other people attractive was also fine. Jealousy over the idea of Katie being in a relationship with someone else wasn't part of Brendan's emotional landscape. Heartbreak, sure, but not jealousy. Like him, she'd dated other people before. Maybe they both would date other people again in the future, too.

What was absolutely not okay, however, was a man talking about Katie in those terms or anything like them.

"Hey, Tyler. Can you maybe fucking not?" Brendan spoke up again, more sharply.

Tyler spun lazily around on his bar stool. When he saw Brendan glowering at him, his mouth opened in feigned surprise.

"Oh, so sorry, Reid. Didn't realize you were there."

"Bullshit, man. Stop talking crap about the girls, yeah? You sound like an even bigger asshole than usual." Brendan knew he was getting loud and, frankly, didn't care. He was stressed and tired and angry, and here was the perfect outlet.

"Like you give a shit what I say about the rest of them. You're just pissed someone else is looking at your girlfriend."

Brendan's hands clenched into fists on top of the table. He didn't try to loosen them; he was too angry. Dimly, he was aware of everyone else at the table staring at him and Tyler and this mess that was suddenly unfolding. "She's not my girlfriend, and I don't need to be dating her to be pissed at you for being a dick."

Tyler rolled his eyes dramatically, impervious to Brendan's insults and oblivious to the awfulness of his own behavior. "I'm sure everyone in the audience tonight was convinced. Watching you two skate is the most public form of foreplay I have ever seen. Except for the part where she won't fuck you. Half the dudes in the arena wanted to be in your place and get into Katie's fine frigid pants. If they only knew!"

"Try to have a little respect, yeah?"

"What'd I say? Knight in shining armor. Too bad she kicked you to the curb years ago."

That was more than Brendan could take. He may have been a figure skater, but that didn't mean his athleticism was limited to the ice. He spent an annoying amount of his life doing strength training. He could lift a fully-grown person into the air, over his head, with one arm, if not easily, at least confidently, with grace, and with small risk to himself or that person.

He was strong. But that didn't mean he was dangerous. And it definitely didn't mean he had aim.

Because without nearly enough thought, he lunged to his feet, took a few steps, swung at Tyler, and missed spectacularly. His fist hit the bar behind his target with enough force to shock his arm numb and possibly break his fingers.

He had only a fraction of a second to process that – and the startled gasps and excited whoops from the people around him – before Tyler landed an only marginally better aimed punch just off-center from Brendan's nose. He stumbled backward, more from surprise than pain, and knocked into a chair, tipping it over.

"Hey. Hey hey hey hey HEY!"

Through the sudden confusion, Brendan was aware that the bartender, a burly, ponytailed guy in plaid, was coming towards them. Before Brendan could get his bearings, the bartender grabbed the back of his jacket and herded him and Tyler out the door.

The cold outside was yet another blow, one that made Brendan stand up straighter, suck in a lungful of air, and put a hand to his throbbing face. "Oh, shit," he hissed.

"You okay, man?"

Brendan looked up to see Tyler standing in front of him, looking much more sober and vaguely remorseful. "You punched my fucking face," Brendan said.

"Yeah, sorry, dude. You came at me, I just…." Tyler trailed off.

"You gotta not talk about the women that way." The heat of the moment had passed, but Brendan was not going to let the perfectly reasonable explanation for his wildly unreasonable behavior go.

"Fucking knight in shining armor," Tyler muttered. "Are you sure you're not Canadian?"

As the rest of their group filtered out of the bar onto the sidewalk around them, Justin and Natalya both had their phones out and were, presumably, recording what had happened.

Great. All I need is for this mess to wind up on social media.

Across the street someone wolf-whistled at them. A fan? A totally random bystander? Brendan didn't know, but the absurdity of the entire situation suddenly washed over him. He met Tyler's gaze, and they both started laughing.

"No seriously man, are you okay?" Tyler asked, grabbing Brendan by the shoulder and shaking him gently. "Shit, you're bleeding. You wanna see the doc?"

Brendan dabbed his nose with the back of his hand. Sure enough, it came away bloody. "Please tell me it's not broken."

Tyler shrugged. "Hell if I know. You don't look as ugly as any of the hockey jackasses I train with, so you're probably okay. Still…."

"Yeah. Sure, and tell her what, that I walked into a tree?" Fighting was definitely going to be an obstacle to future tour-related employment.

"Fuck. We're going to get in a ton of trouble aren't we?" Tyler had apparently just come to a similar conclusion.

Brendan's stomach sank. If he screwed up this opportunity for Katie – or Tyler or anyone else – he'd never forgive himself. "What do we do?" he asked.

"We lie, obviously," Tyler said matter-of-factly.

"And say what? That we just wandered into the middle of a fight because we went to the rough part of Portland?"

"I don't think Portland has a rough part," Tyler offered in a manner which was the opposite of helpful.

"That," Brendan sighed, "was kind of my point."

7

After the Show

Portland, OR

With everyone else out at a bar for the evening, Katie was glad for a few hours to herself. She needed time to process everything that had happened over the last couple of days and to regroup. At least she and Brendan had fixed their issues on the ice. But she was furious at him again – furious, and hurt. If he simply hadn't loved the farm Katie had grown up on, that would be one thing. Farming was hard work and not for everyone. But since she had been nine years old, Katie had been acutely aware of the differences between her and Brendan and the circumstances in which they had each grown up.

Their families lived less than an hour apart from each other, but they'd lived in different worlds. Brendan had been in Minneapolis, where his parents had well-paying office jobs and never had to worry about fitting his skating expenses into their budget. Katie had been out in the country, on a dairy farm owned by her mother, her uncle, and her uncle's partner. Every lesson and costume and

53

hour of ice time was carefully calculated against her family's income. They had never begrudged her the money spent, but Katie had also never stopped feeling guilty and acutely conscious of it. It had only gotten worse the older and better she got. Sure, there were eventually sponsors that took some of the pressure off, but that could never make up for her not being another set of hands at home to help get the work done.

That burden was her own, her choice to make peace with in private, but Brendan's contempt for where she was from was unbearable. Oh, sure, he liked her people well enough, and he was always polite whenever he came over. But who didn't Brendan like? Who wasn't he polite to? He never seemed comfortable at the farm, whether he was there for a few minutes dropping Katie off after one of their road trips from Denver, or for a few hours for dinner on a weekend while they were both home. Brendan, who was warm and so kind everywhere else, was stiff and ill-at-ease on the farm – and so damn cruel when he talked about anything that wasn't a city.

Even if, and it was a big if, they could figure out everything else that was going on between them, Brendan could never love where she was from. Brendan loved *her*, she was sure of that, but only the her as she was on the rink and on the road: Stylish. Ambitious. Determined. One day, maybe one day soon, that version of her was going to end. What would Brendan do with Katie as she was on her family's farm, up before dawn and dirty and daydreaming in ratty jeans and muddy boots?

It doesn't matter, Katie told herself. *Because we are light years from that ever being the most pressing issue on the table.*

Her knee hurt. She needed an ice bath. And she needed to call her family.

She was extra glad Natalya wasn't there as she filled the bathtub with cold water and ice from the machine down the hall. Ice baths were just one of many common unpleasantesses among skaters, but she hated to do it in front of anyone other than Brendan. It felt too much like admitting weakness.

Katie changed her pants for a pair of shorts, pulled on a sweatshirt, and zipped a light jacket over that. Ice was *cold*, whether on the rink or in a tub, and she wasn't going to be working out to make up for the lost heat. She slid into the freezing water as quickly as she could, holding up her sweatshirt and jacket so they wouldn't get wet. With her top half bundled up and her legs stretched out in the cold water, Katie scrolled through her contacts to her Uncle Rob and punched the call through.

She watched as he answered and the video call took a moment to settle into focus.

"Katie! How are you, sweetheart?" Rob asked once the connection was stable.

He was her mother's brother, and Katie had lived on the farm with them and Rob's partner Jesse for as long as she could remember. Her father had left when she was three and had never even appeared out of nowhere to borrow glory when she and Brendan started winning everything.

Rob was a big man, with graying brown hair and a thick beard. He wore overalls and plaid flannel shirts completely unironically. Now, he sat at the table in the kitchen as they spoke. Over his shoulder Katie could see the beams running across the ceiling and hear the chug and mutter of the ancient refrigerator. Katie felt an immediate lurch of homesickness at the familiar surroundings.

"Is this an okay time?" Katie asked. "I know it's getting late there." Farms woke up earlier – and went to bed earlier – than other places.

"For you, it's always a good time. We're just working on the books. Your mom's out at the barn, do you want me to get her?"

Katie shook her head. "No, that's fine." She didn't want

to disrupt their evening any further, not when there was so much work to be done. "Is everything okay?"

"One of the cows isn't feeling well. Nothing serious, she's just checking on her. Now, I noticed you didn't answer the first time. How are you? Unless you don't want to say."

Katie felt herself smile in spite of her rotten mood and cold legs. Rob had that effect on her; his ease and calm made her feel at ease, too. "I'm sitting in a tub of ice, and I really need a hug."

"Aww, kiddo. Your knee again?"

"Yeah."

"You working too hard?"

"Probably. I'm okay, though. How are you all?"

"We're good. We're good. Also, where are you? Wait, no, don't tell me, I have your schedule here somewhere...." Rob propped his phone against something on the table and started shuffling through the papers spread out on it. From this new angle Katie could see Jesse sitting in the chair next to Rob's and waved at him.

Jesse was more slightly built than Rob, wiry where his partner was broad. He too was from a farming family, but he'd gotten a degree in agricultural science from the University of Wisconsin - Madison and had brought a more contemporary sensibility to the farm. Thanks to him, in addition to the milk, the family had a growing business in homemade cheeses, jams, and pies. He'd even set up a website for the dairy.

"Hey Jesse. How's it going?" she asked.

"Good. I'm trying to convince your uncle to start a microbrewery with me."

"Oh? That would be so cool!" *And so much more work.*

Katie felt another tug of homesickness. Her whole life, whether on the farm or with Brendan, had been about a small group of people working hard with a common purpose. The Olympics and her competitive career were over, but the farm, reassuringly, would always be there. She missed it desperately.

"That's what I'm telling him," Jesse said enthusiastically. His gray eyes lit up, and he ran a hand back through his sandy hair.

"And *I'm* telling him he's welcome to, if he wants to deal with drunk college kids coming in on weekends," Rob put in.

"The drunk college kids aren't going to bother driving all the way out from Minneapolis. Right, Katie?"

Katie shrugged. "I dunno."

She'd never gone to college. She'd dropped out of high school to compete and gotten her GED when she was seventeen; Brendan, a year older than her, had managed to graduate from his high school before their skating schedules made juggling everything impossible. Which was one more thing that felt like a secret gulf between them. "According to my roommate I'm missing some awesome hipster microbrew beer tonight, though."

"Because you're in Portland! Of course." Rob finally pulled the schedule, printed off the tour website, out of the mess of papers on the table. "How is it?"

"It's a city." Katie had seen a lot of them at this point in her life. One was very much like another.

"And the tour?"

"It's had its ups and downs." Katie admitted. She didn't want to get into the details, but she was grateful to have a conversation with people who didn't ask her to feign anything: Not enthusiasm, not excitement, not energy. Of course, all of that was true of Brendan as well, but he took up energy in a different way.

"And how's Brendan?" Rob asked, after the briefest of hesitation. Katie knew her uncle liked and respected him, as far as their skating partnership went. He'd been less impressed with – and more wary about – the mess of their off-ice relationship.

Katie heaved a sigh and slumped a little. "We're kind of a mess."

"Ah. Same mess as usual or a new shiny kind of mess?"

There wasn't much about her situation with Brendan her family didn't know. They'd witnessed most of it, after all. "Some of both, and I don't understand it enough yet to complain to you or ask for advice or anything. You should distract me with farm gossip, though."

Rob smiled at her, fond and amused. "They're cows, Katie. They don't get up to much."

"I know," she said. "But I miss them. Fill me in. Also, hang on a second, I need to get out of this tub before I give myself hypothermia."

Half an hour later, up to date on the business of the farm, and finally warm and dry and tucked in bed, Katie said goodbye and ended the call. The happiness that had surrounded her faded a little. She was alone in a hotel in Portland, and she was miserable.

She glanced at the clock on the nightstand; it was getting late. She knew she should take advantage of a night in a bed instead of on the bus, but the idea of sleep seemed elusive.

Much later, having scrolled through social media on her phone, replied to a few fans, and posted some pictures from backstage, Katie was willing to acknowledge that sleep was not in her near future. Upset at him as she was, she felt restless without Brendan. Maybe she should have gone out, for all that staying in had gotten her mind off him.

She opened her text thread with him, and only then noticed the picture he had sent from the bar. Why on earth was there a shuffleboard thing there? *How's the night out on the town?* she texted him. Then she tossed the phone aside and rolled over, her face buried in her pillow. Brendan wouldn't respond, and she could pretend she hadn't given in to a moment of weakness.

But less than a minute later there was the chirp of an

incoming text. Katie lurched for her phone, glad that no one could see her do it.

I've been better, it read. *Didn't even play any shuffleboard. Heading back now. How's the night in?*

All right. Can't sleep.

I'm sorry about earlier, Brendan sent after a pause. *I didn't mean to be a dick.*

I know. You were though. But thank you. Something in Katie's chest loosened a little. Brendan could be carelessly hurtful, but Katie was tired and missed him and wanted to get back on an even keel. She was perfectly willing to accept his apology, even if it was over an issue he'd probably never stop making mistakes around.

Come over when you get back? she typed out. She bit her lip before she hit send.

Brendan took longer to respond to that one. Katie tried not to read into that. He was out at a bar. Other people were around. There were conversations to be had. He wasn't ignoring her, and he wasn't done with her now or once and for all. Any thoughts to the contrary were her anxiety talking.

Finally, her phone chirped again. *Sure. What for?*

Katie typed and deleted half a dozen replies before she settled on the one she finally sent: *We're a mess, and I miss you.* Might as well be honest.

Okay. I can do that. We're almost there, see you soon.

Katie laughed weakly and dropped the phone on the bed beside her. She closed her eyes and tried to relax, but found it was as impossible as ever. She hated not sharing a room with Brendan; having to plan times and places to meet was like having to make plans to meet her own arm. It was just wrong.

A few minutes later there was a gentle knock. Katie kicked back her covers, padded in bare feet to the door, pulled it open – and stopped short. Brendan was sporting a spectacular black eye. And he wasn't alone; next to him stood Natalya, holding a bag of ice and looking between him and Katie with an expression of amused anticipation.

Katie had intended to usher him inside, but she stood frozen. "Oh my God, what happened to you?"

"Um," Brendan said sheepishly. "Got in a fight. Sort of."

Katie's concern shifted to suspicion at Brendan's hedging. He didn't usually avoid questions. He also never got into fights. *What the hell was he thinking?*

"Sort of a fight?" She reached out to touch the bruise, but Brendan flinched back.

"Hey, ow!" He lifted his hand to ward off any further attempts at contact.

"He tried to hit Tyler," Natalya provided helpfully. "He failed. Tyler did not."

"You did *what?!*"

"He was talking shit about you," Brendan muttered.

"So you hit him?" Katie asked. Her stomach sank. What had Tyler been saying? But no. That was not the point. Any freakout about what other people thought of her – and how that could impact the rest of this tour or their next one – would have to wait.

"Tried to hit him," Natalya said again, scornfully insistent on this point. "Here, I got you ice, it will help." She pushed the bag at Brendan, who took it and pressed it to his face with a wince.

"You're going to have to cover that," Katie said with a frown. She'd been lonely and sad and anxious and had wanted ten minutes with Brendan to try to stop feeling all of those things. Instead she'd gotten one more shitty thing to deal with.

"Yes, I'm fine, thanks for asking," Brendan said, his wounded puppy dog expression shifting towards anger. "Jesus, is that what you're worried about? How this whole thing reflects on you?"

"That is not what I said, Brendan. You really want to

show that shiner off to all of America? And the internet?" Katie was beyond tired. She wanted to cry. But she couldn't do that and give Brendan the satisfaction of comforting her again. Definitely not with Natalya watching them like this argument was a particularly engaging tennis match.

"Obviously not."

"I didn't think so. Now would you listen to what I'm actually saying instead of trying to twist it so you can be mad at me?"

"This? Coming from you? Oh, no no no."

"What's that supposed to mean?" Katie asked. Even with Natalya as an audience, falling into an argument with Brendan was too easy. Like breathing. Or skating. And as necessary as both. But this was so far from them getting back onto an even keel as to be laughable.

"What do you think I mean?" Brendan shot back. "All I'm doing is standing here, and no matter what I do, you get pissed at me. I kiss you back, you get mad. I keep my distance, you get mad. I skate with you at four in the damn morning, you get mad. I go out for one night without you, and here you are, still mad!"

"Because you got into a fistfight!"

"The fistfight is not the problem, Katie. I shouldn't have done it, and my face hurts like hell, but I'm pretty sure it is not the problem."

"So you want sympathy now," she said flatly.

"I...." Brendan took a breath and looked away from her. "You know what, I don't need this," he said bitterly, stepping back into the hallway.

"You didn't have to come here!" Katie instinctively stepped forward to follow him. Whether she was on or off the ice, if she wasn't running from the strange intimacy she shared with Brendan, she was chasing it.

The door slammed shut behind her; hopefully Natalya had her key.

"You invited me," Brendan said over his shoulder as he

strode down the hall, his voice rising.

"Because I wanted to get okay with you again!" Katie's voice rose to match his as she followed him. They probably shouldn't be doing this so publicly, but they were in it now, and Katie didn't know how to redirect the conversation.

Brendan spun to face her. "So what's stopping you?"

"You!"

"Me?" Brendan gave a bitter laugh. "I'm the problem, when you're the one who believes we're cursed in some way that prevents us from moving forward together? No. I don't think so."

"We don't *work* when we're together –" Katie began.

"I HEARD YOU THE FIRST TIME." Brendan reached the end of the hallway, glanced around, seemed to realize he'd passed the elevator, and banged through the door into the stairs. "And I don't mean two days ago on the fucking bus, I mean when you broke up with me after Annecy."

Katie pushed through the door after him. "Because we sucked."

"It was our first Olympics!" Brendan yelled. Everything was concrete; his voice and footsteps echoed as he pounded up the stairs. "I was twenty-two! You were twenty-one! You were a non-stop panic attack any time we left the athletes' village, and I was fucking terrified. In that room, just you and me? We were great and happy and delighted and whole. You have no idea if that's why we sucked on the ice. You never asked me what I thought, or what I was willing to give up. You just told me what you thought! Which is what always happens!"

Katie ran up the stairs behind him. She didn't know what would happen at the end of this chase, only that she couldn't stop. Brendan drew her like a magnet. "That is so unfair, I listen to you –"

Brendan grabbed the railing to pull himself around the turn in the stairs. "And then make all the decisions anyway! Whether we're allowed to fuck, the music, the goddamn costumes!"

"You don't care about the costumes."

"I do, actually, but that's not the point!"

"What is the point?" Katie yelled at his back.

"The point." Brendan reached the next landing and whirled around to face her. He was breathing hard and seemed at a loss for words.

Katie stopped on the step below him, inches away. They may have fought nearly constantly, but this, tonight, this was something new and possibly final. Neither of them wanted to be doing this anymore, that much she was sure of.

"The point," Brendan repeated, his voice angry and close. "Is that all of this, everything, every single moment of my life, has been your idea. You came to me after Stockholm and said we should make a comeback. Exactly like when you skated up to me on that rink when I was ten and told me I was going to be your partner. Except way messier. And so much more terrifying. But you always said we could do this. *Together.* I said yes, I showed up, and I did the work, every time, all so you could win a gold medal."

"You wanted to win, too!"

"Sure. And we did! Together! Because we're a team and that's what we do. And should have always been doing without interruption. But you treat me like a thing or a prop you need, and I am done with it!"

Before Katie could respond, the door behind Brendan slammed open, and he startled so hard he nearly toppled down the stairs. Without thinking, Katie steadied him with a hand to his chest. Brendan turned to face whoever had come in. Katie peered around his shoulder.

Leo, the tour manager, loomed in the doorway.

Katie wanted to dissolve through the floor. But the step she was standing on, like every rink on which she had ever fallen, did not oblige by swallowing her up.

"I should have known it was you two." Leo sighed. He wasn't a tall man, but he was strong and compact, and his presence was substantial. He'd been a skater once himself and knew how to project the most subtle emotion from one end of the stadium to another.

"Leo – Katie began at the same instant Brendan started stammering apologies.

He shushed them before he spoke. "Would you care to exit the echo chamber of doom before we address this?" Leo held the door open and looked pointedly at them. Brendan went first, his shoulders slumped penitently. Katie swallowed down her nerves and followed, her own back held straight. They were going to get yelled at, and they deserved it.

Once they were in the hallway, Leo shut the door quietly behind them. With his arms folded, he turned to face them, sizing them up.

"Is there something I should know about?" he asked, looking first at Katie and then at Brendan, his gaze lingering on Brendan's black eye. "Other than what is likely the obvious, that you two are on the outs again and making yourselves into the sort of tour problem I don't want to deal with?"

Katie bit her lip and tried to blink away the tears stinging her eyes at the unspoken threat. They needed this next tour. No matter what complicated feelings she had about it. If she and Brendan had screwed up their chances....

Brendan shook his head. "No," he answered for both of them. "Nothing that's going to impact anyone other than us." He gestured at the door they'd just come through. "And we've survived worse than shouting matches in a hotel stairwell."

"Mm. Somehow, I completely believe you. Are you hurt anywhere other than your eye? Either of you?" Leo asked. He unfolded his arms and took a step closer to examine Brendan's face.

"No," they said at the same time.

"Is anyone else hurt?"

"No," Brendan said, alone this time. "So you know, Katie wasn't there when it happened. I went out with a bunch of the other skaters. She stayed in."

"Well, at least you two are still slightly less of a mess when you're together than when you're apart." Leo sighed again. "I don't think your nose is broken. Good thing too, since a quarter of our audience is hoping they can steal you away from Katie once and for all." He gave them both long, searching looks before seeming to come to a decision. "We'll talk about this more in the morning. In the meantime, do everyone in earshot a favor and go to sleep before the hotel kicks us out and I fire you on the spot. Are we clear?"

"Yes," Katie said at the same time as Brendan.

"Good," Leo said before he left them in the middle of the hallway and went back to his own room, muttering to himself about their histrionics as he went.

"Oh my God." Katie covered her cheeks with her hands. Whatever anger she had at Brendan paled in comparison to her mortification at what had just happened. Sure, they had a ton of issues, but there had never been less doubt that they were in this mess together.

"Come on," Brendan said softly. "Let's finish this now. I don't think we can risk everyone's wrath if we don't.'

Katie didn't disagree. She went willingly when Brendan grabbed her wrist and led her back into the stairwell and up two flights to his room. He let go of her only to unlock the door and hold it open for her. She stood awkwardly in the little entryway as Brendan let the door shut behind them.

The room was, mercifully, devoid of his roommate. Katie had no idea where Justin was, or when he'd get back. All she knew was that she didn't want to be interrupted in whatever conversation they were about to have.

"Now what?" she asked.

Brendan shrugged. "You tell me."

Katie tried not to roll her eyes, but right now, she felt more than justified in her ongoing anger. "You can't yell at me about making choices for you while also asking me to solve all this myself."

Brendan took a deep breath and let it out slowly. "I am so tired of this." His voice was low, every syllable clear and sad. He swiped a hand through his hair. "Look, if you're going to hate me, can you do it from a distance? And keep it off the ice?"

Katie shook her head. How had Brendan gotten to that conclusion? "I don't hate you. I have never hated you," she said insistently. "This would all be a lot easier if I did."

"Would it? Because this is awful." Brendan stepped closer, as if he wanted comfort from her even when she was the very person causing him pain. Katie knew the feeling. "If making you hate me will make it hurt less, I will absolutely sign up for that."

"No you won't," Katie said simply. She had no idea what was going on in her head about a dozen issues – herself, Brendan, their skating career, touring, the horrible things he sometimes said about places like the one she was from – but she knew they could never hate each other. She reached out to touch his hair, an impulse, ridiculously, from their choreography. It was how they projected tenderness all the way up to the cheap seats. He grabbed her hand to stop her but didn't let go.

Katie stared at their intertwined fingers. "I wish you hadn't done that," she breathed. They were far too close now, and gravity was pulling them together.

"Why?" Brendan's voice was a whisper. The air had changed around them, and the hair stood up on her arms.

She looked up at his face, at the perfect bow of his lips and the glint of his green eyes watching her. She couldn't help herself. She went up on her toes and leaned against him like they were on the ice and kissed him.

Brendan opened his mouth to her as if they were the lovers they portrayed in their programs and not the terrible mess they were everywhere else.

Katie's stomach swooped as his hands grabbed her hips – so familiar from their routines and so different in these circumstances – and pushed her up against the back of the door. She had never been so glad not to be in the frozen world that was the foundation of everything between them. If they had been in a rink, it would have been time to spin apart by now, but Katie couldn't go anywhere and in Brendan's arms she didn't want to.

The slightest touch of his hand on the back of her thigh was all the cue Katie needed to wrap her legs around his waist and her arms around his neck. He caught her easily, bracing her weight between his body and the door. Katie could feel his heart beating wildly, joyously, against her own.

Brendan pressed his mouth against her neck. "Kate." His voice was ragged and solemn.

This moment was the only thing outside of the Olympics Katie had ever dreamed of, but it wasn't something she could have. "Put me down," she said abruptly.

He stopped kissing her immediately and pulled his head back. "What?"

"This is too perfect and too much and will be absolutely ruinous." She was starting to panic. Not because she didn't trust him, but because she didn't trust herself...or the universe. "Put me down," she repeated.

He did, instantly, letting her weight come to rest on the floor again as gently and precisely as he did after any lift. He stepped back, out of reach. Katie had been overwhelmed a moment ago by his proximity, but now she was overwhelmed by his absence.

"I'm sorry," she said. "We can't do this." She spun around, pulled the door open, and fled from every bad decision she desperately wanted to make.

8

The Morning After the Screaming Match in the Stairwell

Portland, OR

Before Brendan left his room for breakfast a knock sounded on the door. Justin had already gone, and, unless he had forgotten his key, this was unlikely to be anything good. Brendan hoped it wasn't Katie. If they were going to engage in yet another round of bullshit, he wanted some coffee first. He was tired, his face hurt, and he looked like crap.

He padded over and glanced through the peephole. Leo was standing in the hallway. Brendan's heart sank. Between Leo and Katie, Leo was probably the worse option.

"Come with me," Leo said unceremoniously when Brendan opened the door.

"Uh, sure." Brendan fumbled his shoes on awkwardly while holding the door open with one hand.

Leo led him down the hall to another hotel room whose door was propped open. Inside was Dr. Meyer, her first aid kit sitting on one of the beds.

"First, we're getting you checked out," Leo said. He steered Brendan into the room with a hand on his back, like Brendan might bolt. But Brendan was not about to do anything that was going to make this day worse. "Then, we're going to talk."

Brendan had been through a lot of bad mornings: Mornings after he'd lost competitions, after uncomfortable red-eye flights, after fights with Katie, after girlfriends had broken up with him because of Katie. But this morning was quickly on its way to qualifying as one of the worst. On top of everything else, it looked like Brendan was going to have to face the very reasonable consequences of his actions not only on his partnership, but on his job. He had no idea how bad those consequences were going to be.

He took the chair Dr. Meyer waved him into and sat still while she examined his face, pressing gently on the side of his nose.

"Any headache?" she asked, checking his eyes and nose with an otoscope.

"I mean, it hurts, but no." How had Brendan let his feelings run away with him – first with Tyler and then with Katie? He never let things get out of hand like that. "How bad is it?" he asked, giving Dr. Meyer his best pathetic expression. He couldn't undo anything that had happened, but he could at least try to win some charm points back. It wasn't like he had anything else going for him at the moment.

Dr. Meyer tutted and leaned back in her chair, stripping off her gloves. "You're fine. Nothing's broken. You'll have that shiner for a while, though."

"I gathered." Brendan poked the skin under his eye tentatively. "Ow."

"Stop doing that," she said.

"Yeah, okay."

Leo, who had been sitting back letting the doctor do her

work, sat up in his own chair. "Now, care to tell me how that happened?"

"To be honest, no." Nothing Brendan could say was going to make this any better for himself.

"Brendan."

Brendan took a breath. "A group of us went out to a bar last night. It doesn't really matter who else was there, they weren't involved. Except Tyler. He started saying stuff about the women on the tour. You know…sexually suggestive stuff." Brendan couldn't bring himself to repeat any of it. "I told him to stop, we got into it a little bit, verbally, but then he said something about Katie. I lost my temper and tried to punch him. I missed, but he didn't." Brendan touched his cheek gingerly. "I know I fucked up, and for what it's worth, I'm sorry."

"Well, I suppose that could have been worse," Leo said. "At least no civilians were involved – if you're telling me the truth, and I'm assuming you are. I think you know this already, but I do need to say it."

Brendan braced himself. Were he and Katie about to get kicked off the tour? Brendan didn't think so – their box-office draw was too powerful and people had probably done worse than this in the past – but having to consider the possibility was unnerving. He'd never forgive himself if he did anything to screw up Katie's career.

"You can't do things like this and expect more tours – with a group or with Katie – to be an option." Leo went on. "Pissing off the hotel is bad enough on its own, but fighting on top of that? No."

"There was a noise complaint?"

"You were shouting in a concrete stairwell. You're lucky I found you before there was more than one noise complaint."

Brendan nodded rapidly, more ashamed now.

"But now that I've said all that." Leo looked even more serious. "I'm going to have a word with Tyler. Fisticuffs in a bar is a terrible choice, but I'm not going to tolerate anyone talking about the ladies – any ladies – like that."

"Thank you," Brendan said. He meant it too.

Leo nodded and stood up. "Now, ice that eye of yours. And don't do anything like this again."

"Yes, sir."

Once Leo had left, Dr. Meyer turned to Brendan. "Is there anything else I can help you with?" Her tone suggested she wanted to chase him away, and a large part of Brendan would have been happy to flee. But help he did need. Why not ask someone who was as sick of his and Katie's shit as he was?

"Actually, uh. Yeah. I've got a question. Not about medical stuff. More about the car crash of my life. If you don't mind me asking?"

"At least you're interesting." Dr. Meyer dropped into the chair Leo had vacated.

"You've known Katie and me for like, a long time," Brendan said.

Dr. Meyer nodded. "More's the damn pity."

"Yeah, well. I don't disagree. We're a mess. I mean, more than usual."

"Brendan, we're clear I'm not a therapist, right?"

"Uh-huh. I'm just desperate."

"Then can you please cut to the chase?"

"Right. So." Brendan was grateful for Dr. Meyer's acerbity. It helped him focus, which he desperately needed to do. "Since Harbin we don't know where we stand with each other or ourselves or anything, and I know it's because we're retiring and neither of us really knows what to do without competitive skating. But we're miserable, and I don't know how to fix it." Brendan looked down at his hands on his knees and clasped them together. He could do so many things with his hands: perfect the lines of a spin, hold Katie in a death spiral, catch her in a throw lift. But he couldn't fix Katie's knee or banish her anxiety or repair whatever it was between them that was cracking apart.

"You don't fix it," Dr. Meyer said bluntly. "You don't get to go backwards, you know? You have to do what's next. Which is preferably not getting into another bar fight." She looked at Brendan intently. "What do you want?"

"I don't know," Brendan said reflexively.

"Bullshit," Dr. Meyer said, all gruff kindness again. "No one has very public screaming matches with the person they've been officially not dating for years unless they want to be dating them. So, I'll say it again, *what do you want?*"

"Katie," Brendan blurted before thinking the better of it. "If Katie wants that, of course. But she thinks we're cursed if we try to date and skate at the same time. And now we're not even friends because we've both been so awful. We're not sharing a room anymore. We never used to need space from each other."

Dr. Meyer narrowed her eyes at him. "You want my advice?"

"That is why I'm here humiliating myself. I mean, other than the black eye."

"Well, I wanted to make sure. Because I think your first mistake is in thinking you and Katie were ever friends."

Brendan frowned. "What do you mean? She's my best friend."

"Sure," Dr. Meyer said. "But not like go-to-the-movies-once-in-a-while friends. You're big, messy, epic, people-write-classical-tragedies-about-you friends. Anyone can see that."

That was a whole new grim way for someone to put it, but Brendan didn't see any point in arguing. Dr. Meyer was right.

"We don't really try to hide it," he said. "We use it on the ice all the time. Although I hope it's not that bad in person."

"It is that bad. You've spent most of your lives together, in whatever way you are, since you were children. Now you're approaching a major career change. This is where you have to stop thinking like a competitive figure skating pair."

"What do you mean?"

"Every program you've ever skated with Katie has been about a boy and a girl in love. That's what the sport requires. That's the story you've spent your entire lives telling. So of course you want that kind of happy ending for you and Katie too."

Brendan nodded.

"But maybe that's not the ending meant for you. Maybe you're supposed to be figuring out how to be apart. Not together."

Brendan was shaking his head before he realized he was doing it. Every part of him rejected the idea that he and Katie weren't two halves of a single whole.

Dr. Meyer didn't press the point, just gave Brendan a few moments with his thoughts while she stood and rearranged some gauze pads and sterile wipes in her first aid kit. Her activity reminded Brendan that he couldn't linger. The group would be on the road again soon; he needed to pack and hopefully find something to eat from the hotel's breakfast spread. Regardless of what was going on in his head.

He took a deep breath and stood up. "Hey, thanks for the," he said, gesturing generally at his face. "And for the words of wisdom."

"Anytime. But please figure this out, you're killing me here."

Brendan hardly heard her as he shuffled out of the room and back down the hall to his own. He had too much to think about as he threw his things together quickly. At this point he barely needed to be conscious to find his phone, unplug his chargers, zip his costumes back in their bag, and kneel on the floor beside the bed to make sure nothing had gotten misplaced underneath it. As he went through the familiar motions a cold, unpleasant knot settled in the pit of his stomach. Figure out how to be without Katie? Impossible. It would be like figuring out how to be without half of his soul.

By the time he hauled his bags down to breakfast, the majority of the tour was already there. Lena and David were sharing a newspaper and a plate of scrambled eggs. Justin and Haruka were poking at the waffle maker. Shane was gracefully navigating the closely-packed tables and chairs, three paper cups of coffee held precariously in his hands.

Most of them glanced up when Brendan shuffled in, but he didn't care about whatever interest they were taking in his black eye and the rest of last night's drama. He only had eyes for Katie as his gaze instinctively landed on her.

She was sitting in a corner at a table by herself, her headphones on, and a mostly empty plate in front of her. She had pulled her sleeves over her hands as if already anticipating the chill of the rink, and her damp hair hung around her shoulders. Brendan couldn't help remembering last night; he could almost feel her hands in his hair again, her mouth against his own. There was so much potential between them. Why was it so hard to make things work?

As if feeling his eyes on her, Katie glanced up. She didn't smile or nod in greeting, but the gesture wasn't necessary; Brendan could read the recognition in her eyes, along with sadness, unease, and a cautious hesitation. For so long words had been unnecessary between them. Years had seemingly passed without him ever needing to ask her how she was. He knew by the angle of an eyebrow, the pressure of her hand in his, the tension in her back when he grabbed her for a lift.

But maybe that was part of the problem. Certainly, if Brendan wanted something between them to change, he was going to have to start communicating differently. He crossed the room to her.

"D'you mind if I sit here?" he asked, reaching for, but not touching, the back of the chair opposite Katie. He knew he sounded awkward, but this was an awkward situation.

"No. Of course not." She took off her headphones and tucked them into her bag, but then moved her bag off the chair beside her. That unspoken invitation was louder than her spoken one had been.

Brendan circled around the table and dropped into the seat, Dr. Meyer's words ringing in his head. The worst part was that he couldn't dismiss them completely. He wanted to, desperately. But maybe she was right. Maybe he and Katie weren't destined for the happily ever he had always assumed they would, somehow, achieve.

He'd known for years that his and Katie's relationship was not typical or, by other people's standards, healthy. They sublimated anything they might have wanted from each other and left it all out on the ice. That relationship had worked for them, gloriously, but it had done so in a context that no longer existed. With the Olympic gold medal behind them, it was entirely possible that he and Katie had already been as close as they ever would be.

But Brendan was as capable of wanting things and working for them as she was. He was just better at it when he was with her. If they ended up falling apart – for whatever reason in whatever way – it wasn't going to be because he hadn't tried.

"I'm sorry about last night," he said, his mouth tucked low to Katie's ear so no one else could hear.

Katie gave him a sideways sort of smile. "I imagine you are. Did Leo yell at you?"

"A little. Probably less than I deserved. He said he's also going to tell Tyler off for being a skeevebucket."

Katie grinned more broadly at that. "Good." But then her smile faded, and she looked away from Brendan and stared at the juice machine instead. "What you said last night...."

"I said a lot of things last night."

"When you said you wished you could hate me. If it would make things easier."

Brendan bit his lip. Of course Katie had latched onto that line.

"Did you mean it?" Katie asked. Her voice was small. "Honestly?"

Katie folded her arms across herself. "I sure don't want anything but honesty from you."

"Yeah. I meant it." Brendan reached a hand out and closed it around one of hers. Gently, he peeled her arm away from her body so that he could fold their fingers together under the cover of the table. "But I don't hate you. God. Far from it. I really hope you know that."

Katie nodded but didn't say anything.

Brendan swallowed and made himself go on. "There are a lot of things we have to talk about. Probably sooner rather than later. Because I think Leo's going to throw us off the tour if we do what we did last night again."

Katie scoffed, her shoulders straightening and her tone lightening. "No way. Our box office draw is too good."

"That's kind of what I think too, but I didn't want to say it."

Katie jabbed her elbow lightly into his side. "You're a jerk."

"You started it."

"Okay, we're both jerks." Katie gave him a small, tentative smile.

They were both so good at deflecting and running from this thing. On any other day, Brendan would have let the conversation go at that. Katie was smiling at him. Their tension had, for the moment, dissipated, and they would be able to get the work done. For so long that had been all that mattered.

But not anymore. Brendan squeezed her fingers. "I want us to have a conversation about what we're doing and what we both want and what we're going to do about it. But I also don't want to have it in a hotel lobby with half our friends watching us."

The smile faded slowly from Katie's face, but in its place she fixed Brendan with an intent look. "Okay. Yeah. Of course."

"Good. Okay. Now." Brendan pulled out his phone. "We've got half an hour before the bus leaves and an episode of that makeover show to finish. If you want?"

"Absolutely." Katie sounded relieved, though whether that was because she felt reassured that Brendan didn't hate her or because they had postponed more drama, Brendan wasn't sure.

Katie offered her headphones, and Brendan plugged them into his phone, taking the right while she took the left. As the opening credits of the show started, he felt Katie breathe deeply beside him. Then she nestled her head onto his shoulder.

From a few tables away, Natalya glanced at them angrily. "You two are not even going to talk? You are so boring."

Brendan felt the exhale of Katie's breath when she laughed. He really hoped they could fix this. Life without Katie was incomprehensible.

9

Later that Day

Somewhere on the Road Between Portland, OR and Sacramento, CA

Katie sat and stared out the window at the landscape as the bus rolled down the highway. Today was a travel day, not a performance one, for which she was grateful. She couldn't stretch on the bus as much as she wanted, but at least her knee got a break. With some time before she had to be on the ice with Brendan again, she could work on regaining her equilibrium.

Not that she was avoiding Brendan. If she had wanted to, such a thing wasn't possible on a bus with a dozen other people. He was sitting next to her right now, his laptop open on his knees as he worked on yet more modifications to their Harbin free skate.

He was quieter than usual. Much quieter. Normally when he was working he wouldn't shut up about his ideas, but today he sat with his headphones on, his shoulders a little slumped, listening to the same twenty seconds of music over and over again and writing and deleting the same block of choreography. Even Katie's anxiety couldn't interpret that as anger towards herself; she knew Brendan too well. He wasn't upset. He was sad.

If Brendan were another man Katie might interpret that as a subtle sort of guilt-tripping, indirect puppy eyes to make her feel bad for kissing him and then running away…again. But Brendan was sweet, and he was decent. Whatever was bothering him was surely rooted in the larger complexity of their situation.

So she didn't ask. Any conversation he hadn't wanted to have at breakfast, he wouldn't want to have here. Besides, she wasn't ready. She wasn't sure she would ever be ready. To put words to this thing between them – words that were planned and not shouted in the heat of the moment – was terrifying. Katie hated uncertainty, and she had no idea where such a conversation would lead them. Her life didn't make sense without competitive skating or without Brendan. Competitive skating was already gone. What would happen without him?

Katie closed her eyes and rested her head against the back of her seat. Those questions had kept her up all last night, spinning through her mind while her exhausted body had refused to sleep. If only she could catch up on shut-eye now, but the seats were too uncomfortable, her leg twinged intermittently, and Andrej and David were watching a hockey game in the row behind her.

She shifted restlessly in her seat. The sound of Brendan's typing stopped, and she felt his hand come to rest gently on her leg. She could hear the sound of his breathing, soft but distinct over the chatter of the bus, as his thumb traced soft circles over her knee.

◆

Katie woke up to the lurch of the bus pulling into the hotel parking lot.

"Are we here already?"

Brendan was standing in the aisle, sliding his laptop into his bag on the luggage rack. "If by 'already' you mean 'six hours later,' yes." He smiled, but there was anxiety in his eyes.

Katie didn't want to deal with what needed dealing with, but she also wished they could rip the band-aid off before the tension in her chest ratcheted up any higher. But there was too much to be done for the tour first. They barely had an hour at the hotel to drop off luggage and change clothes before they had to get back on the bus for the venue. They needed to get a feel for the ice and to run through the group numbers.

At practice Katie was, for once, relieved they didn't have anything particularly difficult to work on. As they skated through the pairs number with David and Lena, Brendan was quiet and distant, leading her to wonder whether he was upset with her after all. How much had he meant it, when he said she treated him like a prop to her own career? Did she do that? When it came to skating they needed to be together. That was a fact. Everything else was just logistics. And if Katie had ever pushed Brendan brutally – and she knew she had – he had always pushed her just as much.

She only snapped out of her own head when she and Brendan were both so distracted they nearly ran into David and Lena on a simple footwork sequence. *Get it together, Nowacki.* She scolded herself as Brendan apologized for them both.

✦

Thanks to the vagaries of scheduling, dinner that night was a group event. Everyone from the tour gathered around one long table in the hotel restaurant. Brendan slid into the seat next to hers, as he always did. Being left handed brought all sorts of minor annoyances into her life, and bumping elbows with righties while eating was one of them. At least she and Brendan were in sync enough they didn't have repeated collisions with each other.

"All right, team meeting time," Leo announced once everyone had ordered, only to be greeted by a chorus of groans. "Look, it's a dinner meeting or a four a.m. meeting, and I'm happy to get up at four."

The table, mostly, fell silent.

"That's what I thought," Leo said with a smile. "Okay. First. Yume's birthday is next Tuesday, so everyone, be nicer to her than usual. If you all want to celebrate, by all means, but please, no dramatics," he said with pointed glances at Brendan and Tyler.

Both of them looked embarrassed.

Good. They should be, Katie thought. The bruise under Brendan's eye was a little better today, but still definitely a dark purple.

"You should all have the updated practice schedule in your inboxes, and I've got copies here," Leo went on, brandishing a sheaf of papers before handing them to David, who sat next to him, to hand around. "Points of note. Tyler and Natalya, you're now at eight-thirty with the other singles skaters. Lena and David, you're at eleven so you can do media first thing in the morning. Van will be here to pick you and Katie and Brendan up at five."

"I thought we didn't have to do media 'til the day after?" Lena made a face. Katie could sympathize. She'd much rather spend tomorrow morning in the gym until it was time for their practice slot.

"I did too, but the local outlets changed their mind. And a reminder that we're on the road again tomorrow after the show, it's a long damn way to Denver."

Katie tuned the rest of the announcements out as she became aware that Brendan was staring at her with an odd, distracted look on his face.

"What?" Katie whispered.

Brendan shook his head. "Nothing. Just a thought."

She caught him staring several more times during dinner. Every time she looked at him he would smile, a little guiltily, and look away. Which wasn't like him at all.

When the meal was winding down and people were beginning to stand up and leave, Brendan touched the back of her hand lightly. As soon as she turned to him, he withdrew his fingers.

"Come back to my room?" he asked.

"What for?" Her voice was tight.

"To talk. We agreed we should, and after tonight I don't think we're going to have much time for a couple of days."

Katie nodded. So they were doing this now. She stood up, grabbed her sweatshirt off the back of her chair, and followed Brendan.

She knew it was absurd to be nervous about a conversation. Here she was, walking down the hallway with Brendan like it was any other trip they had taken and they were going back to their shared room…except for the utter uncertainty. She had no idea what happened next. And Katie always knew.

"What about Justin?" she asked as they approached Brendan's door. He paused to fish his keycard out of his wallet.

"He's hanging out with Natalya and Yume, I think. I asked him if I could have the room this evening, anyway. So we're good."

"You asked to have the room?" Katie was somewhere between impressed and appalled. "He, and everyone he tells, is going to think we're fucking."

Brendan scoffed. "They know we're not. Really. I promise." He unlocked the door and held it open for her. In Denver, Katie had a key to his apartment; on the road, they usually shared a room. There had never been a need for one of them to let the other in before. Yet here they were.

"Do you want anything to drink?" Brendan asked. "I have water. And uh, whatever came with the coffeemaker."

"We literally just had dinner," Katie said.

"I know. I was trying to be nice."

"Stop. You're making this feel like a first date." Not that Katie had been on many of those. But this – the awkwardness, the not knowing where to sit or where to look – had been a part of all of them, whether with boys or girls.

Brendan shrugged and toed off his shoes. He dropped into a stretch on the floor by the window, working out the kinks of the day, leaving the bed between them.

How many times had they done this? How many times had they come back from a performance or competition or dinner and been helpless to know what to do next? How many times had they busied their bodies with innocent activities – stretching, brushing their teeth, organizing their suitcases – so that they didn't touch each other? Because Brendan was right. They'd been millimeters from fucking for years. The moment on the bus right before they kissed had been singular only because one of them had finally followed through on the sweet, teasing promise they'd been playing with for so long.

Brendan had one leg tucked in, the other stretched out, and he looped his hand easily around that foot. He wore a short-sleeved V-neck shirt. Stretching like this, Katie could see a good deal of the smooth lines of his muscular chest. She swallowed down the desire to run her fingers across his skin there, to pull aside the collar of his shirt and leave bruising bites where no one could see.

Instead, she circled around the end of the bed and sat on the floor opposite him, just out of reach. If touching was an option, she would sooner or later take it. And she couldn't. Not now. Not tonight. Not before they talked.

For a long time, too long probably, neither of them said anything. But Katie wasn't going to break the silence first.

Brendan had asked her here. Let him start.

Brendan switched legs. "It's been a rough couple of days," he finally said.

Understatement. "I know. And to the extent that's my fault, I'm sorry. Especially for kissing you."

"Jesus, don't apologize for that."

"What I mean is, I'm not apologizing for not having sex with you after I kissed you." Because Katie was not ever going to apologize for that to anyone.

"I didn't expect you to."

"Good." Katie nodded.

"Okay. Fine." Brendan matched her impatient tone. "Do you want me to come out and say you've been unbearable and I'm confused? Because I can do that too."

"I think I've been pretty clear."

"Yeah, no," Brendan said. "You've been upset at me and having anxiety about your knee and convinced we're cursed. Which has left me feeling like I'm supposed to guess at – or worse tell you – what you really want."

If I knew what I wanted, this would all be a lot easier. "We are cursed."

"You're giving me nothing to go on here, Kate."

"What do you want me to say?"

"I want –" Brendan sighed. "I want you to tell me what you want. If you think there are obstacles to that, then I want us to discuss them."

Katie pulled her knees up to her chest and hugged her arms around them. "I don't know."

"You must know. All you do is know."

Katie laughed bitterly. "I really don't."

Brendan was looking at her earnestly, his chin tucked a little and his green eyes earnest. He was gorgeous, and he was perfect, and he had far too much confidence in her. Someday, probably soon, she would let him down. Which would definitely break her heart. She didn't want to break his, too.

Brendan smiled, disbelieving. "You're Katie Nowacki. You decided when you were nine that we were going to skate together and that we were going to win a gold medal. We did, because you are brilliant and committed and the most ambitious, hard-working, passionate person I have ever had the privilege of knowing."

Katie felt her cheeks heat a little at the praise. Something warm stirred in her stomach. "We're not doing press, you don't have to say nice things for the audience."

"Everything good I have ever said about you is completely, totally, one hundred percent true."

She looked up to see Brendan sitting up too, his posture mirroring hers, his eyes fixed on her face. "God, can you not do that?" she said.

"Do what?"

She turned her face away, resting her cheek on her knees. "Just…look. I don't know."

"Katie." Brendan said her name so softly and with such exasperation she had to look at him again.

"What?"

"It's *me*." Brendan reached across the space between them, offering her his hand.

She took it, twining their fingers together. "Sometimes you do this thing and looking at you is like looking at a part of myself. It messes me up."

"I can't help that," Brendan said, his voice soft. "And, if I'm being honest, I wouldn't if I could. Though if it helps, that's how I feel every time I look at you. I always have."

"That just messes me up more."

"Okay." Brendan squeezed her fingers. "There's one thing I need to know."

Katie focused on their hands again. It was easier than looking at his face. "Okay?"

"Do you not want to be with me. Like…do you not want me to chase you? Because if you don't, if that's not interesting or comfortable or whatever. I swear, I will stop this right now and you will never have to deal with anything of that sort from me again."

"No." Katie shook her head.

"No, you want me to stop, or no, you don't want me to stop?" Brendan pressed.

"Don't stop," Katie blurted, then bit her lip. She hadn't planned to say that. But it was true.

"Okay. But you don't want to be with me?"

"No, I don't." Katie pulled her hand out of his. "Not now. Not…yet."

"Okay," Brendan said again, infinitely patient. "Now, you can be mad at me about this if you want. But when Dr. Meyer was looking at my face, I talked to her about some of this mess. A little. I doubt any of it was news. I mean she's known us for ages."

"You did?" Katie asked suspiciously. They so rarely went outside each other when trying to solve their problems. Which maybe wasn't the best conflict management system, but it was what it was.

"I did. She told me that maybe – just, that maybe – that what we're meant to be doing is learning how to be apart. Not together. That made me wonder if all this drama we've had since Harbin, which you think is the universe jinxing us…. Maybe that's all because we're not meant to be together off the ice at all. Regardless of what either of us want."

"Is that what you think?" Katie couldn't keep the hint of panic out of her voice.

"No. But I also don't want to think that's what's going on, so I'm not trusting my own judgment. In fairness, I needed to put it out there so you could think about it too. That advice wasn't just meant for me."

Katie nodded in acknowledgment. The notion took her breath away, and not in any fashion that was pleasant. While she didn't entirely know how to be with Brendan, the idea of being without him was incomprehensible.

"What do you think?" Brendan asked, almost desperately.

That I don't know how to breathe without you.

"I don't know," she said slowly. "I wanted to be Nowacki and Reid forever. When the only thing we could possibly have was skating, nothing else mattered. And truthfully, I liked the world that way." She looked down and tugged at the short pile of the carpet. "I know that's not the answer you were looking for, but –"

Brendan leaned forward and put a hand to her wrist again. Every cell in her body turned its attention towards him, and whatever she was about to say died on her lips.

"I want the answer that's true, no matter what it is." Brendan's thumb circled her pulse. "Tell me what you want, and I will do everything in my power give it to you."

There were so many things that Katie wanted that were not within Brendan's power to provide. She wanted the noise in her heard to be quieter. She wanted her knee to be more reliable. She wanted never to age, and she wanted to go back to Wisconsin. Mostly, she wanted everything she felt for him to be a solution instead of the massive, ongoing problem it was.

"I want time," she said. It was true, in so many ways. "I also want you to stop thinking about what's possible, or what happens next, instead of what's right here. I know desire has always been the thread that holds us together on the ice and right now, I need you not to do anything or ask anything of me that puts that in peril."

Katie watched as Brendan worked to integrate her words into his reality. It was like criticism from a coach. You took it in and no matter how much it pissed you off, you did what you had to do. Brendan was nothing if not dutiful. Sometimes that made the way they cared for each other even harder.

"Okay." He seemed to gulp for air. Katie understood. She too felt like she was drowning in this conversation. "No making out. No propositions. And no thinking ahead of where we are right now."

"Thank you," she said, but Brendan wasn't done talking.

"I'm going to assume that the next move, if and when there is one, will be yours. But I'm not going looking for it. So you'll need to be clear. Small words, complete sentences, possibly hitting me with a two-by-four clear. Can you do that for me? If and when?"

Katie nodded. She would do anything for him. She just hoped her feelings would ever be that clear about anything.

10

The Local TV Station

Sacramento, CA

Getting up at the crack of dawn because Katie wanted to practice was one thing. Getting up at the crack of dawn for a media appearance after a difficult conversation with her was another. Brendan didn't want to perform for cameras; he wanted to be with her. He wanted to heal her body and her heart and all her fears. But no one could do that, for Katie or anyone else. All he could do was stand by her on her terms.

The studio did have at least one major thing going for it: Coffee. Katie seemed cheerful. If last night's conversation had left her feeling better, he was glad of it. He let himself bask in their easy banter.

Makeup took a little longer than it usually did thanks to his eye. He'd covered the bruise with foundation before he left the hotel, but not well enough for TV cameras. He hoped no one asked about it on air. When Katie, seated in the chair next to his, reached out to take his hand – as she'd done hundreds of times for the endless appearances they'd done like this – it seemed like the most natural thing in the world. Brendan exhaled and let himself sink into it.

By the time they were seated at the news desk with the hosts, he was enjoying himself. Brendan loved talking about their sport, loved sharing his passion with everyone watching at home, and loved doing anything at all with Katie. The hosts ate it up when he and Katie bantered back and forth on camera, teasing each other gently and finishing each other's sentences. Brendan knew Katie struggled to be gregarious – she hated to be on camera unless she was skating – but no one watching her could ever tell.

"So, now that the Olympics are over, can you give us any hint about what's coming next for you?" one of the hosts, a woman with her blonde hair styled in a sleek bob, asked.

Katie brushed a lock of her own hair behind her ear. "We're really excited, there's a lot of opportunities out there for us. But right now we're focusing on the tour and taking things one day at a time."

The other host was a man in a suit with a checked tie and a pocket square that didn't match. Brendan and Katie would have commented on that unfavorably had he been on one of the makeover shows they liked to watch.

"Now that the Olympic pressure is off, you must have a little more time for fun," he said. The question was conspicuously leading, but Brendan knew better than to give him what he was looking for.

"A little," Brendan said. "We've gotten to do some sightseeing while we've been on the road. And we get to sleep later than we used to."

"Brendan found a really cute bar in Portland," Katie put in. "It had shuffleboard."

If she had meant for Brendan to be offended by that little dig, she had failed. He knew he deserved it. Also, it was funny.

Undeterred by their dodge, the first host said, with an eager look on her face, "Since you're America's sweethearts, I have to ask. Are either of you seeing anyone right now?"

Brendan held his breath. There was no great secret to keep, but it was such a mess of a question. For a moment he was angry at how intrusive it was, but then he looked over at Katie. He watched as she gave a broad, playful smile that didn't reach her eyes.

"I don't think I understand the question," she said, making it clear she meant exactly the opposite. "I see a lot of Brendan if that's what you mean." The hosts laughed and exchanged meaningful looks. "Other than that, no."

The interviewer gave a knowing smile and looked at Brendan. "And you?"

If Katie thought playing this game was a good idea, who was he to ruin the fun? "A gentleman doesn't kiss and tell."

The words had seemed immensely clever in the moment before he said them, but once they were out of his mouth, Brendan wanted to bury his face in his hands. What he had said had far more specific implications than the way Katie had threaded the needle of that question.

You, Reid, are a human disaster, he thought.

Behind the desk, Katie gently kicked his ankle. Apparently she agreed.

✦

Despite the early-morning media horrors, the rest of the day went well enough. During rehearsal Katie didn't seem on edge. She even suggested they try out more of the modifications to the Harbin program Brendan had been working on.

Brendan was both surprised and relieved; those changes were usually anathema to her, which meant he rarely got the opportunity to test them out. Whatever shift their conversation last night had brought about, they were moving forward, together, as he always wanted to be.

That good feeling continued through that night's performance. They nailed their own routines and during the group numbers Katie was playful and energetic beyond what the performance required.

That good mood faded – for them and everyone else – after the show when he and the rest of the tour gathered outside the venue to board their bus. This was an overnight drive, so it should have been a sleeper bus, with bunks. Except there were no bunks.

"Why is it all seats?" Natalya asked.

Leo looked somewhere between miserable and resigned. "The back axle of the bus we were supposed to get cracked in half. Due to a long series of screwups which are entirely out of my – or apparently the bus company's control – there are no other buses with bunks."

Natalya folded her arms over her chest. "So we have this?"

"'Fraid so," Leo said.

Justin looked around as he climbed on board. "How are we supposed to sleep?"

"Badly," Shane said.

"Do we think the luggage rack could support my weight?" Yume mused. "Because that's like a bunk."

Brendan looked at Katie. "Separate seats or joint seats?"

"Joint," she said immediately.

Brendan sighed in relief, grateful for the logistical solution and their newfound equilibrium. That would make tonight marginally less unpleasant than it could be.

Most the girls could lay down across two seats and possibly be intermittently comfortable. But he was tall and broad and wouldn't fit. Even Katie likely wouldn't have much luck. She was tall for a skater and the tallest woman on the tour. The best they could hope to do was lean on each other.

"This sucks," Katie grumbled as they got underway. She had her knees tucked up to her chest and her shins pressed against the back of the seat in front of her.

"I agree," Brendan said. "Strenuously."

"I'm going to hurt all over tomorrow. Hell, I hurt all over now."

"Is that your knee, or just…everything?"

Katie side-eyed him. "Everything. Definitely everything."

Good. The last thing Katie needed was anything to aggravate her injury.

For a few minutes she looked out the window in silence, the lights along the highway playing across her face. "I wish we were going to any other city but Denver." She spoke so quietly Brendan could hardly hear her.

"Why's that?"

"A hometown show and our official retirement announcement are going to be hard enough without a night like this."

✦

As uncomfortable as they were, at least he and Katie had each other. David and Lena were making do very much the same way, with David leaning against the window and Lena leaning against him. The rest of the tour was faring somewhat worse. Natalya and Haruka were doing competitive stretches in their seats and quickly verging into Cirque du Soleil territory. Natalya was multitasking that with facetiming her mom's new puppy. Towards the back of the bus, an initially friendly argument between Tyler and Shane about video games was growing snappish and unpleasant.

"Okay," Katie finally said, pulling out her phone and unlocking it. "If nobody's getting any sleep anyway…."

She put on one of their warm-up playlists, the one with

European electropop they used when they were dragging and unhappy.

"Really? This?" Brendan rolled his head sideways to look at her. "It's one in the morning. What are you doing?"

Katie grinned and nudged his knees. He had to stand so she could get out of their row, but she didn't slip away. Instead, she stood right in front of him so they were toe-to-toe. "Come and dance with me."

"In the bus aisle," Brendan said, amused.

"We've danced in stranger places," Katie offered.

"I'm not sure that's true." They'd hardly danced at all since they'd broken up after Annecy. Pair skating was arguably a form of dancing, but on the ice there were rules to follow and a job to do, which kept their mutual desire within bounds. Moving together on a dancefloor involved skirting real danger. They'd tried to avoid it.

"Amsterdam," Katie said. "The night the canals froze."

"That was a good night." That had been two years before Annecy, when all their mutual tension had still been entirely unspoken.

"And not just 'cause we won Worlds the next day." Katie gave him a coy smile that made his stomach flip.

"David and Lena's wedding," he said. "In the kitchen at that cabin everyone was staying in."

"Oh God. That was a wild night. You know, I never did find the shoes I lost."

Brendan grinned and cast back in his memory for another time. Katie found it first.

"In the —" She cut herself off.

But Brendan's brain had already completed the sentence for her. *In the shower.* They'd been dating then, if whatever crazed mess of sex and frenzied emotional confessions they'd been doing for those few brief weeks after Annecy counted as dating. They'd come back to Brendan's apartment from practice, sweaty, exhausted, and keyed up and had taken their argument about some piece of choreography right into the shower. Katie had demonstrated exactly what kind of intimacy she wanted them to portray on the ice. The hickeys across his collarbone had taken a week to fade.

Here and now, Brendan could see the look of horror on Katie's face. Not at the past, but at the profound inconvenience of knowing both of them were picturing the same moment.

"That tiny awful bar in Toronto, when our flight to Tokyo got cancelled," Brendan offered. They hadn't really danced, but there might have been some vague swaying and a lot of complaining. It did, however, serve to move the conversation along, which was the right thing to do.

"I'd forgotten that," Katie said. "Thank you."

"You're welcome."

"Now come on!"

Brendan watched as Katie turned from him and walked down the aisle, holding onto seatbacks to keep her balance, game face on. When bad situations didn't freak her out completely this was what she did: make the best of it, without acknowledging that the situation was rotten to begin with. It made her a good team player, but, as Brendan had learned over and over again, could make her impossible to pin down when there was a problem that needed solving one-on-one.

He watched, torn between amusement, concern, and a desire to pull her into his arms as she danced the rest of the way up the aisle, grabbed Shane's hand, and pulled him out of his seat.

"Hey, can we get some mood lighting back here?" Katie shouted.

"Only if you can make sure we avoid a personal injury lawsuit!" Dr. Meyer called back.

Despite that admonition, the lights overhead went out. Brendan waved his phone around in a pathetic attempt to simulate club lights.

"Give me that. You're doing it wrong," Natalya said, hanging up her call with the puppy and snatching Brendan's phone away from him.

She held her own glowing phone in one hand and Brendan's in the other as she waved her arms around rapidly, curling and twisting her wrists.

"Like glow sticks, see?" she said as she continued the show.

Katie laughed in delight and worked on getting everyone else onto their feet. David picked Lena up and twirled her around in the tiny space the bus aisle allowed. Tyler stood and offered his hand gallantly to Yume. Brendan watched in awe as Katie transformed the moment from a desperate attempt to keep people happy to one of genuine joy.

"Is the plan to be so annoying they get us a better bus?" Justin asked as he got to his feet.

"The plan," Katie declared, "is to not be miserable."

All the other skaters were dancing around her now, but Katie was not satisfied. "That means everyone," she called out.

Brendan wanted to join in because it would make her happy, but the whole situation felt like a pile of bad decisions waiting to happen.

She walked back down the aisle to him, weaving between the other skaters, and held out her hand. "Even you."

Brendan couldn't refuse her. With a deep breath he took her hand and waded into the crowded mess at the center of the bus. He had to duck so as to not get hit in the face by his own phone which was still a very active part of Natalya's dance routine.

"Better," Katie said with an approving nod.

He stood there awkwardly, not sure how to take the next, obvious step. But she was right. This – the bus situation and everyone's attitude, but also his own heart –

was better. He loved Katie, and he didn't have her, but they were still together. It wasn't the world as he wanted it, but it was good, even if it never changed. She was miraculous.

"We're going to be exhausted by the time we get to Denver," he said.

"We were going to be exhausted anyway." Katie shrugged.

"That's true," he said. "That's fair." Sometimes it was hard not to repeat himself nervously in front of her, even after all these years. She was just so much. "I guess I'm supposed to dance, but...."

He trailed off. Her own dancing slowed as if in time to the words leaving him. So much remained that could not be healed by this moment. Not Katie's knee, not his sadness, not the uncertainty of their future. Neither he nor Katie knew how to fix any of it. But they had, despite everything, each other. They could, he hoped, figure this out.

Something on his face must have given away the roil of emotions within him, because suddenly Katie frowned, and stepped into his arms.

"I know," she said. "I know."

✦

The bus reached the outskirts of Denver as the sun was coming up. Most of the tour would get a chance to catch a couple hours' sleep in an actual bed, but after a shower and a change of clothes Brendan and Katie were back at work.

Brendan only briefly regretted that they'd elected to stay at the hotel with the rest of the tour rather than their own homes. He really would have liked a little time alone with Katie far, far away from skating, except, of course, his gold medal from Harbin hung on the wall in his living room with all his other medals.

His apartment also had absolutely no food in it, and

Katie had sublet her room while they were travelling. So however odd the choice, hotel it was. But the hotel was far from the most bizarre thing about being in Denver.

No, the most bizarre thing was that their plan to officially announce their retirement from competitive skating had somehow turned into them being presented a key to the city by Denver's mayor.

"I can't believe we had to give up breakfast at our diner for this," Katie muttered, adjusting her sunglasses against the glare. The mayor was giving them a speech welcoming them back and congratulating them on their Olympic win.

"You, as you so often remind me, are the one who wanted to win the most," Brendan retorted. There was no bite in the words. It felt like old times, standing shoulder to shoulder with Katie against cameras and absurdity. "And since we won, the consequences of winning are that people like to take pictures of us. Smile and look grateful."

"I am grateful," she insisted. "But I also really wanted pancakes. Everyone already knew we were retiring anyway." Katie leaned against him, just for a moment.

Brendan was glad she was able to make light of the event. Even he had mixed feelings about making their retirement official. One era of their life may have been coming to an end, but as absurd and exhausting as the bus ride – and Katie's impromptu dance party – had been, it had loosened something between them.

He tuned back in to the mayor's speech in time to hear him thank them for the tourism boost they would provide the city. Brendan didn't think that was true at all. People would come to Denver for the reasons they always came to Denver – skiing, corporate conferences, and legal weed.

He chanced another glance over at Katie. She was smiling, but a muscle in her jaw twitched. She was definitely thinking the same things and, like Brendan, was also trying not to laugh. She turned towards him. Brendan had never been so happy for sunglasses; had he been able to see her eyes, he would have lost it right there.

"Don't make me laugh," he whispered to her.

"Why not?" she asked through her clenched teeth.

"Because everyone's going to think we're high if we're up here trying to stifle giggles."

"I hate you," she hissed.

"You don't."

"I wish I did!"

The words were eerily similar the ones they'd exchanged after their stairwell fight in Portland, but the mood couldn't have been more different. The giggles were starting to slip out of both of them now, despite their best efforts. For a moment Brendan wondered how to cover this – kissing Katie quiet was absolutely out of the question – but she, always media savvy, faked a coughing fit.

Brendan patted her hard on the back, like he was trying to be helpful and wasn't in as bad shape as she was.

"You're a mess," he said.

Katie quieted herself and stood straight again. "Yeah," she said, slipping her hand into his. "But I'm your mess."

11

Before the Show Katie Is Even More Nervous About Than Usual

Denver, CO

Performing on home ice was hard for Katie. The show wasn't at their rink of course, but they were back in their chosen city, performing for a crowd that had rooted for them since she was sixteen. These people had shown up to watch her and Brendan at gala events and tour performances for more than a decade, including through defeat, while they were with other partners, when they were attempting their comeback, and now, finally, in victory. Katie would be grateful to them forever and desperately wanted not to let them down. She changed into her first costume, did her makeup and sat while Brendan did her hair with more nerves than usual.

To her relief, that nervous energy sharpened her skating rather than caused mistakes. Being under the spotlights with the audience cheering wildly for them felt good. After their heart-to-heart and that absurd yet strangely lovely dance party on the bus, everything was working. There was enough unspoken desire between them to make everything flow beautifully, but not enough brittle anger to make their edges shallow or throw their timing off.

"I don't know how you guys do it," David said as he, Lena, Katie, and Brendan stepped back into the tunnel after the joint pairs number. "You two skate so close, I always think you're going to crash. But you're always perfect."

"We are, aren't we?" Brendan winked at Katie, ruining the moment entirely.

She was glad. Otherwise, she would have been tempted to step closer to him, wrap her arm low around his waist, and lean her head on his shoulder. While that would have felt wonderful, it wouldn't have been helpful.

Katie had asked Brendan for time, and he had granted it so graciously. But she wasn't a fraction of the way closer to knowing what to do when this whole thing was over.

✦

After the closing number Katie rushed back to the dressing rooms, put on a short-sleeved black dress Brendan had helped her pick out and touched up her makeup. Transitioning from performance mode to social mode was a challenge no matter how many times Katie had done it.

Brendan met her again in the hallway outside the dressing rooms. He looked model-perfect, as he always did for these things. His dress shirt was open at the collar with one more button unfastened than strictly necessary, his jeans showed off his backside to excellent advantage, and his hair looked artfully tousled instead of what it really was: sweaty and standing on end because he kept running his hands through it.

"Hey," he said. "How are you doing?"

"Honestly? Pretty jumpy." Meet and greets made her nervous. These were people who needed things from her.

While those things were theoretically small and easy to give, there were often vitally important to receive. Katie didn't want to screw it up.

"Why? We've done this a million times before."

"True. But it's Denver."

"Yeah," Brendan said, nodding thoughtfully. "I get that."

"I don't understand why people come to these things," she said as they walked to the room that had been set up for the meet and greets.

"Why not?" Brendan asked curiously. "People like watching us on the ice, and they like meeting people who do stuff they like."

"I get why people pay to watch us skate. I get why people want to meet us too, but autographs? A handshake? Awkwardly posed photos?" She always felt like her understanding of this particular part of her job was just out of reach.

"You never wanted to meet your heroes when you were a kid?"

Katie shook her head. "Not like this. I wanted to meet them on the ice. As competitors."

When she was little there had barely been money for ice time and lessons and coaching. There certainly hadn't been money to shake anyone's hand. She would do that when she arrived. And eventually she had.

Now, she and Brendan had to spend the next hour standing together, smiling and shaking hands and saying thank you for the endless gifts of stuffed animals that would get donated to a children's hospital at the end of the evening. Katie asked little girls about their best jumps, their fastest spins, and the rabbit fur jackets – some synthetic, but too many not – that were de rigueur for the under-twelve skating set.

Most of them would do something interesting and satisfying with their lives, but likely none of them would ever do this. They'd never get the kind of adventures Katie had enjoyed – but they also would get to escape the terrible days, the injuries, the obsessing over scores, and the brutal insecurity.

At least Brendan was having fun. Katie smiled to herself as he signed a young boy's skates, chatting with him about the struggle of choosing figure skating when his friends had all chosen hockey. Brendan would make a good coach. He was personable and charming; of the two of them, he reliably knew what to say to people.

Like when a girl and a boy – Katie thought they might have been thirteen – asked him what his and Katie's secret to success was. Katie never knew how to answer that question without sounding smug or defensive. But Brendan looked between them and smiled.

"You guys a pair?"

The two nodded.

"Do the work, every day. Don't hate yourself if you screw up, because you will. Out there, on the ice, you're your own worst enemy." He glanced over at Katie as he said it.

"A little on the nose there, yeah?" She smiled to take out the sting. She had no desire to fight with Brendan right now, but his words had, she knew, been meant for her as much as for the kids.

"I'm not wrong," he said.

I know you're not. But easier said than done.

"He forgot the most important thing, though," Katie told the kids, with a sidelong glance at Brendan to make sure he was listening. "Find a partner you trust with your life. Even when it's hard. Even when you're not getting along. Find someone you can't imagine skating without. And keep them."

The kids exchanged glances at that, startled and shy. Katie wondered if she should look away; the light bulbs going off over their heads weren't meant for anyone else to see.

They all made small talk for a few more moments, but Katie continued to watch as they walked away. When they reached the doors, their hands slipped into each other's.

"Remind you of anyone?" Brendan asked.

They did, painfully so. She remembered being that age, angry and ambitious and so insecure. She'd been sure of only two things: Brendan and that they were going to win everything together.

"We did not have our shit that much together at that age."

"That's for sure." Brendan slung his arm around Katie's shoulders and squeezed her into his side. "But we figured it out."

We figured out how to win, yes. The rest of it? I'm not so sure.

◆

Staying at the hotel instead of their own homes had been a perfectly reasonable logistical choice, but a less reasonable emotional one. They were in Denver. They should have been hanging out in Brendan's living room, eating cookies from their favorite bakery and gossiping about everyone on the tour. Instead, after the show, they took the van with everyone else back to the hotel. The group stood around the lobby talking until Leo reminded them how early the bus was leaving in the morning. People started to trickle upstairs to their rooms. Brendan and Katie took the elevator up to their floor but then kept talking outside of the elevator bank.

Katie didn't want to leave him yet. Brendan didn't seem to want to go either.

But eventually, he checked the time on his phone and looked at her. "It's almost one in the morning."

Twenty-four hours ago they'd had their dance party on the bus. It felt like a year ago. A very good year, after a string of bad ones.

"So much for getting a decent night's sleep in a real bed," Katie said ruefully.

Neither of them made a move to leave. Which wasn't good. They were either going to have to say goodnight and go their separate ways, or accept that they couldn't. Which would mean crashing together in one bed. Which would be a terrible choice.

Probably.

Before Katie could talk herself further out of – or into – a bad decision, Brendan took a step forward. Katie's heart pounded loudly in her chest. Adrenaline made her limbs feel suddenly cold. Were they going to do this?

"Goodnight, Katie," Brendan said, his voice warm in her ear. He gave her a hug.

Katie could only barely return it. "Goodnight," she replied automatically. Disappointment and embarrassment made her face burn. Of course they weren't going to go to bed together – platonically or otherwise. She'd asked for space and time to think, and Brendan was giving it to her.

She felt him press a kiss to the top of her head before he turned and walked down the hallway to his room. Katie dug in her jacket pocket for her room key so she didn't have to watch him go. *God, what is wrong with me?*

Natalya was already asleep, or at least lying in bed with an eye mask on and her headphones in, when Katie slipped into their room. She was glad. She couldn't have faced her right now.

She toed off her shoes and dug pajamas out of her suitcase, then shut herself in the bathroom. She was too wired to sleep and desperately needed a shower.

Under the spray, Katie tipped her head back, letting the hot water massage her scalp and pound over her aching muscles. The bathroom was pristine white tile, stocked with anonymous shampoo and soap. The whole room was anonymous, with no history and no future. Katie wanted to be somewhere she had both. She wanted to be at Brendan's apartment, taking a shower there because they had dinner plans after practice and it was easier than going to her own place. She wanted the familiar gray and green tile and the little details that made the place a home. His bathrobe on the back of the door. Her spare hairdryer on the counter.

Brendan had asked her if she wanted to move in once, a year after they'd started skating together again. Not, he had hastened to say, as any kind of romantic gesture, but because he had the room and it would be less unpleasant for her than staying in a house with a bunch of other skaters. Besides, she slept on his couch half the time anyway.

All of which was true. But Katie had flatly – and in retrospect, not very kindly – refused. She was still sure that had been the right decision. But she sometimes wished it hadn't been and that she had chosen differently. Like this moment, right now.

Katie gasped and shuddered. Her eyes stung, and not because she'd gotten shampoo in them. She was crying.

She wrapped her arms around herself and turned to face the spray so that it poured over the front of her body, across her chest and down her thighs. She was tired, and lonely, and homesick in the middle of the only city she'd ever come close to loving. She wanted Brendan to be here, his arms wrapped around her instead of her own.

You're just tired, she told herself. *Being on the road sucks. Touring is exhausting. Your knee hurts. Of course you're miserable.*

All of that was true. But none of it was the point.

✦

The next few days were uneventful, at least by touring standards. Off the ice she and Brendan were what they'd always been: Best friends. Seatmates. Dinner companions. But they sat too close. Held hands. Traced each other's fingers when they were lying side by side on a bed in Shane and Andrej's room, watching a movie with everyone. It was maddening, confusing, and absolutely delicious.

They weren't sublimating everything anymore. Somehow, that made the desire that they brought to their performances burn even brighter.

Maybe being together wouldn't be the end of skating, she thought one day at rehearsal, watching Brendan goof around on the ice with Natalya. *Maybe we could still make it work.* It wasn't like she would stop wanting Brendan once she'd slept with him. Desire didn't go away; it transformed.

✦

Somewhere on the road between Chicago and Philadelphia, Brendan and Katie were the only two people awake, lying in bunks across the aisle from each other. They'd started taking advantage of these quiet moments when everyone else was asleep to be together. Now that they weren't road roommates, they had so little time that was just the two of them.

"What would you think of me doing more of our choreography?" Brendan asked.

Katie shifted to get more comfortable on her side. These bunks were terrible. "You're already doing it. It's not like we're adding new numbers to the tour at this point."

"I don't mean for the tour. Not this tour, at least. I was thinking for ours. Or just…whatever else we do." Brendan tucked his knees up closer to his chest. He was wearing basketball shorts and an old T-shirt. Katie wished she could press her forehead against the soft cotton, warm with the heat from his body.

"You feel ready to do that?" she asked in lieu of being able to touch him.

"Honestly? Yeah. I mean, it seems terrifying. But if this

is something I want to do, I have to actually do it."

"But what would you do it for? We don't have another season coming up."

"We don't," Brendan said slowly, like he thought she was being dense. "But we have our tour coming up. And then...whatever happens after that. Before we know it we're going to be in New York dealing with all those meetings. So I want to be prepared. Or at least have some idea about what our next programs might look like."

Our next programs. The words were thrilling. Katie had loved this point in all their other seasons. The anxiety about competing hadn't kicked in yet, and for a few weeks she could simply enjoy working and planning with Brendan. Except they weren't going to compete again. Ever.

"Can I show you what I have in mind?" Brendan asked, when Katie didn't say anything else.

"Sure."

Brendan handed her his phone open to the music app. "First two tracks."

Katie glanced at the screen. "These are good songs."

"I know. Listen to them." When Katie put one of the earbuds in, he went on. "Okay, so here's what I'm thinking...."

He's being so incredibly kind, Katie thought. *So generous.* For her, tour programs could never match the excitement and satisfaction of competition programs. But while she struggled to be more than her dodgy knee and her anxiety, Brendan was trying so very hard to remind her that they could still do so much together. Even if it wasn't what they most wanted.

That thought, as much as her enjoyment of the songs and Brendan's ideas, made her smile. Brendan's mood seemed to lift as she did so. They always were so in sync with each other.

"Do you ever wish," Brendan asked, taking back his phone and scrolling through it to find the song he wanted her to listen to next, "that we had one more season in us?"

Katie squinted at Brendan. "I don't know how to answer that question."

"What do you mean?"

"I mean…of course I want another season. I love this. I don't know what else I could possibly do with my life." Katie paused to try to gather her thoughts. "But also…we won. Once, and gloriously. For a whole five minutes we were the best in the world. We can't replicate that. And it would break my heart to compete again, on Olympic ice, and lose."

"Second place isn't losing, Katie," Brendan said, as if silver or gold were the only possible outcomes for them.

"It would feel like it." No matter how many times she'd put on a game face for the cameras and talked about how pleased she was with their work and their performance, any time they'd come in anything but first she'd felt like a failure, unworthy of anything.

"Seventeenth place didn't feel like losing."

"Are you kidding me?" Katie asked. She remembered her own devastation, watching his short skate and seeing his scores. She reached her hand across the aisle that separated them, as if she could reach through the years and hold his hand on that miserable day too. "You didn't even make it to the free skate."

Brendan closed his hand around hers. "I mean, that part sucked. But we were so far down the list, it hardly hurt. If we'd been closer, like you, I think…. No, I know. It definitely would have felt worse. As it was, I got to go to the Olympics. It's what we dreamed of since we were kids. It was incredible."

"We'd already been to the Olympics," Katie reminded him.

Brendan gave her a scornful look. "It's not the kind of thing that gets old."

"I was so nervous, that first time, I thought I was going

to die." The memory of that anxiety – it had bordered on terror – could still stop her as she walked down the street.

He smiled fondly. "I know. I remember."

Of course he did. Brendan was well-acquainted with her anxiety. After all, he'd grown up right alongside it. In many ways, he accepted it as part of who she was better than she did herself.

Katie looked down at their hands, twined in the dark over the gulf between their bunks. "For what it's worth, you did make it better."

Brendan's fingers twitched in hers, almost as if he were embarrassed. "You just needed to let off some steam. Anybody could have done that for you."

"I wasn't talking about the sex." Katie was relieved they could talk about this, that they could joke about it. "Or, well, not only the sex."

"I'm flattered, I think?"

"I mean," Katie said, keeping the tone light and teasing though her stomach churned with nerves at the words. "I didn't sleep with anyone at Stockholm. You slept with everyone."

"Not…actually, everyone," Brendan said slowly, as if he was trying to remember.

Katie remembered all too well. "Your skating partner."

"Yeah, but we were dating, it doesn't count."

"The Italian ice dancer."

"Okay, her, yeah."

"That Canadian skater."

"And her too. Jeez. Did you make a list?" Brendan asked.

"It's not like you were discreet." Katie retorted. They were, for some reason that made no sense given their conversation topic, still holding hands. She didn't want to let go.

Neither, apparently, did Brendan, who was sliding his fingers back and forth through hers. "C'mon, don't judge.

The amount of sex that goes on at the Olympics is legendary. Me and those girls…everyone was clear about what was and wasn't going on."

"I'm not judging."

"Then what are you doing? Why are you bringing it up?" Brendan sounded a little offended. That was fair. They hadn't been dating when they both were at Stockholm. They were still training at the same rink but hadn't even been speaking to each other. And they weren't dating now. His history with anyone who wasn't her was none of her business.

"I'm…wondering." Katie ran her thumb over the back of Brendan's knuckles.

"Wondering what?" Now he sounded curious.

"A lot of things."

"Like?" Brendan asked, drawing the word out lazily.

"Like what it means that you went out and found people to be with when you couldn't be with me."

"You're jealous?"

Katie shook her head slowly. She was, a little, but that wasn't the point. What would it be like, a world in which Brendan finally got tired of her no's and maybe's and I-don't-know's and started dating someone else? What would it be like to have to watch that? Was Brendan capable of being with anyone else – really, fully being with anyone else? She knew he'd had relationships that had foundered over the bond he had with her, even when they hadn't been skating together. Was Katie everything to him, the way he was to her?

"Why didn't you sleep around at Annecy and Harbin?" she asked.

"Well, at Annecy I was in bed with you when I wasn't on the ice. Happily. Ecstatically. And in Harbin I was with you too, just, in front of the cameras."

"Not all the time," Katie said.

"It sure seemed like it," Brendan said. "Also I had a lot

of other stuff to worry about."

"Like what?"

Brendan ran this thumb over the back of her hand. "It was the Olympics. What do you think?"

Katie narrowed her eyes and hummed.

"I'm not lying!" Brendan protested.

"I didn't say you were lying. Just omitting."

"About the sex?" Brendan asked.

"No. About the worrying."

"Well, I don't have to worry about most of those things anymore."

"Really?"

"Got the medal, didn't we?" Brendan said casually, like it had been skating and not their own precarious relationship under discussion.

To her own annoyance, Katie felt a cold weight of disappointment sink in her chest. But what, really, had she expected Brendan to say? That he'd been preoccupied with their off-ice relationship while at the peak of their on-ice careers? She knew he had. He knew she knew. And they'd fairly beaten the subject to death since.

"We should go to sleep," Katie said. She pulled her hand out of Brendan's grasp and rolled to face the far side of her bunk. *I'm the one who told him that we weren't discussing this. Time to not discuss it already.*

✦

The bus arrived in Philadelphia the next day in time for the skaters' official appearance at a 76ers game. Katie didn't understand why they'd been invited; basketball and skating couldn't be farther apart. But a night out was a good break.

"Hey, which of us have ever actually been to a basketball game before?" David asked when they took the bank of seats the team had set aside for them.

Brendan raised his hand. Everyone else stared at him, hands very clearly not raised. Katie resisted the urge to roll her eyes. Of course Brendan would be the one to have spent the time and money watching other people play sports.

"What? Don't you people have lives?" he asked.

"It is called skating and living on a tour bus with you," Natalya said.

Katie was glad, as it stopped her from saying something much sharper to Brendan about what the lives of people who didn't have his privileged upbringing looked like.

"Okay, basketball is easy, how it works is –"

Natalya cut him off. "Don't be condescending. All your failure players come to Russia and are very successful. I know how the game works, I just don't care. But it's nice they brought us here."

Katie laughed. She was glad she'd had the chance to room with Natalya and get to know her a little better. Someone else having Brendan's number, and calling him out on what a good-natured nuisance he could be, was exactly her idea of a good time.

"What sport do you like?" Brendan asked Natalya. *Always so nice.*

"Hockey," she said, lifting her chin, like she expected him to laugh at her. Brendan, of course, did nothing of the sort.

"Because skating?" he asked.

"No. Because fights. Which you are not very good at," Natalya reminded him.

"See, this is a wise woman," Justin said. "Fights would be so much better."

Brendan huffed and, having a lack of actual insults at the ready, called everyone losers.

Katie patted his shoulder. Watching Brendan interact with people who weren't her made her feel more grounded, like maybe someday she, too, could learn how to have a life outside of skating.

"Are you going to make fun of me too?" he asked, turning his puppy dog eyes on her.

She felt incredibly fond of him and laughed. "Only if you want me to."

She rested her head on his shoulder. When the jumbotron zoomed in on their group to recognize the Olympic skaters, she had to restrain the impulse to pull away from Brendan and whatever assumptions people were going to make about the gesture. Physical closeness at a rink was one thing; that was where they lived. But here, in public, invading each other's personal space felt like a statement she wasn't ready to make. Yet, it also felt like one she wanted to make, that it felt right to make. She'd always trusted her gut about skating; maybe it was time to do so about Brendan too.

Twenty thousand people watched live as she waved, but kept her head right where it was. For the first time, maybe ever, that was okay.

Up on the giant screen she saw him glance at her and smile.

12

The Second to Last Day of the Tour

New York, NY

None of the buses broke down again. Neither did Brendan and Katie, but Brendan suspected that was only a matter of time. What they had going now wasn't quite a détente so much as it was an extended game of public edging. They hadn't truly solved anything between them, but Katie seemed willing to be present and figure it out, which was enough for now.

They were in New York City, with only two performances left. Soon, the rest of the skaters would go their separate ways, but he and Katie would stay on here for a week. They had what felt like an overwhelming number of meetings scheduled to discuss opportunities from memoirs to product endorsements to licensing deals.

After the first performance, the entire group went out for a farewell dinner. Everyone was tired, wired, and ready to be done, yet somehow still up for one last bout of camaraderie before the final performance.

They took up the back room at a Chilean restaurant and

ordered a ridiculous amount of food. Brendan sat next to Katie, as he usually did. While he began the night chatting and bantering with the rest of their tour mates, as the night went on, his focus narrowed to Katie.

He didn't have his own inclinations to blame for that, either. At least not solely. Halfway through dinner Katie leaned over to say something to him and put her hand on his leg. Higher than was strictly appropriate, had they been just friends. Higher than she would have a few short months ago.

Brendan folded his hand over hers. To stop her? To question her? To welcome her? He wasn't sure. She tensed slightly, and Brendan's hopes were confirmed. Her gesture had neither been platonic, nor intended to be. Brendan had caught her out. He knew she was afraid, both of her own boldness and of Brendan making them talk about things again. But Brendan loved her boldness and felt no need to press a conversation tonight.

Before she could pull away, he shook his head and wove his fingers through hers. The normalcy of sitting there holding her hand like they were absolutely sure what they were to each other was somehow worth more than responding to her tease and flirtation.

After the restaurant everyone went out to a bar, where there was a lot of hugging and promises to stay in touch and absolutely no fist fights. Tyler and Brendan even shook hands, and Brendan wished him good luck next season. Most of the skaters on the tour would see each other back on the competition circuit, but Katie and Brendan would not be among their number.

Natalya found him and Katie where they were sitting side-by-side and too close at the bar.

"Katie. My surprise roommate. I have something for you."

"You do?" Katie looked confused and flustered. Brendan grinned to himself. He wasn't the only one she didn't know how to accept affection from.

"Do you two want me to give you some girl time?" he asked, getting up out of his seat.

Natalya shook her head. "Oh no. You should see this too," she said before turning back to Katie. "I will miss seeing you at competitions next year. So I got you this."

She handed Katie a small tissue paper-wrapped package. Brendan watched as Katie, looking uncertain, carefully pulled off the tape and unrolled the paper from whatever was inside.

A Russian nesting doll fell into her palm.

Katie smiled. "Thank you, Natalya. It's beautiful."

Natalya scoffed. "That is not the whole thing. I customized it. See, open it."

Katie did, opening each doll in turn and lining them up on the bar. There was something written on each one in gold ink. Katie read them out loud as she went, her cheeks reddening as she did so.

"Stupid boys…bar fights…knee problems…kissing drama…bus falling."

"They are all your woes," Natalya said. "So you can tuck them all up together and keep an eye on them."

Katie threw her head back and laughed. "Thank you," she said, sliding off her bar stool and hugging Natalya. "These are wonderful."

"You're very welcome." Natalya looked pleased. After she let go of Katie, she turned and gave Brendan a hug too. "I will also miss seeing you at competition. But I know that you are one of Katie's woes. So I hope you fix that."

"Me too," Brendan said fervently. "Me too."

After that, Brendan tried to stay engaged in the conversations going on around him, but it was impossible. Katie was too captivating. She had turned on every bit of her charisma, and had focused it all on him.

Brendan was still stunned, twenty years and who knew how many programs later, how much meaning Katie could put into a look, a glance over her shoulder, a flick of her wrist. The chemistry that commentators loved to wax poetic about, the detail that elevated their programs from excellent to superb; none of it had ever been an act. It had always just been them.

God, Brendan wanted her. And tonight, Katie clearly wanted him. That much was crystal clear. She wasn't hitting him with a two-by-four, but she might as well have been.

All right, then.

Back at the hotel, everyone poured into the lobby, exchanging more hugs and shouting goodnight's and I-love-you's to each other. It took a couple of elevators for everyone to get up to the floor their rooms were on. Brendan and Katie hung back by a mutual, unspoken agreement to be among the last upstairs. When they finally reached their floor, Katie started off down the hall towards her room, but Brendan caught her around the waist.

"Just a minute," he said, ignoring Justin's pointed eyeroll as he walked past them.

Katie looked up at him through her eyelashes. "Oh?"

"Wait 'til everyone's gone," he said.

Barely a minute passed before all the doors had banged closed up and down the hallway and they were alone again. It felt like eternity. Once the prying eyes were gone, Brendan took Katie's hands and stepped backwards until he met the wall.

Katie, both bold and uncertain, followed his lead until she was nearly pressed against him. "Now what?" she asked. Her eyes were wide and there was a flush high on her cheeks.

Perhaps all the space between them was finally, permanently, going to disappear. Brendan watched the pulse leap under the skin of her throat. Oh, how he wanted to press his tongue there. His own breath caught in response.

"We said we'd talk about us after the tour," he breathed. He kept his back against the wall. He needed it to stay standing. He needed Katie to come to him.

She put her hands on his shoulders and pressed herself against him. The warmth and feel of her was familiar from a hundred skates and yet was completely different in the here and now.

"The tour's over," he said, his mouth brushing the soft shell of her ear. He wouldn't ask the question, but he needed her to answer it.

"Not yet it's not," she said.

"It might as well be." Brendan ran a hand down her arm. "And we're doing whatever this is." He traced his fingers over her lips, which parted slightly in a small and gorgeous gasp. "But I need you to tell me what's next."

Katie tipped her head back as if she didn't care that they were in public. Brendan ghosted the pad of his thumb over the pale column of her throat.

"Well, there's us, this version of us, at any rate," Katie said. "And there's the next tour. Ours."

"And then?" Brendan was nearly afraid to breathe. Katie, and everything they could be together, was so close.

Katie said, "I don't know."

Brendan pulled away from her slightly, as much as he could anyway with his back to a wall. How could she not know, standing here with him like this, breathing with him here like this? "You don't know?!"

Katie shook her head. Her eyes widened, like that should have been obvious. "I told you before. We had a whole conversation about it."

"Yeah, we talked, and you asked for time to figure things out. Since now we're here, like this, I thought you had?" *Did I misread her*? The possibility was horrifying.

She shook her head again, this time more sharply. "I didn't figure it out."

"Like, you don't have any idea what you want? With

us? With skating? With anything?" Brendan knew he was repeating himself, but he was terrified of getting this wrong.

She fisted her hands in Brendan's shirt and for a moment pressed her forehead to his chest. "How could I? I had one dream, and I got it." She looked up at him beseechingly. "I don't know how to have a second one. Or a third, or a fourth. You keep offering me such beautiful things, all of which I wish I had the courage for, but I don't know how any of them could compare to what we've already done."

Brendan covered her hands with his own, as gently and non-possessively as he could. She rubbed her cheek against the back of his wrists, like she was seeking comfort as much as anything else. Brendan wished he knew how to give it to her.

"We got to the Olympics by making a choice," he said. "We won the gold by making a choice. All you have to do now is decide what you want your life to look like and make a choice."

Katie pressed the most fleeting of kisses to the back of Brendan's hand. "All I ever planned for was winning, Brendan. You know that. That was do or do not do. Now there are all these shades and possibilities and so many more things that could go wrong than losing. I don't know how people do that. I don't know how I'm supposed to do that."

"By being scared and doing things anyway." Brendan had no idea what was happening in Katie's head. She'd always been so determined. So sure. He knew her anxiety made things hard, but he'd assumed – perhaps erroneously – that post-competitive life would be easier on her.

"That's all great and abstract, but like…I don't even know how to get a job!"

"That is definitely your anxiety talking. Jobs are going to come to both of us. People are going to help us. We've got this week of meetings and a ton of opportunities. You have to know if we put the word out we wanted to coach or choreograph...." Brendan tried.

"Don't those meetings scare you? Because they terrify me."

Brendan shook his head. "No. We're good. We're in demand. People who are experts in their work the way we're experts in skating are going to do their best to make sure that benefits all of us."

"But the things we're talking about – it's getting paid to be us. And live some sort of glamorous lifestyle which is the opposite of the reality of skating or the tour bus or the costs and –"

Is that what you think comes next? Brendan thought. *Is that all that you think is left for us? A public life with no private joy? Oh, Katie....*

Brendan tightened his hands around hers. She was, he knew, close to having a panic attack. He didn't have to understand why – hell, she didn't have to understand why – for him to do what he could to help her through it. "Shhh. Shhhhhh. Breathe," he said. "Just look at me and breathe."

She bit her lip and nodded.

"We'll find a way to do what's right for us. We'll figure it out. It will be okay, I promise."

Katie pulled back and shook her head roughly. "You can't promise that. No one can promise that. And it's not fair or kind for you to try."

Brendan stared at her, and finally, *finally* started to get it. She wasn't being stubborn. She had no idea what the world looked like – or if it could even continue to exist – after this tour ended in less than twenty-four hours. Of course she was terrified. Who wouldn't be?

"You're not kidding," he said in wonder and a growing horror. "You really have no idea what happens next."

"No I'm not kidding! Why did you ever think I was kidding? Am I ever kidding about anything?"

She was growing frantic. Brendan felt like the ground was slipping away underneath his feet. "No! Which is why I'm so puzzled. Did you forget how to do things?"

"No, Brendan," Katie said slowly, as if she were speaking to a small child. "I can't have forgotten how to do it, because I never knew how. We're being asked to launch a business, by ourselves, by a bunch of people I don't know or trust or know how to evaluate!"

Brendan gulped for air as his brain struggled to keep up. "I don't get how this is any different than what we've been doing all along, but if you don't know how, why haven't you asked?"

"Who was I supposed to ask?"

"Me!"

Katie shoved away from him. "You don't know anything more about the real world than I do! It's not as if you've got your life figured out. A shrug and 'oh yeah I guess I'll coach' isn't a plan!"

"I'm pretty sure it is, and even if it isn't, I'm still doing better than you!"

"Seventeenth," she hissed.

Brendan rolled his eyes. Nothing could be less relevant right now. "Newsflash, the only one of us who cares about that is you."

"You know what? I don't need this. These whacked out arguments are why every time you've almost got me convinced we should be together, it becomes wildly apparent that we don't know what we're doing and are never going to figure it out!" She stormed off down the hallway.

Brendan willed himself not to reach after her. This wasn't going to get better. Not tonight and maybe not ever. His hands were shaking slightly, and he pressed his palms against his thighs to stop them. "Where are you going?"

"To get my head together for our big finale tomorrow! That, I know how to do."

Brendan sighed and slouched against the wall. He was a mess. Katie was a mess. And this situation was a disaster.

13

The Last Day of the Tour

New York, NY

Katie woke up with the same riot of emotions she'd gone to bed with: She was shaken and disappointed in herself, but profoundly grateful for Brendan giving her space, even if it had ended with them yelling at each other. Again. She couldn't imagine ever feeling competent enough to deal with the choices that loomed in front of her.

As she went through her show day routine at the arena – stretching, ice for her knee, small high-protein meals, and more stretching – Brendan was nowhere to be seem. That was fine. He wasn't required to be there until rehearsal, and she probably needed the alone time.

Last night had been a disaster, and more than anything she felt ashamed. Her brain was a mess and her body wasn't much better. Those things could be corrected, but dealing with them seemed as overwhelming as any other decision about her – and Brendan's – future. Their few weeks of tentative truce and slow, possible drifting back together had ended as she had feared: with another fight.

They were running out of time in which they could keep doing this, and Katie wasn't sure they knew how to do anything else. At this rate, once they were done with skating, there would be nothing to keep them together at all.

When Brendan showed up for their rehearsal slot with barely a second to spare, Katie narrowed her eyes and immediately took her starting position for their solo number. What was the point of scolding him about being on time here on the last day of the tour?

"Wait, no, hey." Gently, he touched her wrist, encouraged her to lower her arms.

"What?" she barked.

"Do you want to do this?"

"Fight? No. Rehearse? Yes." She was tired. So very, very tired. Of the tour, of numbers she hated, of feeling lost and adrift.

Brendan shook his head. "No. I mean, tonight's the last hurrah. Do you want to do this program?"

"I never want to do it. But what's the alternative?"

"The one that won us gold in Harbin."

Katie stared at him. "Have you magically figured out how to fix it so you're comfortable with me skating it?" Brendan was a good choreographer, but Katie was long sick of hearing him talk about taking the challenge out of a program she so desperately loved.

He shook his head. "Nope. But what you do with your body is your business, not mine. How's your knee?"

Katie shrugged, though her heart was thudding in her chest with hope, with the possibility of skating their absolute best again. "Same as it's been."

"Okay." Brendan's face was excited and so earnest. He wanted to give her this.

Why is he so wonderful even when we're such a mess?

"So do you want to give our big moment one last spin tonight?" he asked.

Of course I do. "What's the catch?" she asked. Brendan was up to something.

He shook his head. "No catch. Last night was awful. Maybe tomorrow will be awful too, I don't know. But I do know no one should take what we are out here from us…not even each other." He reached out and took her hands "So one more time? Whether it's forever and ever or just in case?"

Katie nodded. "One more time."

✦

They ran the program once in rehearsal to prove to everyone that her knee could take it. It could, and they had skated clean. Now they just had to do it again.

"I can't believe we're doing this," Katie said hours later as they waited in the darkened tunnel for their names to be announced. She couldn't believe Brendan had talked Leo into letting them do this. Hell, she couldn't believe Brendan had talked himself into it.

One more one-more-time. She'd never felt this excited about a non-competitive skate before. If touring could always be like this, she was all in with this being the future of her and Brendan's careers.

Beside her, Brendan found her hand and squeezed it.

"I'm fine," she said.

"I know. I just wanted to be nice or something."

"You're always nice. Except when you're awful. Like me."

Brendan laughed.

Katie glanced at him sideways. "Thank you for this, by the way."

Brendan swung their hands a little. "No thanks necessary. With our meetings next week, the least we can do is take this moment to figure out who we are." He paused, then pulled her against his side. "I know you don't know what's coming," he said into her hair, wrapping his arm around her shoulders. "But something good is going to happen for both of us. I'm sure of it."

"I hope you're right." She leaned against him, but didn't trust herself to say anything else. For all the fits and starts and disasters of their relationship, this skate, this moment, this return to their Harbin program against all good sense was the most romantic thing he'd ever done for her. She knew no way to repay him other than to give it everything she had. This needed to be their performance of a lifetime.

The announcer's voice crackled over the sound system, calling their names.

Brendan turned his head; Katie could feel his breath on her cheek and then his lips as he pressed a soft kiss to her temple. "We're gonna kill it," he murmured.

She hoped he was right. They hadn't practiced enough, she wasn't mentally prepared at all, and, worst of all, there weren't any obvious stakes.

Except my whole future and this perfect mess with this perfect man.

The audience buzzed as they took the ice.

"With me?" Brendan asked.

Katie smiled at the familiar words. "Always."

When they took their starting positions, which were entirely different from the other program, the sound from the audience changed. It became louder. More insistent. More confused. Happier. The audience knew, and they wanted something they didn't believe they could have.

So do I, Katie thought. *So do I.*

Her focus narrowed away from the audience and to herself and Brendan. She couldn't see the people in the stands, but she could feel them. When the music started the whole arena froze.

Except them.

Katie tried not to tense up as they approached the side-by-side triple axels. It had been so long since they'd done these, this afternoon's practice aside. But nerves and doubt would kill you long before your muscles let you down. So she took a deep breath, kept Brendan at the right distance, and let herself trust.

They landed them perfectly. The crowd erupted into cheers.

Brendan caught her hand as they went into the sit spin. Their eyes locked; his face was incandescent with joy. Maybe now he could understand all the things she was so afraid to give up.

As they pulled out of the spin and into some footwork, Katie felt her expression shift from a performance smile to a real one. This, right here, was what they'd spent their lives learning how to do. And they were still perfect.

Brendan's body against hers, the ice under their blades, the very air itself felt charged. Katie slid her face against his as they went through the steps they'd first memorized so many months ago in Denver, the movement almost a kiss. The crowd gasped, and maybe it was exhibitionist of Katie but their reaction made it better. For these four and a half minutes the ice was theirs, and no one could look away.

Splaying his hands wide across her back, Brendan guided Katie into position for the twist lift. She spun three times through the air, and Brendan caught her, but her knee ached oddly when he set her back on the ice. On the next side-by-side jumps, the triple lutzes, it twinged painfully when she landed. It only got worse as the program continued, but Katie had no choice – and no desire – to do anything but go on. She pushed the sinking feeling of *something's really wrong this time* to the back of her brain, letting the music, Brendan's body, and her own fierce desire to carry her through.

They struck their ending poses with the last dramatic beat of the music. There was a collective moment of indrawn breath, and then the audience roared.

Brendan pulled her upright into his arms with a crushing hug, kissing her hair.

Katie panted into his shoulder, clinging in both victory and relief. They'd done it. And it had been so, so good. But she was in pain. A lot of it. She wasn't sure she could get off the ice while continuing to hide it. She needed to tell Brendan, but she didn't know how. Speech in the sea of applause and pain and emotion felt beyond her.

"I love you," he said.

She had no doubt he did. He always said that after they nailed an important skate. She'd never been more grateful for it than she was right now.

"They're standing," Brendan said, his voice awed. "It's a standing ovation. We should do our bows."

Finally she made herself say it. She pressed her mouth to his ear. She didn't want to chance a camera catching it. "My knee really hurts."

Brendan froze. "Shit. Shit." He started to push away from her, to see her face or to check the injury, she didn't know.

"Stop it!" she hissed. "Be normal. Help me hide this."

"But –"

"Do you want the solo tour? Keep your fucking hands on me and don't make it look like you're carrying all my weight."

She spun out of his grasp and kept her weight on her good leg as she curtseyed. They turned and bowed three more times, once to each side of the rink, making sure to acknowledge every bit of their incredible audience. And then Brendan scooped her up into his arms.

"Time to break the internet," he whispered.

Katie didn't know whether to laugh or cry. So she did the only thing she could – both.

✦

Brendan didn't make a scene once he'd gotten them off

the ice, which was a minor miracle for which Katie was desperately grateful. Now that the shock of whatever had happened out there had passed, the pain was ebbing enough for her to get backstage and to the ice therapy machine.

"Do you want me to get Dr. Meyer?" Brendan asked as he knelt by her side, wrapping the cuff of the machine into place. Katie could have done it herself under normal circumstances, but her hands were shaking too hard.

She shook her head. "I want you to figure out what I'm doing in the group finale so it doesn't look weird when I skip the jumps." Tears, which she thought she had been done with, sprang to her eyes again. She balled the fabric of her skirt in her hands and bit her lip. She had to change before the final number, and she didn't have much time.

"Are you sure you want to go through with that?" Brendan pushed his hair off his forehead and looked up at her, his green eyes kind and his brow furrowed in concern. He deserved better than this, to be stuck at the side of a partner who couldn't skate.

"I can be injured tomorrow," she said firmly. "Or next week. In secret. I cannot be injured tonight. Now help me figure it out."

"Okay." Brendan pressed a hand to her thigh, like he was going to use it to lever himself up, but he stayed there, his elbow resting on one knee, his other knee on the floor, his eyes intent on hers. "Okay. I will."

✦

Somehow, Katie got through the rest of the show – and the meet and greet – and back to her room. She had it to herself tonight; Natalya was catching a late flight out of JFK. Which would have been perfect, if Brendan was staying with her. But he wasn't, at least not for the night. After he made sure she was settled, asked repeatedly if she wanted him to get Dr. Meyer, and offered to get her anything she needed from her suitcase, he finally left with a kiss to her cheek and a worried frown.

Katie almost asked him to stay. The tour was over, her knee was no longer a problem she could pretend was going to go away, and maybe nothing mattered anymore. But she needed to figure out what to do. She didn't want Brendan there to fret over her or complicate whatever her decision was.

In the morning, Katie found herself taking one of Brendan's main suggestions from the night before and was relieved to find Dr. Meyer still in her hotel room.

"Katie," she said in surprise when she pulled the door open at her knock. "Is something wrong?"

"Can I come in?"

"Of course." Dr. Meyer stood back to let her in. "What is it?"

"My knee," Katie said, twisting her fingers together. "I don't know what I did to it last night, but it's way worse. I need to find someone to take a look at it. Now. Like, today. And I need to be discreet about it because we're about to start negotiating our tour. If you have any favors you can call in...." She took a deep breath and finished in a rush. "Please don't tell anyone."

She nearly cried in relief when Dr. Meyer steered her into a chair and reached for her cell phone.

✦

In less time than Katie thought would be possible, she was back from the doctor's office and sitting in her and Brendan's first meeting of the day. She didn't know which was worse: having the imaging done on her knee or the meeting. She didn't have much to say, which was only partially because she was waiting for a phone call to give her the results of the imaging, worrying about the surgery she might need, when she could possibly get it done if she did need it, and when she was going to tell anyone about it.

Katie had spent lots of time in meetings before, but they had been about things she understood: Jumps. Lifts. Spins. Music. Costumes. Arcane ISU politics. Even sponsorships. All things about which she had deep knowledge and strong opinions.

But now she was overwhelmed by all of the people they were meeting and all of the information they carried. Everyone had job descriptions that didn't seem to involve actually doing anything. And sure, she knew ghostwriters were a thing, but writing a book she wasn't going to actually write? About exercise tips or self-esteem or achieving your dreams? Not her speed. At all. The type of success she and Brendan had found wasn't about smiling and believing in yourself, it was about blood and bone and a brutal ruthlessness. Who would let her write a book about how to come from nothing and sell your soul? No one, she was pretty sure.

This wasn't her world. Brendan could nod along and ask all the right questions and pretend he was comfortable in fancy offices, but this wasn't his world either; his world was at the gym and on the ice. Here, he was faking it all the way and everyone could tell. Somehow watching him left her more exhausted than her own feeling of being wildly out of place. She wasn't used to not being an expert or her own career. She wasn't used to her background showing. She wasn't used to talking about her body instead of talking with it.

Her knee made everything more complicated. By discussing a tour without being honest about her health, Katie knew she was negotiating, if not in bad faith, at least not totally openly. Her conscience was soothed somewhat when she started to realize how long a tour would take to organize. Would she be able to comfortably address her knee issues in the interim created by logistics? Very possibly. But she knew she was considering any number of highly calculated risks. She didn't only need a doctor, she probably needed a lawyer too.

As for the rest of the work being discussed, Katie could hardly consider it work. In the past, sponsors had paid for them to train and compete in exchange for her and Brendan wearing the right logos and filming an ad now and then. Now, companies would be paying them to smile and sell and pretend that the right hair care products had made their defunct skating careers possible. Katie knew it was the norm for retired athletes, but that didn't make the prospect less repulsive.

You okay? Brendan scribbled on the corner of his notepad.

Katie gave a minute shake of her head. Of course she wasn't okay. Her knee hurt. She was waiting for the doctor to call her back with his verdict on the imaging. That news wasn't going to be good so much as a matter of how bad. She hadn't told Brendan where she'd been early that morning and needed to figure out how. Her body was falling apart, and she was going from being a world-class athlete to being a doll.

That wasn't a metaphor; there was a discussion of a doll. Little girls would carry it around like a good luck charm, dirty and dangling from their skate bags. It wouldn't even have knees that could bend.

◆

Now that she and Brendan were being courted by managers and agents and entertainment companies, shared rooms and overnight buses were a thing of the past. They had moved from the hotel they'd been in with the rest of the tour to another fancier than anything they'd had on the road. Here, in New York City, that was saying something.

Katie knew each of their rooms could pay for a ridiculous amount of ice time. Instead, she got huge windows splattered with rain and a view of a sea of concrete that paid tribute to the types of ambitions she had never possessed.

Between her appointment and all the meetings, she and Brendan didn't get a moment to themselves all day. Even their meals were business meetings. Their one break, which only happened because a representative from a sportswear company had been running late, had been interrupted by a call from the doctor. The news was what she dreaded: Her knee was definitely damaged in a way that couldn't be corrected with rest and therapy. Given her medical history surgery, followed by months of recovery and physical therapy, was inevitable. Would she skate again at a level worthy of a post-Olympic athlete? Possibly. With hard work, time, and no small amount of luck.

I can work hard. But I can't control the clock.

She needed to tell Brendan. But after dinner, their meetings finally done for the day, he went to make one of his regular but infrequent calls to his parents. Katie retreated to her room alone. She showered, changed into pajamas and sat on the bed, her bad knee stretched out in front of her. The solitude, for a second night in a row, was alien. Her whole life had been roommates to ignore or Brendan, too close and holding her hand.

Brendan. She needed to tell him about her knee. Before they went any farther in these negotiations, he needed to know everything so they could be a united front. She glanced at the clock; he'd be off the phone by now. He never talked to his family for long.

She slid on her flip-flops, grabbed her room key, and padded down the hall.

Brendan answered her knock wearing sweatpants, a T-shirt, and a puzzled smile. "What's up?"

"Can I come in?"

"Sure." He looked skeptical. *With good reason*, her mind suggested traitorously. Still, he stepped back to let her in. "What's going on?"

She opened her mouth to tell him about her knee, but couldn't get the words out. To buy herself time, she gestured at the room and his own massive bank of windows. "All of this. New York. These meetings. I just...I wanted to talk to you somewhere that's not a boardroom or an office or some business dinner. I'm not used to this."

"Neither am I," he said.

"I'm not made for it," she clarified.

"And I am?"

Yes. No. Maybe. "I'm really freaked out about the doll." The doll was far from the only problem, but it sure summed it all up.

"You can say no to the doll."

Katie frowned and sat down on one of the room's beds. She assumed it was the one Bredan wasn't sleeping in because his stuff was piled all over it.

"Are you jealous?" she asked.

Brendan laughed. "Nah. You're the prettier one. People don't turn up at things to look at me."

"They do, actually," Katie said. Brendan was gorgeous, and she knew there were plenty of fans who shared her opinion on that. His green eyes that looked so soulful in pictures were even more striking in person. His thick dark hair, that she loved to run her fingers through in choreography, was every bit as soft as it looked. And she was far from the only one who appreciated the lean, muscled lines of his body that his simple costumes only accentuated. There weren't many men in the world strong enough to lift a grown woman over their heads with grace and a smile. Brendan could. That feat alone would have made him attractive.

"Maybe." Brendan sat down on the other bed facing her. "But I always knew I wasn't getting a doll."

Katie frowned. "What does that mean?" She was genuinely curious. Brendan didn't often talk about what was going on in his head if it didn't relate to whatever task was directly in front of them.

Brendan turned his face to the side a little and didn't quite meet her eyes. He seemed...small, somehow. "Did it ever occur to you I keep talking about coaching and about the tour because that's all I get?"

Katie shook her head. "I don't understand."

Brendan gave a small, almost imperceptible sigh. "This is where our paths diverge in so many ways," he said quietly.

"But –"

"Make-up contracts. A line of workout clothes. The doll. Books about self-esteem for young women. Little girls dream of being ballerinas or skaters. You can work this for the rest of your life and turn it into anything you want. I can do exhibitions, and I can coach."

"I thought you wanted to coach," Katie said, her voice softening to match his.

"It's the option I like most of the ones open to me," Brendan said.

Katie felt absolutely ashamed. For so long she'd been focusing on her own pain and panic and grief at leaving competitive skating behind. Brendan was always so calm and together – at least, he seemed to be – that it hadn't occurred to her that he might be as heartbroken at this transition as she was.

If only they could be as good at communicating with each other off the ice as they were on it. But they weren't, and here at what felt like the end of everything, maybe they never would be.

"A lot of athletes go into politics," she offered. She hated herself that she didn't have anything more useful to say.

"Yeah. Football players." Brendan grinned ruefully.

"I'm a figure skater who got a black eye in a bar because I attempted to prove my masculinity by defending your honor. When I tried to hit the guy, I missed."

Katie laughed. That night had been awful, and she knew she'd only made it worse. She couldn't fix anything else, but maybe she could make up for that a little. "I love that you missed. And as mad as I was at you, I kind of love that you tried. Thank you."

"You're welcome."

She smiled fiercely. "I wouldn't have missed."

"I know."

"What do you want to do?" she asked, even as she realized it was far too late for such a question. And she still hadn't told him about her knee.

"See what our options are – all our options – and choose the ones we can stomach. Do them, save money, and then do whatever we want after that I guess. You've always steered us, you've always set our goals and made sure we met them. I guess I took that for granted. I know I kept yelling at you for not having a plan, but I guess I've been pissed at you for not having a plan with me."

"Because you love me?" she asked. Brendan admitting to weakness and uncertainty was very nearly breaking her heart. He was half of her being, and she hadn't known.

"Because you're getting a doll and I'm not."

Now was her moment to confess. But she couldn't. Brendan's words left her feeling raw, like a scab she hadn't known she had scraped open. She didn't know how to move forward from here. She also didn't know how to move away.

"Can I stay here tonight?" she asked.

Brendan raised an eyebrow.

Katie pointed at the bed she was sitting on. "I sleep here. You sleep there."

"Why?"

He didn't usually challenge her when she asked for

things like that. But the question, like his skepticism when he let her into his room in the first place, was entirely fair. Katie knew she'd been, at best, mercurial over the last few days. *Weeks. Months. Years.*

But Brendan was home; he was where she felt safe. None of the words she needed were coming to her, so she said the only thing she could.

"Because I can't think when you aren't breathing next to me."

◆

Katie lay on her back in the dark, watching the lights of New York play on the ceiling. Brendan couldn't sleep either – she could hear his quiet breathing from the bed next to hers, and the occasional rustle of the sheets as he turned over.

"This is terrible," she said, flinging an arm out from under the blankets to reach for him.

Across the gap between the beds his fingers found hers, just like they had in so many hotel rooms after so many competitions all over the world.

"What is?"

"The lights," she said. "How does anyone sleep?"

"I'm pretty sure they draw the curtains." He was judging her. She could hear it in his voice.

"Even if you draw the curtains, it's still there."

"Do you want me to respond to that?" Brendan asked.

"I'm not lying here because I want you to be quiet."

Brendan shrugged. "Maybe you want to talk. I want to give you space if you do."

"What does it feel like for you? Here?" she asked. What else didn't she know about the person who had been her whole world for so long?

"Where?" Brendan sounded uncertain.

"New York City," she said.

"That I'd rather be seeing it than being stuck in all these

meetings. Why? What does it feel like for you?"

"Like a TV show that I'm trapped in. Like it knows I don't belong here. Aside from everything else, I miss home."

Finally, cautiously, Brendan spoke. "So you do want to come back to Denver…?"

Katie made a noise that she hoped didn't entirely sound like disgust. "Home home. Wisconsin home. The middle of goddamn nowhere home. Home where you only get out by being good at something impossible. Home where you eventually have to go back because that's what it costs and that's who you are."

Brendan squeezed her fingers lightly, like he did when she had too much sharp energy going into a skate and he was encouraging her to gentle herself. "That doesn't sound like missing a place."

"It wouldn't, to you." Of course Brendan wouldn't understand. He never could.

"What's that supposed to mean?"

Katie shifted under the covers. "You're from Minneapolis."

"…yeah?"

"No. I mean like, you're from a city. I grew up on a farm," Katie said.

"I know. I've been there."

"A farm doesn't work if you don't work. There's no vacations or days off. I had to work really hard, all the time. Not just for skating, but so I could skate. So the barns didn't flood. So the cows didn't, you know, shrivel up and die."

"You're not painting a more appealing picture, there."

She felt crushed by his lack of understanding. "Home needed me, Brendan. Needs me. I miss that."

✦

Katie woke to sunlight reflected into Brendan's room

by the building across the street. She felt like an ant set up to burn under a magnifying glass.

She looked over at him in the other bed. She'd woken up with him so many times in the last two decades. All the times they'd shared a room on the road, all the times they'd shared a bed just to be close, all the times they'd crashed at each other's apartments. Despite her attempts to date over the years, she'd never been able to make sense of everyone else's expectations about relationships. But she could imagine waking up next to Brendan every day.

That wasn't going to happen in this life, though. She hadn't managed to tell him about everything that needed to happen surrounding her knee. Shame settled as a cold, uncomfortable weight in her stomach. Their shared space should have been lovely, but she needed not to be here.

Katie slipped out from between the covers, put her flip-flops back on and padded to the hotel room door. Brendan stirred as she opened it. She hovered there for a moment, as if between one life and the next.

"Wha...?" he asked, turning towards her and less than half awake.

"I've got to get ready for whatever is happening today," she said softly. "I'll see you at breakfast."

He made a noise of agreement and flopped back down.

Katie left. She was glad that no one was around to see her wandering in pajamas from her partner's hotel room back to her own at seven in the morning.

Inside, she stared at her half-packed bags, her skates in the corner, the Russian nesting dolls Natalya had given her, and the notes she had taken at the doctor's office. The problem hadn't been waking up in Brendan's room this morning. It was being in New York at all. While she was here, she certainly wasn't going to get over her concerns about the unappealing marketing options in front of her, about her knee, or about her terror of letting Brendan down. She needed to make some choices instead of only fretting about them.

She felt a stab of doubt as she threw the rest of her things in her bags. She was leaving Brendan to the wolves and without his partner in crime and in business. The tour was probably going to be a non-starter without her there to be part of the conversation. As for the rest of it…it was like what Brendan had said about the doll. From here, their paths diverged regardless of what either of them wanted.

It was time to leave him to it.

✦

Katie didn't start trembling until she was in the cab on the way to the airport. Any minute now, Brendan would make his way downstairs for breakfast and she wouldn't be there. A little while after that he would realize something was wrong.

Except Brendan knew her better than she knew herself. He might realize what she had done immediately. And then he might panic. *Wouldn't that be a change of pace,* she thought bitterly. Sometimes she really hated her brain. But whatever else she was doing, she didn't want to scare him. She pulled out her phone and opened their text thread.

Hi. I need you to cover for me one last time. Yes, it's my knee again. And my head and everything else. I'm going to turn off my phone after this, so don't worry if you can't get ahold of me. I'm okay; I just need to go home. For whatever it's worth, I'm sorry.

She didn't know when the next flight to Minneapolis-Saint Paul was. And wasn't that ironic? She had to go through Brendan's home to get to hers.

PART II

14

Three Months After Katie Left Brendan in New York City

Denver, CO

Brendan was jolted out of a very pleasant dream by the sound of an air raid siren. He rolled over and slapped awkwardly at his alarm clock, stuffing his head under his pillow once he'd finally managed to turn it off. He wished he could close his eyes for five more minutes without running the risk of falling asleep and being late for his first session of the day.

Get up, Reid, he told himself. He shoved off the covers and dragged himself out of bed.

He'd never been a morning person, and he'd never had Katie's built-in alarm clock, though he had certainly benefited from it whenever they'd been on the road together. At least so far as getting woken up at the crack of dawn by the sound of Katie getting dressed counted as a benefit.

One day, I'm going to wake up and not have my very first thought be about Katie.

Today was clearly not that day.

Brendan wasn't angry with her all the time anymore. He had been, those first hours in New York City after he'd gotten her message. He'd thought about following her to yell at her for leaving or to plead with her to stay, but he hadn't known which airline or which airport. Besides, getting to any of New York's airports was a nightmare. Most importantly, even if Katie was an asshole for standing him up at a series of important business meetings, she of course had the right to leave.

So he'd lied and dissembled for her, signed his own deals where he could, and watched as the entertainment machine that had wanted them crumbled before his eyes.

Brendan had slunk back to Denver, to the apartment that had been a gift from his parents when he'd first moved out there. Katie had always hated not the apartment itself, but the fact that he'd had it. As Katie's radio silence drew on, he'd grown to hate everything about it too.

He drove to the rink without any music on. All his playlists were filled with songs they had practiced or competed to, and he didn't have the heart to listen to any of them. Making new mixes felt a little too much like defeat, an acknowledgment that Katie really was gone from his life for good.

"You are pathetic," he told himself aloud as he parked at the rink. Why break his newfound morning routine now?

Working at the same rink he and Katie had trained at for so many years was surreal. Everything looked familiar but felt different. And not in a good way. If he'd been smarter, he'd have gone somewhere else. But he had a community here, the town knew him, and packing up his life and moving somewhere else for the sake of something new held zero appeal.

Plus, he liked the kids he was working with. He wasn't a fully-fledged coach yet or even close. He was working with a coaching staff for two different junior-level figure skating pairs, assisting with choreography and the artistic aspects of their programs. As much as he'd planned on coaching after his retirement from competition, he was surprised by how much he enjoyed the work. He was in love with skating and always had been. Watching his skaters strive and improve meant as much to him as if their progress had been his own.

Tomorrow, one of the pairs – Shelby and Miguel – was leaving for a competition in South Bend, and the stakes were about to get higher. If they placed high enough there, they would advance to the next round of competitions. At that point this would get a lot more serious for all of them. He really needed to get his head in the game and give his kids the best he had in him.

✦

Brendan hadn't expected travelling as part of a coaching staff to be so different from travelling as a skater. But here he was in Indiana with a hotel room to himself, way less luggage, and no one to freak out to.

The last part was the worst, he thought as sat at the desk with his laptop going through his notes and making sure he had absolutely everything in order for tomorrow. Not because he necessarily needed to freak out – he was nervous, sure, but his kids were as prepared as they could be. But because whenever he'd travelled for a competition, ever since he was ten, Katie had been right there with him. Even in those terrible years when they hadn't been partners, he'd always known she was somewhere in the same city and skating on the same ice.

Before he closed his computer for the night he refreshed his inbox one last time, another ritual he'd started since he got back to Denver. There was, as usual, nothing from Katie. Brendan sighed, snapped his computer shut, folded his arms on top of it and buried his face in them. He had to assume Katie had given up skating forever – or that her knee had forced her to do so. He'd texted, emailed, and called her in the first couple of weeks after she'd fled New York, almost frantic for wanting to know if she was okay. But the more time that went by without a response from her, the more evident the answer became: Either she wasn't okay and there was nothing Brendan could do about it, or she was fine and she wanted nothing to do with him.

Brendan shook his head and stood up to get ready for bed. He needed to not think about Katie, and he needed to sleep.

✦

Shelby and Miguel nailed their short program, as Brendan had known they would. He managed to keep thoughts of Katie mostly at bay until they were about to do their free skate the next day.

Before their names were called, Brendan leaned his elbows on the boards to give them one last pep talk. They had an actual coach who was more than capable of doing this for them, but in the last few months they had gravitated towards Brendan. He wasn't sure what made them trust him so much, or from where he drew the words to calm their nerves and build their confidence, but he was glad of it, whatever it was. Glad, and also humbled. Brendan had been in their shoes once and knew how much faith they were placing in him. He couldn't let them down.

Shelby's eyes were huge. Miguel looked grimly determined. They reminded Brendan so very much of himself and Katie at that age. The nerves would never go away, but with luck, support, and the right resources they'd become part of the process instead of a barrier.

"Hey," he told them both. Shelby reached for the box of tissues and blew her nose, still looking like a deer in the headlights. "You like skating, yeah?"

The two looked at Brendan, looked at each other, and looked back at him in perfect unison. Their faces said plainly that they thought he'd lost his mind.

When they didn't answer, though, he lifted his eyebrows and repeated the question. Learning how to communicate their needs as athletes meant learning how to actually communicate. Out loud. He wasn't going to let them fall into same bad habits as him and Katie.

"Yes," they said together.

"Then don't worry about what comes after. Go enjoy the shit out of the next three and a half minutes."

That got a smile out of them. Their names were announced, and he gave them each a last hug over the boards before they pushed off, hand in hand, for their starting positions.

Brendan knew someone's camera in the audience would find him either because they were curious as to how he was handling his transition to coaching or because it was an excuse for the internet to wonder what had happened to Katie. He folded his arms and told himself very sternly not to bite his thumbnail. He had every bit of confidence in his kids; they were a moment away from becoming extraordinary.

He didn't breathe until the song was done and Shelby and Miguel struck their final position. Neither they nor Brendan needed the judges to tell them they had absolutely nailed that program. Stunned, relieved smiles broke out over their faces, and they threw their arms around each other.

Fuck. Brendan missed Katie. The old, familiar sensation of her absence was suddenly painfully sharp. He found it hard to breathe as it lingered, staying with him as Shelby and Miguel got their winning scores, through the congratulatory hugs, and during the medal ceremony. So many memories were tied up in the rituals of the day. Without Katie at his side he felt like he was missing half of his body.

In the arena parking lot he waved goodbye to Shelby and Miguel and their parents, then leaned against his rental car as he watched them go. They were headed for a celebratory dinner, almost effervescent with their delight in their victory. Brendan was going back to his hotel room. He needed to review the tape of today's performance and make notes for the kids and for his own work. He needed to reply to the emails he'd gotten today from his other team, still at home in Denver. But he also needed to make a plan.

Time and therapy alone were not cutting it. He needed to solve things with Katie once and for all. Even if, after that, they never spoke again.

✦

He waited to call Katie until he arrived back home the next day. He dropped his mail on the kitchen counter and looked around at the rest of his apartment. He was hardly ever here; his life was spent mostly at the rink or the gym. Without Katie crashing here on weekends and the odd weeknight, it looked more empty and bare than ever. A couple of dishes were sitting somewhat sadly on the draining board. Aside from his medals and a few framed photographs on the wall, the place looked more like a hostel than a place where anyone actually lived.

This was not a home he could share with anyone, his previous invitation to Katie to move in with him notwithstanding. She'd been right to refuse that offer for so many reasons. His place wasn't – and had never been – the home of a person who was ready to have someone in their life.

What the hell am I doing here?

Such a mood was, perhaps, not the best one in which to reach out to his ex-skating partner…his ex-everything, really. But he needed to do this. Brendan scrolled to her number in his phone and hit call.

He stared at his phone as it rang. His heart pounded. He told himself sternly that the worst that could happen was that Katie would hang up on him. If the last three months hadn't killed him, that certainly wasn't going to finish him off now.

He let it ring until it clicked over to voicemail, but he was unprepared to leave a message, so he hung up. He'd write something out that made some sort of sense and call her back later. That way, if her voicemail picked up again, at least he'd be prepared.

The second he set his phone down on the counter, it rang.

Katie.

Calling him back.

Suddenly, he hated her all over again. By which he meant that he was totally in love with her all over again and in a total panic.

Fuck.

He answered the phone. And said nothing.

Katie mirrored his silence, although he could hear her breathing. He wondered if they would hang up without speaking a word.

Finally she spoke. "Hi."

"Hi."

She took a deep breath that sounded like all the ones before the music started. "I know you didn't call just to say hi."

"No." *God, I missed your voice,* Brendan thought. There was so much he wanted to say, but now that Katie was there on the line, he didn't know how.

Isn't that always the problem with us, though? The chance that they would be able to fix things between them suddenly seemed remote.

Katie sighed impatiently. He'd missed that sound, too.

"I'm not hanging up on you," she said sharply, 'but I'm

also not playing twenty questions. What do you want, Brendan? It's almost my bedtime."

"It's eight-thirty." Where did she get off being angry about him calling, when she had been the one who left him in New York and had never even answered an email?

"Do you know what time cows get up?"

After all the years they had spent together, Brendan suspected he should. But if she had told him before – and she probably had – he had forgotten. *Ugh.* "What time do cows get up, Katie?" he asked snidely. Then he kicked himself. Whatever his case was, he wasn't helping it.

"Four."

"That's really fucking early." *As early as skaters get up.*

"Yeah, I'm not making small talk with you about cows."

"They won," he blurted.

"What?"

"One of the junior pairs I've been working with. They won. Today."

"Congratulations," she said tartly.

Brendan wondered if she resented his bringing up skating. But what else was he supposed to do? Like she had said, making small talk about cows was definitely not an option.

"Is this a nostalgia call?" she asked.

"No. It's not." *What does she want me to say? What do I want to say?* "Are you okay?"

"I'm great," Katie said. She sounded like she meant it.

"Really? Because –"

She cut him off with an exasperated noise. "Why is that so hard to understand?"

"Because you weren't okay when you left. Because I'm not now. Because my kids won yesterday and all I wanted to do was get in a car and get to you."

He could hear Katie's sharp inhale. "But you decided that would be a creepy, shitty, stalkerish thing to do?"

"Yeah. Of course. Christ. I'm not trying to make your life harder." He ran a hand through his hair. "Now that I've stopped being pissed at you all the time –"

"I'm sorry about New York," she cut in.

Brendan could hear the nervous edge in her voice, could imagine how she worried her fingers together. She always did that when she was afraid she had disappointed him. He didn't want to ignore that, but right now, he had to. *Put your own oxygen mask on first,* he told himself sternly.

"Now that I've stopped being pissed at you all the time," he repeated, needing to work up the courage to say the next, horrible, necessary words, "I want this shit between us to be over. Once and for all. Officially."

A pause. A breath. "You're going to break up with me over the phone?" she asked incredulously.

He stammered. How could Katie give him so much hope and be so utterly dire about their future all at the same time. "I…uh…*what?!*"

"You can't break up with me; we're not together," she said in a rush.

That wasn't any clearer. Brendan imagined her tossing her ponytail as if she didn't care. But he knew she did. There was no way she couldn't. Even if a permanent, official end to all that they had shared was what they both wanted. Because if she hadn't cared on some messy, complicated level, she wouldn't have run three months ago.

"Okay, but we seriously need to talk. Preferably in person, I guess."

"You can't drive to Wisconsin to break up with me."

"Would you stop saying 'break up?' You're freaking me out and making this more complicated. Also, seriously, would I do that?"

"I don't know. Maybe."

Brendan exhaled. "Look, can I come see you or not?"

"I'm not letting you drive fifteen hours so we can have

an awkward coffee while gossipy strangers stare at us."

That didn't appeal to Brendan, either. "I'll come to the farm, and when we're sick of each other – whether that takes an hour or a day or…whatever – I'm sure my parents will be glad to see me."

"Really?"

"They do like me, yes."

"That's not what I meant." She sounded incredulous. That was fair. The farm, whenever he'd been there had unnerved him. He'd been boorish and had acted like Katie should hate it too. Of course, she never had. She had every right to set this as a test.

"Yes, I'll come to the farm," he said clearly.

Katie hummed like she was considering it. But Brendan could tell that was a performance. Whatever her answer, he was nearly sure he would be getting in his car. And soon.

"All right," she said. "Pack a bag, get ready to work, and be excited for cow time."

15

The Morning After Brendan Called Katie and Katie Finally Called Him Back

Star Prairie, WI

Katie woke up at three-forty-five, rolled over, turned the alarm on her phone off, and flopped back down on her pillows. As always, she'd woken up automatically fifteen minutes before she actually had to. She'd spent years travelling the world for competition and glory, but this – a few extra minutes in bed in her room at her family's farmhouse – was what felt like luxury.

Her room didn't look much different from how it had when she was a teenager. The walls were the same eggshell white, the carpet the same dark green. The trim had been newly scraped and re-stained in another improvement made by her uncle Jesse. It was now a deep brown that showed off the grain of the wood. The curtains, made years ago by Katie's mom out of worn bedsheets, were light blue. The furniture – the bed, the dresser, and the little vanity under the dormer window – had been in the family for generations. Jesse had offered to re-finish those too, but

Katie had turned him down. She liked the worn edges and the pale rings on the wood from where she'd left water glasses as a child.

Here in this room with the sky still dark outside the windows, the call with Brendan last night felt like a missive from another world, tenuous and perhaps frightening. But whether that was good or bad, she didn't know. Her heart had leapt to see Brendan's name flashing across her phone screen, but just as quickly it had clenched and sagged in misery. He'd called so many times the first week or two after she'd left him in New York. She'd never picked up and never listened to any of his voicemails. Eventually, he had stopped calling. Why on earth he would be reaching out now, except to make one more attempt to yell at her for her disastrous choices, she didn't know.

But he hadn't yelled. He'd been sad and uncertain and, as he so often was, so damn earnest. Now he was coming to visit. After twenty years of friendship and whatever else they were to each other, Brendan was still something she did not understand – ferocious, feral, patient, and too kind. She was finally going to have to deal with him off the ice, in the real world. That was new. And terrifying.

What would Brendan think of the farm? Of who she was now? What about her knee? Or how she'd abandoned him? Katie wanted things to be okay between them, but if they couldn't get there, that would probably be her fault – for running away, for ignoring his attempts at communication for so long, and for not being honest.

Her knee was, unsurprisingly, no better than it had been when she left New York City. In some ways, also unsurprisingly, it was worse. Her local doctor had confirmed that surgery was unavoidable, and every day was a day closer to absolutely needing to have that done. She just couldn't quite bring herself to pull the trigger. In the meanwhile, she was doing physical therapy in hopes of buying herself time.

Katie glanced at her phone; her moment of laziness was up. She climbed out of bed, straightened the covers, and arranged her pillows. Her mind churned as she pulled on a pair of jeans with the knees almost worn out and a sweatshirt that had been washed so many times the original color was in doubt. It might have been Brendan's; she couldn't remember. It had been here, in her dresser, waiting for her when she'd come home.

What are we going to talk about? Katie wondered as she jogged down the stairs to find Rob in the kitchen making coffee. She and Brendan didn't have skating in common anymore. He was working with his skaters. She was milking cows. There was a lot to be said for the monotonous, peaceful rhythm of life on the farm. It was about as far from life on the competition circuit as it could be, and Katie loved it. Brendan didn't; he'd shown that before.

But still he was coming to visit.

◆

Katie couldn't shake her distraction as she went through the usually soothing routine of the morning chores. Her mood must have shown. Halfway through milking, Jesse glanced over at her from where they were disinfecting the cows with iodine.

"What's going on with you?"

"Nothing." Katie knew she sounded like an incompetent teen trying to avoid trouble, but what could she possibly say? Jesse had often been less judgmental of her and Brendan's tumultuous relationship than the rest of her family, but that didn't mean he wasn't going to roll his eyes at the latest installment in the drama. Katie did, however, suppose she should warn her family about an incoming house guest.

"Mhmmm." Jesse looked suspicious and unlikely to let

his inquiry drop. He could be as determined as Katie and as ambitious in his chosen profession. Which was probably one of the reasons they got along so well. "You're not as good an actress as all those skating commentators say. So 'fess up before I ask again in front of Rob and your mother."

Katie reassessed how much she liked Jesse. He would absolutely carry through on that threat. She pulled a handful of freshly laundered cloths out of their bin to wipe down the cows with. "Brendan called."

"How did that go?" Jesse asked mildly.

"He's coming to visit."

"Is he now?" He looked surprised at that. "Not that we don't have room, but...."

Katie turned towards the cows so she didn't have to look at Jesse. "He said we needed to deal with our mess once and for all."

"And you said?"

"That he wasn't allowed to break up with me on the phone."

"Wait." She could feel Jesse stare at her. "Were you –"

"No," Katie said sharply. "We were dancing around it. Or I was. Or something. I don't know." She took a shuddering breath. "I also don't know what I want or why he's coming or where we stand. I just know this is it. If we can't make things work now, I'll never have him in my life again. And I don't want you to give me any advice, please, because then I'll be pissed and confused about you too."

"Okay. That's fine." Katie finally dared to look over at him, but he was studiously attaching a milker to a cow. "We'll keep pretending like your life is normal."

"Can you not be obnoxious about this?" All Katie needed to make this situation more fraught was for her family to start meddling.

"I'm not," Jesse said placidly. "I am, however, saying that in order for me to support you in dealing with your incredibly complicated life, you can't keep pretending it's not happening."

"If I were pretending it wasn't happening, would I be back in therapy and seeing a physical therapist about my knee?" Katie asked sharply.

"No. You wouldn't. But you also haven't scheduled your surgery. Or told me when Brendan's getting here. If I hadn't asked what was bothering you, you wouldn't have warned any of us he was coming."

"A couple of days. I think." It was a fifteen hour drive, to be sure, but more than that, Brendan didn't have a life he could just pack up and leave.

Like I did.

She thought about it as she and Jesse finished the rest of the milking. Brendan would have to post-mortem the competition with his skaters and the rest of their coaching team. That meant going over their scores looking for places to improve and finding changes to make in the program that would give them more points or feel more right. She'd done it with him hundreds of times.

He'd also have to find someone to take over his responsibilities while he was gone. For however long he was gone. Skaters, like cows, weren't just something you could abandon. And if Brendan did leave without making whatever arrangements they needed, Katie would think the worse of him. It would be days, at the least, before he arrived.

16

One Week After the Phone Call

Denver, CO

Brendan sat in his car in the parking lot of his apartment building and texted Katie to let her know he was on his way. He'd sent her identical texts countless times over the years, but never when the stakes were as high as they were now. He considered the possibility that he was out of his mind.

Of course I'm out of my mind. Sane people don't win Olympic medals.

He put the car in gear and pulled out onto the street.

+

Brendan had done this drive many times, most of them with Katie. Their routes home were basically the same, and carpooling made the most sense. Together they'd drive down from the mountains and across the endless plain of Nebraska, spend the night in Omaha, and cut northward home through Iowa the next day.

They had grown up within spitting distance of each other, at least as far as the great wide parts of the Midwest were concerned. But he'd been a city kid in Minneapolis, and she'd been living a farm life on the other side of the state border. They'd been lucky to find each other. Or rather, he'd been lucky that they'd gone to the same rink and that Katie had decided he was going to be her partner before they'd ever spoken two words to each other.

He wasn't sure he'd been ambitious before meeting Katie, but he'd never admit that to her. Largely, because she'd shown up, aged nine, and told him how the world was going to be. He'd thought she was hilarious, shrugged, and done as she said. Until he started having ideas of his own.

Denver had been one of them. They'd needed whatever edge they could get once their first Olympics had started to seem possible. Katie was the absolute last of anyone involved to get on board – principally, because she hadn't trusted his motives in dragging her away from the farm.

At the time Brendan had cared about winning, not about distancing himself from the cows. Yes, the farm had freaked him out whenever he'd visited as a kid. But why Katie thought that was his motive regarding Denver, he'd never understood. But she'd eventually said yes, so he hadn't needed to.

And then this miserable drive had become a routine.

✦

For Brendan, Omaha was a place of eternal nothingness and vague dread. Which wasn't Omaha's fault in the least.

He had passed through it at least a hundred times over the last decade and a half. Yet he had never stayed in it for longer than twenty-four hours, if he stopped at all. Usually he'd had Katie with him, and it was always where they'd broken the tiniest of rules – sleeping late, eating wildly unhealthy food, skipping workouts. After their failure in Annecy, the stop in Omaha had been the last time they slept together before Katie announced their relationship and their partnership was over.

Once they'd reunited as platonic skating partners, Katie had advocated trading off at the wheel and driving through the night whenever they made the trip home. Brendan hadn't minded, not really. At least Katie preferred night driving.

◆

Staying at his and Katie's usual hotel – or at least, what had been their usual hotel eight years ago – would have been the easiest option. But that was also where they had broken up. It had been a long time ago, but Brendan didn't want to deal with the place. The memories of being with Katie were more vivid than those of every other relationship attempt he had ever made. Whatever was going to happen at the farm would be hard and confusing enough without muddying his head more.

He kept going on I-80 and found a motel a few exits past the city. Alone in his room, he thought about texting Katie to update her on his progress but decided against it. He didn't have anything specific to say, and until or unless he did, he didn't want to risk rupturing whatever fragile peace had allowed her to invite him in the first place.

He found it nearly impossible to sleep. He kept tossing and turning, expecting to open his eyes and see Katie's dark hair spread over the pillows. When he did finally fall asleep, he slept so soundly the first three alarms he had set, just in case, completely failed to wake him.

He finally jolted awake when a car horn blared outside.

Shit. I wanted to be on the road earlier than this. He pushed back the blackout curtains and looked out at the sun already peeping up above the horizon, bathing the grubby parking lot in warm, golden light. Katie was certainly already awake and would have nothing but judgment for him sleeping in.

He threw what little he'd unpacked back in his bag, grabbed a bagel and a cup of coffee from the lobby, and got in his car. Holding the bagel in his teeth, his coffee in one hand, and his phone in the other, he texted Katie. *Leaving Omaha now. See you tonight.*

Katie finally replied when he was close to the Nebraska border. *Fucking Omaha.*

He laughed aloud, feeling strangely unencumbered. They could still say so much to each other with so few words. Maybe that was a bug in their relationship, but it felt delightful.

◆

Omaha should have been the halfway mark, but stops, traffic jams, construction, and maybe his own nerves meant that what should have been a seven-hour drive turned into twelve hours on the road.

The sun was low in the sky, tinting the green fields with amber as it sank towards the horizon. The land was flat, startlingly so after the mountains of Colorado. Hours of driving across it hadn't been enough to get used to such an open horizon. As such, Brendan could see the house long before he reached it. It had white siding and a red roof, with gable windows looking east and west across the fields above a wraparound screen porch. Beyond it were the barns and outbuildings.

There were lights on, beckoning warm and inviting. At least, Brendan hoped they were inviting.

He parked his car next to another sedan and two mud-spattered pickup trucks and turned it off. The music he'd been listening to fell suddenly silent. There was only the ticking of his cooling engine, the soft whirr of insects in the grass, and the sound of his own breath.

As he got out of the car, Brendan felt immensely self-conscious. Stepping out onto the ice in front of thousands of spectators was not as bad as walking across the drive with, as far as he knew, no one watching.

He had to open the door to the porch, which screeched horribly on its hinges, to get to the front door. Brendan winced at the sound, convinced anyone within a half mile of the house had heard it. But when he knocked there was no response. He rocked on the balls of his feet, his stomach squirming unpleasantly. Should he knock again? Was he being pointedly ignored?

He had just pulled out his phone to text Katie when he heard footsteps. A moment later the door was yanked opened by Katie's uncle Rob. He was as sturdily built as ever, his greying hair and faded overalls threatening to converge into a single steely non-color.

"Brendan Reid," he said in a low, perfectly terrifying voice.

"Mr. Petersen. Hi."

"I expect you're here for Katie." Behind him, Brendan could hear the clatter of dishes

"Um." *Get it together, Reid.* Brendan had never, in all his years of competing and performing, experienced what other people called stage fright. But he was pretty sure he was now. His tongue was tied, and his mind was blank. He could think of nothing to say to justify or explain his presence.

Suddenly he heard Katie's voice from inside the house. "Is that him?"

A second later she was walking towards him down the front hall that led from the kitchen, and then she was standing there in the doorway behind her uncle. She wore jeans and a sweatshirt with fraying cuffs. Her hair, hanging over her shoulder in a messy braid, was longer than

Brendan remembered. It was also more noticeably two different colors than when he had last seen her. She must have decided to grow out the dark, almost black color she dyed it once and for all.

Brendan reminded himself to breathe. He'd worked beside her all day, every day, for nearly two decades. He'd always thought she was beautiful. But three months had passed without seeing her at all, and now she was standing right in front of him. She was even more lovely than he remembered.

"Hi," Brendan said again, because apparently his vocabulary had been reduced to monosyllables.

"You're staring," Katie said unhelpfully.

Of course I'm staring. You left me three months ago. That's the longest I've gone without seeing you since I first met you.

"Do you want me to chase him off?" Rob asked Katie.

Brendan was almost sure he was joking. Mostly because if Katie had wanted him chased off, she would have done it herself. Rob knew that as well as anyone.

Brendan really, really hoped he wasn't about to get chased off. Katie lifted her chin and looked him up and down, clearly evaluating. She wasn't doing anything to put him at ease, which he knew was deliberate. He found it infuriating, but what could he do? He was on her doorstep and at her mercy.

"Did you bring a bag?" she finally asked.

"Yeah," Brendan said uneasily.

"Go get it."

Katie and Rob looked at him expectantly when he hesitated. Since there was nothing else for it, he slunk back to his car and got his suitcase out of the trunk, feeling their eyes on him the entire time. When he was standing on the porch again, Katie nodded at her uncle and they stepped back to let him in.

"He's here to work," Katie said, not to Brendan, but to Rob. "As long as he does, he's fine. He'll be up at four with everybody else." Her eyes might have flickered to Brendan, but he couldn't be sure. "He can stay in the guest room."

With a twirl of that two-tone braid, she vanished deeper into the house. As far as Brendan was concerned, she took his heart with her. He'd spent the last week and the whole drive trying to figure out what he wanted to happen once he got here. And now he knew. He didn't care what it took: He was going to figure out what he had to do to have Katie by his side always – on or off the ice.

Brendan was startled out of his newfound clarity by Rob making an exasperated noise after Katie. Apparently, she was as much of a handful here as she could be on the ice.

"Sorry about that," Rob said as he picked Brendan's suitcase up. "Follow me."

"I can get that," Brendan protested.

"I know you can, but you're a guest regardless of whatever Katie's decided." Rob smiled at Brendan. "Let's get you settled and fed."

✦

Katie's uncle's kindness had assuaged Brendan's most significant concerns about this adventure until he was jolted out of sleep the next morning by the unholy blare of his alarm.

He fumbled for his phone to silence it. Four a.m. *Dear God.* He was used to early mornings with skating, but this was next-level. For a moment he reassessed how much he wanted Katie.

He stumbled around in the dark getting dressed; he didn't think his retinas could take the glare of a lamp this early. Even the muted glow of the very charming hurricane lamp on the bedside table was too much. He tried to guess what would be useful to wear for farmwork. At least he didn't have to worry about whether his clothes matched.

Katie had seen him in far worse shape.

She was in the kitchen when he arrived downstairs, holding two coffee mugs. "You're up," she said.

"You sound surprised."

"It's really early." She gave him the hint of a grin. Brendan's sour mood evaporated faster than he would have thought possible. He would have gotten up a lot earlier than this for that smile.

"Here," she said, pushing one of the mugs at him. "Coffee. Now come on, we've got work to do."

The morning passed in a semi-delirium of cold, caffeine, and cows. Brendan was relieved that Katie's mom, Samantha, and her other uncle, Jesse, were as unphased by his presence as Rob seemed to be. Not that it made the work easier. First, they had to prepare the cows' food, although they wouldn't get that until later. Then milking happened and was a process which involved a great deal of science fiction technology and way more cow interaction than Brendan was strictly comfortable with. And, despite Katie's warning, Brendan somehow managed to get iodine all over his hands.

"That'll stain," Katie said from where she was crouched next to him, showing him how to disinfect a cow's udder.

Brendan did his level best not to give away how worried he was about being stepped on. "Can't be worse than a black eye, yeah?" he said.

Katie cracked a faint smile. "Just don't get it on me."

Which was as close to a dare as anything he'd heard from her in ages, but he wasn't about to start roughhousing around farm animals.

There were *so many cows*. Every time Brendan thought they had definitely milked every cow on the planet by now, another group would appear, lined up by Katie's mom, ready to go. Outside it was slowly growing light, the landscape turning from black to grey to pale green and bright gold.

There was something to be said for glancing up and seeing the sunrise in between tasks. The experience of morning here was different from being at their home rink – aside from the cows, of course. There you never knew what time of day it was; everything was lit with ghastly overhead lights and windows were few and far between. But here, Brendan could never forget that a world beyond what was right in front of him existed.

After the milking was done, it was finally feeding time. Once that was finished, Brendan was ready to collapse in a heap in any corner of the barn. He was more than a little relieved when Katie tilted her head at him and asked if he was ready for breakfast.

"You mean it's not noon already?" He was joking. Mostly.

"Seven-thirty. Come on. Once the cows eat, we eat. Rob makes some killer pancakes."

They walked side-by-side back to the house, not touching or speaking. Brendan was exhausted, sore, and more freaked out by cows than he had been yesterday. But he'd survived the morning, and he was always proud of himself when there was work to do and he could do it.

That said, he had no idea when he'd finally have a chance to talk to Katie about the issues that loomed between them. The chores were obviously intense and continuous. And Katie's mother and uncles were always around. Brendan liked them fine, but he wasn't prepared to have any sort of conversation that might turn into a shouting match in front of them.

"How are your folks, Brendan?" Samantha asked, startling him out of his reverie as they all sat around the dining room table for breakfast.

"They're good." He knew he should say more, but he was no more able to speak fluidly this morning than he had been last night.

"Did you see them on your way here?"

Brendan was sure it wasn't appropriate to say *No, I almost drove all night just to see your daughter, I didn't want to stop and see my parents.* "I didn't get a chance, yet. On my way back, maybe."

"We talked to them the night you and Katie won," Samantha said, with a smile for both him and Katie. "They're very proud of you, you know."

Brendan glanced sideways at Katie, who looked as surprised as he felt. He hadn't known that, actually. His parents had talked about coming to Harbin to watch them, but had never followed through. They'd congratulated him on the win in a series of enthusiastic voicemails, but Brendan always felt uneasy about the way they sometimes ignored everyone else who helped make it possible – very much including Katie.

He hadn't known that their families were on any kind of current speaking terms. His parents had been cordial with Katie's family when they were children. But after their breakup a gulf had opened he assumed would never close for so many reasons, matters of class and culture among them.

For the last year Brendan had been so wrapped up in skating, and in the all-consuming issue of him and Katie, that he'd never thought about how the two of them would navigate existence in the world outside the ice. For the first time, he began to understand a fraction of what had terrified Katie so badly back on the tour.

"We're very proud of you, too," Samantha said. "Both of you."

"Thank you." Brendan was too touched to be any more articulate than that.

"I'm sorry we couldn't make it out for one of your tour stops," Samantha went on. "We tried, but none of the cities were close enough – taking days off is hard around here."

"We watched all the videos we could find online, though," Jesse put in.

"Yep," Rob added. "Had all the neighbors over. Got the projector up and everything."

"We had some questions about those lifts." Jesse teased. "And not about the physics of them."

"Oh my God." Katie put her elbows on the table and buried her face in her hands. "Please tell me you didn't."

Is she blushing? The idea of video of the two of them playing out jumbotron-style over the living room wall was enough to make his cheeks go red too.

"Of course we did." Samantha was smiling broadly now. "Hometown girl and boy make good. Everybody wanted to see."

"Why didn't you ever tell me about this before?" Katie demanded, her voice muffled by her hands.

"You didn't seem to want to talk about skating," Samantha said.

"And I do now?!"

"Brendan's here," her mother said simply.

Katie dropped her hands to the table and looked helplessly at him. He looked as helplessly back. She was feeling the same thing he was, Brendan was sure. Which was less embarrassment over their lifts than surprise that the world had continued spinning while they'd been lost in their drama. That their families had, somehow, at some point, returned to being on speaking terms with each other was even more confusing. How had he not known? How had he never thought to ask Katie or his own parents whether their families were in touch?

"Okay. Brendan and I are going now." Katie stood up from the table and tugged his shoulder.

It was the first time she'd touched him since they'd held hands in New York the night before she left. And it was the first time she'd wanted to be alone with him since he'd arrived. Brendan's heart sped up.

She led him into the kitchen, where she turned her back on him to fidget with the coffeemaker. Brendan leaned against the counter, uncertain. *What am I supposed to do?*

If they were on the ice, he would have known how to draw the answer out of her. But they weren't in their shared world, they were in hers. Because Brendan had wanted to come here, and he wanted to make things work. Right now, that meant being in Katie's world with her. Not just tolerating it, but *being* here. Like she'd asked him to in a hotel back in Sacramento, he needed to not focus on the future. With patience and contentment, he needed to stand with her in this kitchen with the worn countertop, the loudly whirring refrigerator, and the cheery yellow curtains that stirred in the summer breeze coming in the open windows.

Katie grabbed the carafe from the coffeemaker, spun sharply as she turned to the sink, and winced. The movement was a tiny one, but Brendan was instantly on alert. He hadn't asked for an update on her knee, hadn't dared. But now he studied her leg carefully while she had her back to him and couldn't see him do so. Would she ever tell him what was going on in any detail?

"Not a word about skating," she said as she rinsed out the carafe. "Not a *word*."

"They started it, not me."

"Did you know our parents still talk to each other? And that it's still a mess?"

Brendan shook his head. "No. I didn't know either of those things." At least if he'd been in the dark on that, he'd been in the dark with her.

"Oh my God," Katie said, shaking her head.

"Are you embarrassed?" Brendan said, in lieu of knowing how to ask her anything useful.

"I don't have anything to be embarrassed about," she grit out.

"You're right," he said. "You don't. Neither do I. I mean, other than the stuff with the lifts."

Katie groaned.

"I think it's sweet that they tease you about it," Brendan said. "And that they care so much."

"Of course you would," Katie said scornfully. She carried the carafe, now full of water, back to the coffeemaker and poured it in.

"What's that supposed to mean?" Brendan tried not to feel hurt. They had been on the same side for five whole minutes, and now they were back to wherever they'd been before.

"It means you didn't grow up where there had to be family meetings about who was going to drive me to skating practice and who was going to travel with me to competitions," she hissed. "Any time off the farm meant more work for everyone else."

"Do you feel guilty?" Brendan was sure she did, but they'd never talked about it.

Katie glanced at the clock over the stove. "It's almost eight-thirty. What do you want to do next, chickens or baby cows?"

She was changing the subject. As much as Brendan wanted the rest of this conversation to happen, he knew the kindest thing to do was to follow Katie's lead. "Uh. Baby cows?" At least he was already familiar with cows after the morning. Chickens would likely be a whole new sort of horror.

✦

The baby cows, Brendan had to admit, were pretty cute, and they were as excited to see Katie as particularly large and gangly puppies. But that was a brief respite in a day of otherwise overwhelming work. The chores didn't even have the advantage of monotony yet, at least for him.

Living creatures were unpredictable, and Brendan had no idea what he was doing. Katie or her uncles or her mom had to keep answering his questions. Katie might have said he was here to work, but he sure didn't feel like he was being of much help or passing whatever tests she had set for him.

And, as was becoming rampantly clear, those tests weren't just about cows and farm work. He couldn't stop churning over the conversation during breakfast. There was so much that he was finally starting to understand about Katie and the massive wounds she'd been carrying around – without him even noticing them – since they were children. About his city existence versus her farm life. About the coldness of his parents towards her. About her anxiety. About her need to be the best, always, which Brendan had thought was about the sport and now was realizing was maybe about everything but the sport. He was starting to see how all of that had collided in the most spectacular and disastrous way the morning she'd decided to leave him in New York.

But understanding didn't make him less hurt – or less furious – about that. Katie effectively trusted him with her health, not to mention her life, every time they got on the ice together. Why hadn't she talked to him?

By the end of the day Brendan was absolutely beat, physically and mentally. There was no way skating was harder than this. And skating was hard – falls, and bruises, and bleeding feet hard. But it came with music, and most days, one sort of victory or another. He couldn't see that in farming. Not now, not yet, and, he suspected, maybe never. With all the data he was finally getting from Katie, he was starting to realize that might be the fatal deal breaker between them. At least when the end came, he would understand what had happened.

He was climbing the stairs to go take a shower when he heard Rob ask Katie, "Aren't you being too hard on him?"

Brendan stopped with one hand on the railing. Eavesdropping was bad form, but after the day he'd had, he wasn't in the mood to be scrupulously polite.

He could imagine Katie shaking her head when he heard her reply. "He knew what he was getting into."

"I'm not sure that's true."

"Give him a few days at least. He'll come around or he'll leave."

Katie, I love you, and I have fucked up more than once when it comes to you, Brendan thought as he resumed climbing the stairs. *But I am not the only problem around here.*

✦

The next three days were more of the same: Chores, meals, sleep, repeat. Katie was no more forthcoming than she had been, and while Rob, Jesse, and Samantha were all friendly with him, he knew Katie still viewed him with suspicion and distrust. Which, as the days went on, Brendan was getting increasingly tired of. He wanted to work things out with her more than anything, but he wasn't going to be able to do that if she never gave him a chance.

After dinner on the fourth day Brendan wanted nothing more than to crawl into bed, sleep for twelve hours, and wake up somewhere else. But Katie asked, with that look of cool challenge in her eyes, if he wanted to have a beer and watch the sunset with her. Brendan couldn't say no.

For the first time since that brief conversation in the kitchen, they were alone. The entire situation felt too much like the first awkward months when they had started skating together again after their separation. Whatever he said, Katie would surely take it the wrong way. He couldn't entirely blame her.

The sunset was lovely, probably, but Brendan was too tired to appreciate it. His gaze kept wandering to Katie, sitting on the porch steps next to him, her legs stretched out, tendrils of her hair escaping its braid.

Katie took a sip of beer. "It looks like trash, doesn't it?" She didn't turn to him as she spoke.

"What?"

"My hair. Growing out. Like I can't afford to keep up the dye."

"I wasn't thinking about that." He hadn't been at any rate, but he filed it away with the growing list of Katie's hurts that maybe he had never noticed because they'd both been so focused on just one thing.

"I tried to color correct it, so it wouldn't be all chunky, but then it streaked and the ends didn't take." She shrugged. "I gave up worrying about it. But I've seen you looking at it."

Because I like looking at you. Because you're always beautiful. "You want to know what I was thinking about?"

"Enlighten me." She was sharp for being the one who had offered to sit with him and share a drink.

"I was thinking that you were the one who left me high and dry in New York. Yet, here I am, busting my ass, like I'm the one who fucked up."

"It's only been four days."

"Well it's been a really long four days. The question stands. What am I doing here?"

"I don't know, Bren. You're the one who called me. We've both done an awful lot of fucking up over the years."

"I don't disagree. But I was really, really pissed at you."

"I know. I said I was sorry."

"Jesus." Brendan sank backwards to lean on his elbows.

"If you came to try to talk me into anything, you can leave right now," Katie said sharply.

"Who says I came to talk you into anything?"

Katie didn't bother to respond, fixing him instead with a sharp gaze and an arched eyebrow.

"The only thing I came for was closure, and I'm starting to feel like you won't even give me that, on the phone or in person." When she continued to say nothing, he went on.

"I'm making a life. Without you, thanks very much." A life he'd maybe been a fool to leave behind.

"Then why did you bother coming?" Katie demanded.

"I don't think you want me to answer that right now." He was tired. Physically. Mentally. Of Katie's ongoing inability to say anything that mattered or give him the least chance.

"Fine." Katie tucked her knees up to her chest and wrapped her arms around them.

"Fine," Brendan echoed.

17

After Katie and Brendan's Tiff on the Porch

Star Prairie, WI

Katie didn't expect Brendan to be up at four again the next morning. She assumed he would finally balk at his rude introduction to farm life and would sleep in or, worse, split in the middle of the night. She would have deserved it, too. But there he was, standing in the kitchen, fully dressed and pouring coffee into two mugs when she came down the stairs.

"You're still here," she blurted.

"I am," he said placidly.

She was surprised and had no real idea what to make of it. "How'd you sleep?" she asked simply because the silence demanded filling.

"We're doing small talk now?" Brendan handed her one of the mugs.

"We are at this hour, yeah."

Brendan shrugged. "Let's say the work means I didn't notice the springs in my back as much I could."

Katie bristled. But before she could snap at him,

Brendan held out a placating hand.

"Hey, no. Not like that. I appreciate the hospitality. I appreciate that we're trying to figure this out. Maybe I shouldn't talk at this hour either."

Katie's anger, if it didn't deflate, shifted from him to herself. She needed to stop thinking the worst of him. But she probably also needed to stop thinking the worst of herself.

She doubted if what she'd done over the last few days counted as anything but testing behavior. But all the therapy terminology in the world wouldn't make that knowledge useful. She either needed to give Brendan the benefit of the doubt, or she needed to tell him to leave.

She didn't want him to leave.

Beside her, he glanced at the clock on the kitchen wall. "We should get going, yeah?"

Katie nodded mutely. She walked beside him as they made their way to the barn to start mixing the cows' food. She kept being impressed. He'd floundered at first, but was undoubtedly finding his feet, with the work and with her.

How did he keep doing this? Here he was, months after she'd abandoned him, worming his way into the parts of her life he had always hated, like an alchemist. Or a thief. And it was good having him here, better than she wanted it to be. Brendan right beside her, his body so familiar, so a part of her own imperfect one, was overwhelming.

She felt immensely guilty for the secret she was still carrying about her knee.

✦

Later that morning Katie updated some of the cows' medical logs they kept in the small addition at the back of the house that they used for an office. As she left she found Brendan laughing in the yard with Rob. She had missed the joke, but she didn't miss the way Brendan's whole body lit up when he laughed. His hair was standing on end where he'd run his fingers through it, and there were streaks of mud and probably manure on his jeans. Katie had never expected to see him like this, so easy and happy, off the ice and unaware of her. She had to stop in the office doorway to stare.

Suddenly she could picture the rest of her life looking exactly like this, dirty and happy and strong. But that was fantasy. Brendan would get tired of the animals eventually, if he wasn't already; they could be difficult and strange and as full of heartbreak as they were of love. If it wasn't the animals, it would be the dirt, or the work that never ended, or life out here, so far from a city. And if it wasn't any of those things, it would be her knee.

And then where would she be? Alone, in a way that would be impossible for anyone else to ever understand. Because his limbs were her limbs, and his victories were her victories. Which is why that damn seventeenth place in Stockholm had always made her so mad. He was better than that. He'd been better than that. Even apart, he was supposed to be better than that.

But maybe, right here and right now, for this one moment, fifth or seventeenth or first…none of it mattered anymore. Katie felt something unspool inside of her, as if a life in the world was somehow, suddenly possible.

"What?" Brendan had caught her staring. Rob gave them both a knowing look – Katie hoped Brendan didn't see it – and strolled away.

She shook her head, but it was clear he wasn't going to let it go. "You're starting to look like you belong here instead of like you showed up for a photoshoot."

"I didn't –"

"You did." Katie levered herself upright from the doorway and started to walk away. She needed space to process this.

"Where are you going?" he called out to her.

"We're not the lone survivors of a zombie apocalypse. I need to drive into town. Meanwhile, chickens need feeding. Berries need picking. When you're done making friends, make sure someone gives you some work to do."

◆

There was something about getting on I-94 and leaving the farm behind with Brendan in its care that Katie found exhilarating, assuming he was still there when she got back. But she couldn't focus on that now. These hours in Minneapolis weren't about their issues. They were about focusing on herself and getting stronger and happier, regardless of what Brendan did or did not do.

The physical therapy regimen for her knee was not as aggressive as it could have been, but she wasn't getting ready for a competition or looking for a non-surgical fix. Rather, she wanted to keep the pain down and the functionality up, buying herself time until she could get her head around the necessary, but nerve-wracking, medical intervention. She was unsettled enough by her competitive career ending; the looming surgery only made her feel worse about it.

Despite all that, Katie looked forward to her physical therapy appointments as much as her therapy-therapy appointments. Not because she was particularly sanguine about the more challenging parts of self-care, but because they gave her the opportunity to get on the ice without anyone in her family having to know about it.

Like most days when she came in after a PT session, the rink was crowded. Public ice time in the summers meant the rink was often swarmed with people, many of whom were just trying to cool off in the mosquito-laden heat.

Katie didn't mind. Her leg wasn't in any condition to do anything flashy, and she didn't want to draw attention to herself. She was happy to skate a few laps around the rink before going into the center to practice her spins and do a few single and double jumps. It wasn't the freedom of doing the impossible that she so loved in her Olympic career, but it was hers and hers alone. In these months of trying to accept the state of her life, body, and relationship with Brendan, being on the ice without her partner had been a real help.

Physical therapy also enabled her to push through her obstacles and relinquish some of the constant worry she gave her body. Even for an hour a week, that was usually a blessing. But today, she struggled with handing that over.

Brendan been sleeping in her family's guest room for almost a week now. He got up in the dark and did every single task she set in front of him, almost entirely without complaint. Even when he knew, had to know, that she had half set them up to drive him away.

He deserved better from her, and that was going to have to start with the truth. About her leg and about everything she was afraid of. She wasn't sure she was ready yet. But she knew, for the first time, that she would be soon.

◆

The dinner hour was long past when Katie returned to the farm. She might have been stiff and sweaty, but she was also ravenous and was looking forward to devouring leftovers while standing over the stove. She had one last round of work with the cows before she was done for the day, but food had to happen first.

Katie did not expect her access to leftovers and the stove to be blocked by empty glass jars scattered over every surface and Brendan wrestling with a multi-quart pot of jam. The eastern sky outside the window was velvety blue with twilight, and the old glass-shaded lamp over the kitchen table glowed warmly.

"Oh no," Katie said, dropping her bag and keys by the

kitchen door. "Who let you do this?"

"What?" Brendan tried to blow his bangs out of his eyes. "Your mom showed me."

"You're going to give everyone botulism."

"I have been informed, presumably reliably, that the natural acids in berries are enough to ward it off. And your recipe has lemon. So it should be fine." Brendan was right, of course, but he didn't sound particularly convinced.

Katie sighed loudly. Brendan was charming. This bullshit situation wasn't, however. "All right. You're approaching this as a hobbyist. But this is part of our business, which means this kitchen shouldn't look like a third grade cooking class exploded in it. I'm going to get this organized, you're going to not burn that jam, and later we're going to find a way to get back at my mom for inflicting this on both of us."

Brendan, she realized when she stopped talking, was staring at her slightly starry-eyed.

"What?" she asked defensively.

"I missed this."

"Do you have some culinary past you never told me about?" she asked as she pushed past him to rearrange the jars waiting for jam into neat rows. She could hear the sound of the TV drifting in from the living room and felt like she was a teenager again with a boy over, her family keeping a quiet eye on them from a distance. Not that she ever had anyone other than Brendan over to begin with.

"No. I meant me trying to figure out something new and you trying to make it perfect."

Katie was glad she had work to do. She couldn't face his kindness or affection right now, wouldn't be able to until she told him about her knee. She promised herself she would get there. But first both she and the cows needed to eat.

"You know what would make this actually perfect?" she asked.

"What?" Despite her brusqueness Brendan was still smiling at her.

"You getting out of my way enough that I can stuff some food in my mouth before I have to go visit those cows."

✦

Beer at sunset on the days Katie didn't have to go into the city became a ritual. Her mother, Jesse, and Rob left them alone for it, and Katie was grateful. Especially after the jam incident. She was relieved not to have to deal with knowing looks or sidelong glances every time she sat down next to Brendan on the old steps, close enough to touch. They didn't, though. No matter how much time they spent in proximity with all the easy, casual physical interactions necessary to the chores, they kept space between them here. But it was charged, electric, and growing more so every day.

Sometimes they talked about small things: The little events of the day. The weather. What to make for dinner the next time it was their turn to cook – her family had shamelessly added Brendan to her roster in that regard. One day, when a cow lost a calf after a particularly hard birth, Brendan sat in silent commiseration next to her, both of them sniffing occasionally before splitting one more beer.

Brendan never questioned her absences from the farm when she went to her therapy appointments. Katie had overheard him talking to his skaters on the phone or over Skype, offering advice and what assistance he could from a distance. But he never talked to her about those calls, never volunteered any details about the life he'd temporarily left behind in Denver. Eventually, Katie realized he wasn't going to do either of those things, not unless she let him in and gave him permission.

She found, almost to her own surprise, that she wanted

to know. Brendan may have wormed his way into her life here, but she missed skating with him and the world she'd left behind.

"Do you like it?" she asked one evening a week and a half after Brendan's arrival. The sun had sunk below the horizon and the sky in the west was a vivid red, fading to the purple of an old bruise.

"What's that?" Brendan looked sideways at her.

"Whatever you've been doing the last three months. Choreography, I guess."

"Oh!" He smiled. "Yeah. I like it a lot, actually. I only don't talk about it because I thought you wouldn't want to hear."

"I'm sorry. About that. It's…been hard. But you're also just saying that because your kids won," Katie said, cautiously teasing.

Brendan shook his head. "No. I'd love it if we didn't win. Or if they didn't even compete at all."

"What's it like?" Katie asked the next evening. The clouds were spectacular, streaked with gold and amber. She wished she could have a costume that looked that vivid.

Beside her, Brendan stared out at the view with at least as much awe. "You know how you knew exactly what the judges wanted?"

Katie nodded. He was right. She always had.

"It's like that," he said. "But knowing what other skaters need."

"How do you know what you're doing?" Katie asked the evening after that.

Brendan shrugged. "I don't."

The following night a storm came in, low and slow from the northwest. Lightning was visible for miles, and Katie and Brendan sat at the table in the kitchen, watching the thunderheads roll their way across the sky. It had been a hard day, and her knee was a dull ache that pulsed in time with the thunder.

"Do you think I would like it?" Katie asked between strikes.

Brendan shook his head. "Choreography? Probably not. But I think you might like working on the technical elements."

He answered her questions, and he never answered anything but her questions. He didn't push or assume or give her more information than she asked for. That didn't feel like fear. That felt like respect. He wasn't here to convince her of anything.

Katie stood abruptly. If she was going to ask Brendan about his work, if she was going to dig deep and finally see the appeal of his post-competition life on the ice, she owed him the truth about her own circumstances.

"I need to tell you something." She tugged Brendan out of his chair and towards the door.

"Rain's coming," he protested.

"We won't go far," Katie said, even though she knew he was probably afraid of getting caught in a serious squall in the big emptiness of the farm. Especially with lightning on the horizon. Which was reasonable. "I just…I just need some air and actual darkness. Or I'm never going to get the words out."

She dragged him across the grass in the dark towards the main barn. She could hear the cows stirring. At this hour, they should have been quiet, but the impending storm and the sound of people who might be bringing more food must have had them on alert.

"I can't see anything," Brendan said, stumbling behind her in the dark.

"Good."

Brendan stopped walking. Katie felt him twist his hand in her grip right before he grabbed her wrist in turn and tugged. She stumbled into him and caught herself with her hands on his chest.

"You said we wouldn't go far. What's going on?" Brendan demanded. The horizon flashed with lightning again and a cold wind blew up around them.

"You're messing up my moment." Katie didn't feel ready. She had planned to keep walking until she felt ready.

Brendan drew in a breath that sounded like a hiss. "And you're messing up my life. This wasn't where I planned to spend my summer vacation. What is going on?"

And that was it, the rejection she'd known was coming from the moment he'd arrived. "I thought you were starting to enjoy it here." She curled her hands in the fabric of his shirt, as if by hanging on tightly enough, he would always be with her. "I hate you sometimes, did you know that?"

"Crystal, goddamn clear, Katie. Now are you going to tell me why we're out here, or are we going to get struck by lightning?"

Lightning, for a moment, seemed preferable, but then her anger kicked in, and it was beyond useful. If he really was going to leave, she had nothing to lose. Suddenly she was no longer worried about disappointing him with the failures of her body. Not when she could hurt him with them.

"I need surgery," she said loudly so he could hear her over the sound of the wind. "On my knee. Probably before the end of the year. I don't want to. And I'm scared. I don't know how things will be after. Maybe good, or maybe not. And until you got me so furious with you, I was worried about letting you down because of it, even when we weren't talking. But here we are." She threw her hands up in the air in frustrated disgust.

She couldn't read Brendan's face in the dark, which gave her one more thing to be angry about – her own pointless plan for this confession.

Lightning flashed too close, and the hair on her arms

stood up. The thunder came, too fast. The rain, gentle in a way that wouldn't last, started falling.

Brendan looked up at the sky and then at her. "Can you run?" he asked. "Because I think we need to run."

✦

Rob was standing at the door when they returned to the house, soaking wet and shaking with the exertion of their sudden sprint.

"Goodness, you two. Are you all right?" he asked, frowning and pulling the door closed behind them against the now-raging storm.

Katie nodded mutely; Brendan did the same. She wasn't okay, far from it, but she really did not want to talk about it. With anyone.

"Did you find them?" she heard Jesse's voice call from the direction of the office.

"Yeah, I've got 'em. Still in one piece."

Are we, though? Before her family could fuss over them any more, Katie escaped upstairs.

✦

She was surprised to find Brendan still there in the morning. Apparently he was sticking out this ruined summer vacation, though God knew why.

The next few days were quiet. They didn't talk much, just kept their heads down and did the work. It reminded Katie of those fragile, awful, hopeful days after the disaster of Stockholm when they had reunited on the ice but hadn't settled into their natural rhythm yet. Brendan wasn't leaving. She wasn't chasing him away. Something was about to happen. She just didn't know what.

"I'm going into the city this afternoon," she told him at lunch.

"Yeah?"

"I have a physical therapy appointment. I – thought you should know."

Brendan didn't blanch at the reminder that she was injured, and Katie no longer felt the need to hurt him with everything she couldn't do anymore.

✦

Katie got back home from her physical therapy appointment – and another secret hour of skating – after sunset. This time, there was no Brendan making a disaster of the kitchen with his jam-making. As she covered a bowl of leftovers so they wouldn't spatter and slid it into the microwave, she heard his voice call from the living room.

"Is that you?"

She didn't need to ask who he meant. Having him here was so comfortable. But how to make that comfort last? "Yeah, just a minute."

She walked into the living room a few moments later, holding her bowl of chili with her fingertips so it didn't burn her hands. The sky beyond the windows was a riot of gold and orange, but inside the room was dark, lit only by a lamp in the corner. Brendan was in the armchair next to it, his laptop open on his knees.

"What are you working on?" Katie sat down on the couch, adjacent to his chair. "Stuff for your kids?"

Brendan shook his head. "Um. Not exactly."

He sounded – not guilty, but wary. Of her. She'd caught him out at something.

"Are you watching porn?" Katie was sure he wasn't, but it was fun to watch the tips of his ears go red.

"In your mom's house?! No."

"Then why are you being weird?" Katie dug into her chili.

Brendan seemed to consider something for a moment.

Then he stood up, laptop in hand. "D'you mind if I…?' he gestured at the couch.

"Sure." Definitely curious now, Katie set her bowl on the end table as Brendan sat next to her, the screen of his laptop angled so she couldn't see it.

He took a breath, like the ones he took before they were about to attempt something new and potentially dangerous on the ice. He turned the laptop around so she could read the screen.

Katie squinted at the document he had open. It was full of the notations Brendan used when he was choreographing, a mixture of ISU notation and his own shorthand. It was definitely a figure skating program. But if it wasn't for the kids he was helping coach….

"I started working on a program. For us."

Katie stared at him. Goosebumps broke out up and down her arms. Something in her soul thrilled. She never thought she'd hear Brendan say those words again.

Brendan squirmed a little in her silence. "Look, don't get mad. This is mostly fantasy anyway. I don't have any expectations. Of you or us or your knee. This isn't me asking for anything. But we always were my favorite pair to choreograph for."

Katie wasn't mad. Not at all. But she definitely had questions, and she desperately wanted to see what Brendan was imagining for them.

"What song is it?"

"Oh. Right." Brendan clicked a couple of keys, and music started to play.

Katie smiled. "This is one of the ones you were listening to on the bus that one time."

Brendan looked cautiously pleased. "You remember that?"

"Of course I do. I ran away; I didn't suffer a memory lapse." Katie's voice was sharp, but there was a teasing edge to it. Brendan's smile grew wider in response. So she wouldn't have to face that smile and the way it made her stomach flip, she turned back to the laptop.

She was expecting something pretty, but easy. Something that would coddle her knee. And she was prepared to be upset about that. At best, maybe there would be some single and double jumps. But what was actually on the screen....

She knew Brendan was good at choreography. But either his three months helping with the junior teams had polished his skills, or he'd never let them fully loose before. This program was – or at least it had the potential to be – art. And it didn't even lack for jumps.

Katie looked up at Brendan. "You put in triples. There's even a quad."

He nodded.

"How is this possible?"

Brendan pointed to some of his notations. "To be honest, I'm not sure it will be. But if you do surgery and rehab...who knows what's possible. I was thinking too we could switch our takeoff and landing feet, change our direction of rotation."

"That won't be easy," she said in what was possibly the understatement of the century. For a skater, switching jumping directions was approximately like trying to learn to write with their other hand.

"No, and we never had time to think about working on anything like this while we were on tour, or I would have tried it. But now, the circumstances...if nothing else, they give us time."

The jumps weren't the only challenge in this program. There were lifts, lots of them, all longer and more intricate than what was allowed in competition.

Brendan pointed at one. "Also, for these...they won't be easy. For either of us. I know I'm not in good enough shape for some of them right now. But they'll keep your feet off the ice. I know they'd look amazing."

Katie, picturing the lines their bodies could make together, could only nod in agreement. "We're not skating together anymore," she said sadly. She felt an uncomfortable stab of guilt. First she'd lied – or at least omitted – to Brendan about her knee. Although she'd finally come clean, he had no idea she was still skating on the sly.

"Yeah, I know." Brendan nodded. "Like I said. This was just for fun. But...."

"I knew there was going to be a *but*."

"If we ever did skate together again. For any reason. And this is not me asking," Brendan said firmly. "But if we did...I know you never loved tours. I know you miss the challenge of competition, the judging and the scores. But just because we're getting too old to compete doesn't mean we can't still do incredible things. If someone says tour, you see an easy skate to a pop song you don't care about. Lots and lots of big jumps probably aren't in our future, at least not the way we used to do them. But once you get surgery, with the work you're doing on your knee...I know how driven you are. When I think about a tour now, I think of four a.m. ice times and going back to the gym and being absolutely brutal together with you, the way we were when we were at our best. Not to win. But because we want to and because we can. Although. Like I said." Brendan took the laptop back. "This is academic. I'm really not asking for something."

Good, Katie thought. *Because if you did right now, I'd say yes.*

Which was only a problem because she was happy here on the farm. Her family needed her. She could never go back to skating full-time, and Brendan would never want to share his time, or her, with the cows.

✦

In bed that night, Katie couldn't sleep. She was tired

from chores, from her therapy appointments, and from skating, but her mind wouldn't stop racing. That, on its own, was familiar enough. She'd spent plenty of sleepless nights worrying over competitions, scores, music choices, a lift they couldn't get right in practice. More recently, she'd worried over Brendan, the cows, the rest of her life, and her inability to stop worrying. But this wasn't her anxiety plaguing her.

She'd made a mistake in listening to the song Brendan had picked for the program he absolutely wasn't asking her to skate with him. Now she couldn't get it out of her head. And so she was lying here, her headphones on and the song on repeat, imagining what they would look like if they ever did do that routine together.

She missed skating with Brendan. She could admit that now, in the privacy of her own room. Her own sessions on the ice were good. Necessary. Skating without Brendan had helped teach her to feel like a mentally healthier person who could also live without Brendan.

The thing was…she didn't want to live without him. She felt secure enough now in her own self, and in her own independence, to be able to acknowledge what she still missed: Him, beside her.

After all, alone on the ice, she would always be half of a whole.

If they did what Brendan was suggesting – pursue sport for sport's sake, accept their limitations, but see what other boundaries they could press up against and break – they would be incredible. Glorious. They had always been able to do things other people couldn't do. Maybe that didn't have to end.

She could see it now, in her mind's eye: skating with Brendan again, just the two of them, their arms around each other as their blades cut through the ice. Brendan's hands woven through hers as they practiced footwork. His fingers splayed across her back for a spin. Digging into her hips for a lift.

She imagined the mood shifting as they let themselves play. She could picture practicing their emoting and chemistry so they could sell a love story that had never – despite all the times they'd denied it or tried to ignore it – been fictional at all.

Fantasizing like this was a bad idea, but Katie couldn't stop the hot spike of want that coursed through her at the idea of being on the ice again with Brendan's hands on her.

They'd skate so close they'd practically be in each other's faces – one of them pursing forward, the other skating backward. They'd risk tripping over each other except they always knew exactly where the other was. Brendan would press his forehead against hers, slide his nose along her cheek, his mouth so close to hers but not kissing her. He'd done that in so many routines, and she wanted to die from wanting him every time.

In her mind's eye they breathed the same air as Brendan grabbed her waist and dragged his hands up her sides. She dug her hands into his shoulders, making him hiss with pain and the promise of pleasure. At that point they should spin apart, to continue the dance of will-they-or-won't they that captivated audiences.

Having sex of any sort on a skating rink was a really terrible idea both practically and professionally. In reality, Katie would never. But that didn't mean she wasn't going to fantasize. She imagined Brendan backing her up against the boards, slipping one hand under the waist of her pants and pressing the other against the front of her throat to feel her breath catch and her pulse speed up.

Maybe she shouldn't be entertaining these thoughts, maybe it was awkward, with Brendan asleep in the room down the hall and so much still unspoken and unsolved between them. But she wanted him too badly. Wanted what they could be together, in the perfect world where all the parts of all their lives fit together.

She twisted in bed, shifting to slip her own hand into her pajama bottoms. She hadn't had sex with Brendan in eight years. But she knew him better than she knew anyone else on the planet. Closing her eyes, she could almost feel the heavy weight of his body pressed against hers, the warmth of his mouth on her skin, and the stretch of her most secret parts as his fingers worked inside her.

With her unoccupied hand she pinched her own nipples, pulled her own hair. She hated Brendan that he wasn't there to do any of those things himself. Katie worked herself to orgasm efficiently and fiercely. When she came, she shuddered and turned her face into her pillow. She didn't want to risk being heard any more than she wanted the sensation to end. Her lungs heaved with the effort and joy of it all, like she had just finished a skate with Brendan. But then, in some part of her mind, she had.

She lay in bed awake, alert, and alone in the dark, waiting for shame or embarrassment about having masturbated to fantasies about her theoretically platonic skating partner to creep in. But they didn't. There was only warmth and contentment and, under it all, the thread of desire that had always tied her and Brendan together…and, maybe, always would.

18

Three Weeks into Brendan's Farm Adventure

Star Prairie, WI

Brendan wasn't ever going to love farming the way Katie did. But three weeks into this strange sojourn, he had to admit there was a contentment to be found out here with the fields and the cows. He felt like he was beginning to understand what it meant to Katie to be here and work towards a goal that wasn't skating but was just as important.

As wary and angry as Katie had been when he'd first shown up – and as angry as he had been about her mistrust in return – things were better now. Not easy, not perfect, but good and getting better. She had let him into her world. Brendan wasn't afraid she'd run away again, and not just because she had nowhere else to go. Whatever he was still doing on the farm, she wasn't testing him anymore.

They'd actually managed to talk over the last few weeks. They'd fought too, but then they always fought. The difference now was that this time their fights had actually led to them solving issues. They'd covered important ground: Their families. Brendan's choreography work. Katie's knee. The last few days had been honestly lovely. But there was one conversation left: What were they going to do about *them?*

Brendan didn't know how that discussion was going to end. He had no idea how to start it. But one of them was going to have to, and soon. July was melting into August. The days were growing almost imperceptibly shorter. Brendan's life was full of flexibility, but he couldn't put it on hold indefinitely. Video calls to the kids he was coaching were helpful to them, but no substitute for him being at the rink with them and the rest of their coaching team every day. Eventually he'd have to go back to Denver, his skaters, and his obligations.

The clock was ticking. Time, as always, was against them.

✦

Katie's family and their neighbors had a stall at the farmers market in Saint Paul. Katie had spent the occasional day there, but had never invited Brendan along until now. And so, early on a Saturday morning, Brendan loaded up the back of Katie's pickup with home-baked pies, eggs, crates of jam, and boxes of berries. He wondered what had changed in her head to make her ask him this time.

For now, though, he needed to focus on the task at hand. Which was providing the perfect counterpart to Katie's charming farm girl shtick. Brendan had made sure to dress for it. Over the last few weeks his clothes had migrated from his suitcase to the closet and drawers in the bedroom he was staying in. At his request, which hadn't seemed awkward until he said it aloud, Katie had dug through them for something appropriate to the occasion. So he was wearing jeans and a checked button-down over a white T-shirt. Katie wore a wine-colored sundress, the blonde part of her hair mostly hidden under a broad-brimmed straw hat. She looked miles away from the girl in battered jeans and a worn T-shirt shoveling manure.

Once everything was secure, Brendan climbed into the passenger seat. "For a second, I thought you were going to make me ride in the back."

"Why?" Katie said as she buckled her seatbelt. "It's a safety hazard and no one's going but us."

Brendan shrugged. "Eggs and pies are fragile?" he offered.

"You packed them right. You tied them down right. It's fine." She paused and frowned. "You don't think these last couple of weeks have been about me punishing you, do you?"

He considered his answer carefully. "I think they've been about a lot of things. And I think you are not always aware of how much you need it to hurt when you want something."

Katie laughed and winked at him. "I think you underestimate me."

Whatever response Brendan had been expecting, it hadn't been that.

◆

After the relative solitude of the farm, the bustle and noise of the market took Brendan by surprise. He reveled in it, though. The early morning combined with the organized chaos of people unloading trucks and setting up their stands reminded him of nothing so much as the exhilarating hours before a competition. Talking with the dozens of people who came to their table was like all the most enjoyable parts of media and coaching rolled into one.

Katie gave him a sideways smile after he finished up a particularly involved conversation with a grandmother and her granddaughter about the joys and pitfalls of growing strawberries. He wrapped up their purchases and handed them to the little girl, who placed them carefully in the tote she was carrying and waved at him as they walked away.

"You're having fun."

Brendan grinned back at her. He surely was. But he hoped it wasn't news to Katie that he could enjoy this life with her. "You sound surprised."

"I'm not. Just impressed."

"It's like doing meet and greets. Only about farm stuff. Although I'm not going to lie, it is nice knowing what to do for a change."

"You're really good at it. You should use this part of your brain with me more."

There was an invitation in there, or at least a question, but in the middle of a Saint Paul farmers market was not the place to dig further. Brendan contented himself with brushing his fingertips along her waist, then turned to talk to the next potential customer. Behind the cover of the table, for the briefest of moments, Katie twisted her fingers into his.

✦

When the market closed, Brendan didn't feel ready for the day to end. He was as tired as if they'd been practicing on the ice or doing media for twelve hours. But it was the good kind of tired that came with landing all the jumps and having all the right answers.

"Want to stop somewhere and get dinner?" Katie asked as he hopped up into the passenger seat next to her. "I'm starving."

"Sure," said Brendan, delighted at the prospect. Spending more time with Katie was exactly what he wanted, now and probably forever.

They didn't have to get up for the first shift with the cows tomorrow morning – that was part of the deal within

Katie's family, the consolation prize for whoever had to trek out to Saint Paul for the market. Which meant they could stay out tonight as late as they wanted.

Brendan felt like a kid in high school again, missing curfew to hang out with Katie just a little bit longer. Maybe they should have stopped at an actual restaurant and gotten real food. But they ended up sitting in the cab of Katie's pickup in a parking lot, eating greasy burgers and sharing an ice cream sundae out of a styrofoam cup. Brendan thought it was exactly perfect as he and Katie kicked at each other's feet and smiled at each other almost shyly as they fought each other for the last french fries.

When they were done, Katie threw a packet of handi-wipes at him so he didn't get grease all over her truck. *Was this what it would have felt like*, he wondered, *if we'd dated when we were younger, instead of doing whatever the hell we were doing?*

Despite how difficult so much of their time together had been, Brendan realized he didn't have any regrets. Their tension and conflict had made them what they were, as individuals and as a pair. Their struggles through the years also made him appreciate quiet moments like this: driving home together as the sun set behind them, the windows open. Katie's hat was discarded on the seat between them, and her hair was coming loose from its braid.

Twilight was fast fading into night when they turned off the county road and up the drive to the farm. Brendan hopped out of the truck as soon as Katie parked it and moved around to the back, ready to unload the empty crates and coolers. To his surprise, Katie shook her head as she stepped down from the driver's seat.

"Leave it," she said.

"...what?"

"It'll keep 'til morning."

Brendan folded his arms on the tailgate. "I've never

heard you say that in your life. Ever."

Katie gave him a smile that was sly, challenging, and determined all at once. She'd often used it on the ice in their more brutal programs. Brendan was glad he had the tailgate for support. How had he done this dance with Katie for so long without losing his mind entirely?

"We missed sunset and beer," she said. She walked towards the house, swinging her hat in one hand. Halfway there, she stopped and looked back over her shoulder. "Well? Aren't you coming?"

✦

Katie's remedy to missing their evening date on the porch was, apparently, to get a fire going in the pit out back between the driveway and one of the sheds. She'd pulled a sweater on over her dress. As he approached the fire with a six pack, a bag of marshmallows, and grilling skewers, Brendan frowned.

"Is that my sweater?"

"Yes."

"You stole my sweater!"

"Not for the first time and I very much doubt for the last." Katie crouched next to the fire and rearranged a log with a poke from a long stick.

Brendan wanted to make any number of comments about that statement, but he didn't want to put her on the defensive. Not when today had been so pleasant. So he dropped cross-legged into the grass and opened a bottle of beer for each of them.

Katie took hers and clinked it off of Brendan's as she sat down. "Today was nice."

"All of this has been nice," Brendan said.

"I didn't chase you away, you mean. You don't have to pretend."

"Who says I'm pretending?"

"I've known you for twenty years. Coming up on twenty-one now, I guess. You're pretending."

Brendan looked at her incredulously. "Are you sure about that? Or is it easier to assume that nothing ever changes between us, so we don't have to deal with who we've become?"

"Ahhhhh, and here it comes."

Brendan shook his head. "That's it. That's all I've got. No theories, no arguments. I needed this. I needed the break. I needed the hard work." He took a breath. He didn't know how to start this conversation, but he didn't think Katie did either. He might not get a better chance than tonight. "And I needed you."

For a moment, Katie's eyes went wide, but as Brendan watched they hardened again. She scoffed. "So you can go back to Denver or Minneapolis or wherever and win more gold medals with your kids."

Why, why do you always do this Katie?

Brendan wasn't going to rise to that bait. Today had been wonderful, and now Katie was scared, as she so often was, of the sweetness and vulnerability between them. Brendan knew she was frightened, but he also knew that if she could take a breath and give them a chance they could work through this.

"Maybe. Maybe not," he said. "They're their medals. Not mine. I'm actually pretty clear about that."

"I don't believe you."

Brendan chuckled. He wasn't going to rise to that bait either. "I don't need you to understand. But it's probably not dissimilar to how you're okay out here. It feels good, familiar, like you're accomplishing something. I may have hated your cows and your mud and your terrifying chickens when I was twelve, but that doesn't mean that I don't see what it does for you or don't get that it matters."

"Do you still hate it? The farm?" Katie's voice was small and her hands fussed in her lap. That, perhaps more than the question, shocked Brendan.

"No. Of course not. I meant what I said."

"But you did. Hate it. Before." She wasn't asking. She was declaring a fact, and she wasn't wrong.

Brendan didn't think there was much sense in torturing himself over stuff he'd gotten wrong as a child. But right here and right now, he was cursing his younger self for making this mess he was trying to dig himself out of twenty years later. "I was a kid. I didn't grow up around animals and machinery like this. The calves being born in the middle of the night and all this intense stuff that you just took in stride – I didn't hate it, Kate, not really. I was freaked out by it."

"Oh." Katie's voice was soft. Stunned. As if, after all these years and all their fights, she'd finally let herself listen to what he was saying.

"Yeah, oh." He sat in silence, trying not to be angry about all the ways their communication – when it wasn't perfect – was always completely messed up. "Maybe I didn't express myself well. I'm sure I didn't, but you really thought I hated the farm?" This wasn't how he had thought the conversation about their future would go, but he could tell they were rounding the corner into it.

"Yes. No. Maybe." Katie tore absently at the grass and clover her beer rested in. "I thought you were ashamed of me."

"What?!" If Brendan had ever been ashamed, it had been at his inability to keep up with Katie in every stunning facet of her excellence.

"Ballerinas and princesses don't come from places like this," she said. "And that's what little girl skaters get told to be. I was better than you. I had to be. Or you skating with me was going to mean I was a charity case."

Brendan wanted to groan in frustration with Katie, with himself, with the world. "Please, please tell me you're joking."

"Why would I joke about that? I've been carrying it around with me my whole life. Every time we won, every time we had to talk about our early years to the press, every time I'm reminded that since Annecy our families only talk when there are unavoidable Team USA niceties to be performed."

"That's changed, apparently."

"Not much! And it was miserable, for ages." Katie was still looking at her hands.

Brendan wanted to grab them between his own, to make her look at him, to convince her with his touch of what he had failed, for so long, to convince her of with his words. That she was brilliant. That she was his world. That they were meant to do, together, things other people could only dream of. Always.

He made himself stay where he was. "There are a million ways you've always been able to break my heart, but the possibility that we've been a mess forever because as kids I was afraid of cows and you were afraid of what – me? kindness? pity? – might be too much to bear."

"I never meant to break your heart."

"Which is why you dumped me in that mess after Annecy."

Katie's posture changed to something straight and fierce. "That was completely unrelated and totally necessary."

"But *why?*" In all the arguments they'd had in the four years since their comeback, he'd never been able to get a straight answer from her on that.

Katie set her jaw. "We didn't work when we were together."

Brendan frowned. "Do you want to know what I think?"

"You know I wait on your every word with bated breath." Sharp like before. But fonder now. Like maybe, just maybe, she was ready to listen.

Brendan took a deep breath. Time to say what was necessary and, after so many years of struggling and miscommunication, suddenly so incredibly obvious. "I think the problem was never that the universe didn't want us to be together, or was punishing us, or whatever you thought was going on. I think the problem is that when we slept together – or so much as kissed – you stopped trusting me."

"You sound hurt," Katie said.

"Of course I'm hurt!" Brendan dug his fingers into his hair. "I've spent more than half my life learning to pick you up. To throw you across the ice. To do spins without cutting you. To keep you safe. So why is sex when you stop trusting me?"

"Oh, like you've never dropped me," she said scornfully. Still, Brendan couldn't look away from her.

"I did. I have. But you let me do it again and again and again until we were perfect. So why didn't you let us do the work off the ice too?"

"I knew the costs if we lost. I didn't know the costs if I lost you."

Brendan looked at her earnestly. Again, he had to restrain himself from reaching for her hands. In her current mood Katie would probably pull away. "You could never lose me."

"I did. For four years. And it was terrible."

"Because you broke up with me!"

"You think I don't know that?" Katie said in frustration as she tugged a knife out of her boot. She flipped it around and offered him the handle. "You keep staring at it. Cut it off."

"What?" Brendan tried to adjust to the sudden change in topic and also the knife in Katie's hand.

"My hair," she said, like it was obvious.

It really, really wasn't. The conversation had shifted beneath him wildly. He was sure it made sense, somehow, but he didn't know how to follow it. The look on Katie's face only confirmed his suspicions. "H-h-how much?"

"The dyed part. A little quicker on the uptake please?" she said, clearly exasperated.

"What the fuck, Kate?" he demanded.

"I know we've always wanted each other, no matter how much our lives and our other choices made that hard or impossible or, just, the absolute worst idea. But if you want this thing between us to have the remotest possibility of working, then you need to want me as I actually am, and not just as the girl who figured out how to win you a gold medal by being incredibly different than she actually was."

Brendan reached out a hand and, when she didn't withdraw hers, closed it around her wrist. "What if I told you I've always wanted both of them? That there's never been a difference to me? That I knew what you were doing – *always* – and I loved you for it, public and private."

Katie dropped the knife into his palm and undid the elastic at the end of her braid, shaking her hair out. "Well then. Let's see."

Brendan was intensely grateful for all the years he'd spent helping Katie do her hair for competitions and performances. They meant an impromptu haircut was not, perhaps, as strange as it might have otherwise been. Even sawing through her thick hair with a knife was not as difficult as he'd expected.

"This is really sharp," he observed.

"Sharp knives work better. And they're safer. Of course it is."

Trust Katie to turn even this into a lesson in practicality. Brendan smiled to himself.

The next few moments were silent except for the wind moving in the grass and the soft sound of their breath. When he'd cut away all the dark hair, Brendan ran his fingers through her hair to comb out the last loose strands. Katie shivered, which did nothing to help his equilibrium.

"All right, all done," he said.

She turned her head over her shoulder to look at him. Her gaze was sharp and her hair was messy, hanging unevenly at her chin. But it was all honey blonde now, the color it had been when they were kids.

Without another word, Katie looked away from him to bend and twist, gathering up the dark hanks of her dyed hair that had fallen in the grass. She threw them in the fire. The flames hissed and cracked, and for a few seconds smoke, acrid and chemical, billowed out of the pit.

Something animal in Brendan recoiled at the smell while something human in him recoiled at the sense of magic that pervaded the darkness.

"It looks good," he said. That was true, but he was mostly speaking in hopes of feeling less frightened.

"Does it?" Katie was peering at him again, less unkindly than before.

"Yes."

She seemed to make a decision. She stood from where she was crouched, feral, by the fire, brushing her hands off on the sides of her dress, as if there was more than hair there, the residuum of a spell Brendan didn't entirely understand. "You should prove it to me then."

Impelled to follow her, he rose to his feet without thinking. "I really want to kiss you," he said breathlessly. "Can I?"

19

Seconds Later

By the Firepit

Katie nodded, relief and want washing over her like a wave. The air around them had grown so strange since she'd pulled out that knife and burned her hair.

"I have no idea what we're doing," she said as a wild laugh bubbled up from her chest.

"Neither do I." Brendan wrapped his hand around her wrist. His fingers were strong, his hands rougher than they'd been before he'd done so much farm work. His voice was filled with gentle wonder that seemed to chase away whatever Katie had summoned with her impulsive decision about her hair.

Suddenly, she felt like she had the freedom to do what she wanted, and, for the first time in months, she knew exactly what that was. Her eyes went hard, like they sometimes did on the ice when she and Brendan were at their best. She yanked out of his grasp.

Brendan took a placating step back.

That's not what I want at all. Katie followed him and

grabbed his face as hard as he had grabbed her arm. His evening stubble pricked against her fingertips as she went up on her toes to kiss him.

His mouth was soft and warm and yielded eagerly to hers. But then he tried to say something.

Katie pulled back a millimeter. "Is there anything I need to know?"

Brendan shook his head with a comical eagerness.

"Excellent," she said. "Because unless you have an objection, I'm going to need you to shut the hell up."

"Oh, thank God." He laughed as he seized her around the waist with one arm and dug his other hand into her newly-cropped hair.

It hurt, in the very best way, and Katie gasped into his mouth. Brendan had turned the tables on her so easily.

"Good?" he asked.

Katie growled. Her body being weak for him had always, only, made her stronger and hungrier – for joy, for victory, and for her own perfect pleasure.

"Good," she said.

She and Brendan echoing each other happened on the ice all the time. Katie hadn't expected it here, but there was no reason for him to stop knowing her, inside and out now that they were about to go to bed with each other. She just had to trust him. And herself.

He kissed her again, roughly, his tongue sliding along hers and their mouths fitting together as if they'd been made for each other in all their many facets. She loved Brendan when was kind and pretended he needed her in order to be ambitious. But she also loved Brendan when he was a man who could throw her around and be proud of it. Sometimes, she thought he was afraid of the fiercer version of himself, and that fear got in his way. But maybe that was why he was also so simply and damnably decent, and why she was able to be here with him now.

Tonight, she didn't want Brendan's sweetness or

gentleness. She wanted him to devour her. She wanted the all-consuming desire they portrayed on the ice to play out here and now.

Unable to tear their mouths away from each other, they stumbled towards the house. Katie was glad; she wasn't going to have sex with Brendan for the first time in eight years in the grass. But she was almost dizzy with desire. The house seemed awfully far away.

Suddenly Brendan spun her and pressed her against something. Her eyes flew open in surprise, and she glanced over her shoulder to see what she'd landed against. Her truck.

With her head turned, Brendan pressed his mouth to the side of her neck. *I'm not the only one who's impatient,* she thought victoriously. The kiss stung as he grazed her skin with his teeth. Her pulse pounded in her ears, and she dug her fingers into his back.

"House is too far away," he mumbled against her skin.

"I agree, but are you seriously going to fuck me against the side of my truck?" Her voice quavered as Brendan dragged his nails up the side of her thigh.

"Would that work out for you?" he asked.

Oh, game on.

"Sure." She hooked a leg up over his hip to show she meant it. They'd had a spin in their Harbin free skate that was supposed to suggest what this actually was. On the ice, the space that was barely between them, the anticipation, the possibility, had won them gold. But this, and the dissolution of that space to come, was better.

Brendan slid his hand further up her leg, bringing her skirt with it, his palm warm and firm against her bare skin. "Condoms?" he asked.

"Glove compartment," she said against the salt of his neck. A girl had to be prepared. Although it was basically an accident that she was prepared. Her fantasies hadn't looked like this.

Brendan pulled back and stared at her. "Seriously?"

"Seriously what?" Her leg was still wrapped around his waist, and she could feel the hard length of him pressed against her. The last thing Katie wanted right now was a conversation about anything.

"You gave me all that grief about hooking up at the Olympics and you have condoms in your glove box?"

Katie rolled her eyes and pressed her hips against Brendan's, to see his breath catch and his eyelids flutter.

"It's a good thing I know you're not serious," she said. He needed to stop complaining and do as he was told. The payoff was going to be great once he did. "Can you just go get them?"

Brendan pulling away from her, even to yank open the door of the truck, was torture. She shivered from the absence of his touch and listened impatiently as he rummaged around in her vehicle.

There was a pause, a moment of complete stillness, and then she heard him start to laugh. She grinned to herself. It was her favorite sound in the world, and she knew exactly what he was reacting to.

Brendan came around the back of the truck, holding a strip of condoms emblazoned with the Harbin Olympic logo. "Okay…I have to ask…again…." He struggled to get the words out, he was laughing so hard.

She reached out reflexively to him as she started to dissolve into hilarity herself. Brendan dropped the condoms into the truck bed behind them and took her hands in his. Still laughing, he kissed the back of her wrists. Their eyes met, and Katie felt herself melting. This, right here, was what made them such a good match: Their ability to take any moment, any emotion, and be in it so fully together.

Not always fun, she thought, *but always perfect*.

She pressed her forehead into his chest as they both heaved for breath and tried to quiet themselves.

"I can't believe you took Olympic condoms for a souvenir," Brendan said. Katie could feel the vibrations of his voice in his chest.

"Yeah, well, I wasn't going to let them go to waste because we were too busy winning to do anything else. Just because I'm prepared," she added, "doesn't mean I've had a ton of opportunity."

Brendan grew serious and cupped her face in his hands, his thumbs stroking the skin beneath her cheekbones. "You always had opportunity with me."

Katie shook her head. "Please don't make us talk about the past right now."

"Not remotely on my agenda." Brendan ran his hands fiercely down her sides and rucked up the loose skirt of her dress. When he went to his knees, he took her black cotton underwear with him.

"Hey, uh, warning," Katie said, stopping him with a hand to his shoulder.

Brendan looked up at her. "Yeah?"

His brow was creased, his gaze distracted. He didn't look like he remotely cared about anything except touching her. Katie wondered why she just didn't let him. But some guys were assholes, and while she was pretty sure Brendan wasn't – at least not in this particular way – better to know now than in about two seconds.

"You know how I didn't keep dying my hair?" Katie had no idea why she was being delicate about whether she shaved or waxed or *whatever* when she was hopefully about to have Brendan's face between her legs.

"...yeah?" His fingers traced circles behind her knees.

"That's not the only skating queen maintenance I stopped doing."

"Oh. Okay...wait. Why is that a warning?" He looked genuinely confused. Katie loved him so much.

"In case you care." *I hope you don't care.*

"I care about getting my mouth on you in every

possible way," Brendan said firmly.

"Okay then." She shrugged. He better have meant it, or she was going to be angry. She didn't have time for anyone, even Brendan, being squeamish.

He flipped up the hem of her skirt and pressed his face against her. He slid his cheek and lips across the hair there. "See?" he said. "I don't mind."

"Well thank goodness for me." That established, Katie was done waiting.

She stepped out of her underwear and put one booted foot on his shoulder. He looked up at her, his eyes bright and delighted and needy. This moment was like skating, too – not this exact pose; among other things she'd have cut his shoulder with her blade – but the charged air between them and Brendan ready to serve her with whatever she needed.

Brendan's face said he felt it too. Katie's eyes met his and their gazes locked. Her heart pounded in her chest and her pulse echoed between her legs, waiting. As Brendan frowned in concentration, Katie brushed her fingertips across the fine lines on his forehead. Neither of them moved, poised with anticipation. Katie could hear their breath as it synced up in the calm evening air – like it always had when they were about to do something incredible together.

Before Katie was prepared for it, Brendan grabbed her bare ass with both his hands, digging his nails into her flesh. He nosed against her sex, and she could feel the rush of his breath against her. He moaned like he was drunk with the scent of her. Katie echoed him, overwhelmed as she was with arousal at the very idea.

She shivered at the first soft touch of Brendan's tongue on her. The contrast between the cool of the night air around her bare legs and the wet heat of his mouth was overwhelming. *Breathe*, she reminded herself, but her lungs didn't want to comply. The sensation, already, was too much. She gasped sharply.

Brendan pulled back enough to pant against the skin of her hip. "Good?" he asked.

Obviously.

Katie did what she'd wanted to do for so long. She dug her hands into his hair until she could feel the strands tight around her fingers and pulled his mouth back to her. The sound he made was half gasp, half needy whimper. She wanted him to make that noise again and again and again. She dug her boot more firmly into his shoulder.

As she gripped him tight, Brendan ghosted his fingers up her thigh, across her stomach, and down, telegraphing his intent. Katie bit her lip. She was about to shiver apart from his touch and the anticipation.

Brendan worked one finger into her, then another. Katie closed her eyes in relief. His hands, that she'd known and trusted and wanted for so long, were on her and in her, exactly where she needed them to be. His tongue was hot, wet, silky, against her.

The sky above them was dark and full of stars, but her awareness of anything other than Brendan was fading; Katie could feel it happen, the same way her awareness of the audience and the judges vanished right before a skate. The world kept narrowing around her until it contained nothing but the man kneeling at her feet.

She hovered at the edge of orgasm for what felt like hours, Brendan's tongue warm and perfect, his fingers sure and skilled. He was tormenting her, keeping her right on the edge, and he was absolutely doing it on purpose.

She hated him, and she loved him, and she had no idea how she'd gone so long without him.

With one last flick of his tongue, with one final twist and thrust of his fingers, Brendan finally let her come. Katie twisted her head to try to muffle the cry that escaped her throat. Her legs were shaking; her heart was pouncing. Her skin was too fragile a barrier to contain everything she felt.

If Brendan's hands hadn't been digging into her thighs, if she hadn't been braced against the truck, she would have fallen.

She looked down, and Brendan met her eyes. Falling wouldn't be so bad.

"Done?" he asked.

She scoffed. The question would have been appalling from anyone else, but Brendan was just being ridiculous and dear and making sure she had exactly what she wanted. Which she didn't. Not yet.

When her legs felt like they could support her weight, she swung her foot back to the ground and pulled Brendan upright by his shirt. She kissed him – his face wet and messy from her pleasure – like she needed him to breathe. The faint taste of herself on him was like lemons and salt.

Their hands tangled as they hurried to unfasten his jeans and shove them down. Katie undid the buttons of his shirt with shaking hands. She needed his skin under her palms as much as his cock inside of her.

Katie laughed as Brendan leaned into her and over the side of the truck to retrieve the condoms – best souvenir choice *ever*.

"Do you want help with that?" she asked.

Brendan shook his head and ripped the packet at the end open with his teeth, quickly sliding the condom down over himself. "Ready?" he asked her.

"Yes," she said. "Finally."

She gasped as Brendan curled his hand under her thigh and pushed her knee up, encouraging her to wrap her leg around his waist again. His hands were sure as he pressed her back against the truck, encouraging her to brace her weight there.

For a moment, he teased her opening with his cock, but neither of them could bear it. She felt her walls stretch as he pushed into her. Her body had been waiting for him for so long, and she urged him on with breathless curses.

Brendan held her hip with one hand and pushed the other into her hair. "Someone will hear," he whispered against her lips.

"So make me be quiet."

He sealed his mouth over hers. Which was good, because at the same time he pulled on her hair. Hard. Katie felt her whole body convulse with the pleasure of it. A cry tore from her throat and filled Brendan up.

Everything they'd ever done with each other had been a dance, like two stars orbiting each other faster and faster until they crashed. Locked together like this, they pushed each other as hard as they ever had on the ice. Katie squeezed her walls around Brendan, and he twisted her hair tighter around his fist. Again and again, they played this game, neither of them willing to let up. Eventually he lowered his free hand to her clit. He stroked against her in circles that were too hard, too much, and exactly what she needed as he thrust into her again and again.

She could tell when Brendan was about to come – his hips stuttered, his rhythm became irregular, and his breath was wild and ragged. He pressed his face into her shoulder and bit the already-bruised skin there.

"Wait for me," Katie whispered.

"Always," he said as they came together, laughing in shock.

✦

Katie dropped her head to Brendan's chest. Out here in the dark of a country night there wasn't much light beyond the stars and the dying fire. Still, she felt better shielding her eyes from it against Brendan's body. He put a hand on the back of her neck, his palm warm and his touch soothing. Katie rubbed her face against his skin and his open shirt. The fabric was damp. She was crying, her whole body trembling.

"Are you all right?" Brendan asked.

Katie felt more than heard the words and nodded frantically. The last thing she needed was for Brendan to misunderstand emotions she could barely catalogue herself. It was so much all at once.

"Yes. Of course. Just. I feel…." She trailed off. She had no language for what she was. She was relieved. And untethered from everything that had held them back for so long. Absence – even of anger, want, hurt, and fear – was still a loss after so many years.

"I know," Brendan said, kissing her hair and holding her tighter. "I know. Me too."

✦

Eventually, Katie recovered enough to realize she was really damn cold. Even with Brendan's arms around her.

"I'm freezing," she mumbled into his chest. "Want to go back to the house?"

"Oh, thank God," Brendan said. "My ass is an ice cube."

He stepped back and staggered as he tripped on the jeans that were still down around his ankles. Katie caught him as he flailed to regain his balance, and just like that, they were laughing again. Everything had changed, but they were still perfect. Still them. Katie helped Brendan pull up his jeans and re-fasten them, and Brendan fumbled around in the grass for her underwear and the trash that needed to be discreetly disposed of.

"I'm not putting those back on," she declared when he found the bit of black cotton. "The dew made them all damp and they're gross now."

"Fair enough." Brendan stuffed them in his back pocket then tugged her skirt straight and tried to smooth out the wrinkles.

"Pretty sure that's hopeless," Katie told him.

"I know. Just didn't want to stop touching you."

"Well here, then." Katie took his hand in hers and

pushed their fingers together. Brendan's answering smile was like the sun coming up.

Marginally put back together, they walked hand-in-hand to the house. Katie was still shaking a little. From the tremors in Brendan's hand she knew he was, too. Cool as the country evening was, she didn't think either of them were shaking from the cold.

Katie didn't ever want to be done with Brendan. That had always been true, even when she'd been afraid, even when she had pushed him away – on the tour, in New York, and all those years ago in Omaha after the disaster of Annecy.

They'd have to talk about that eventually, and she dreaded it. For all the ways they were inextricably linked, they were also radically, terrifyingly different, with intensely different visions for their post-Olympic lives. But whatever issues they needed to deal with – and however much her anxiety would always be a part of her – her fear was gone.

◆

"My room or yours?" Brendan whispered as they crept up the stairs, still hand-in-hand.

Katie squinted at him in the dark.

Brendan looked steadily back at her. "Unless you want to be by yourself," he said calmly, his voice soft.

"I don't."

"Didn't think so."

"My room," she said. Brendan's room was still a guest room. Hers was home. Also, she really did have the better mattress.

"Your family won't mind?"

Katie shook her head. How could her family mind? They all managed their lives exactly as they wanted regardless of anyone else's opinions. "If anything, they'll be relieved."

Somehow letting him in her room was as intimate as everything they'd done outside. She flipped on the light switch, and they both blinked against the dim light of the lamp on her dresser.

"I haven't been in here in years," Brendan said, dropping her hand and turning so he could look around.

"I haven't changed it much." Katie sat on the bed to take off her boots. When he'd visited as a kid they had hidden out here together, but as they'd grown older it had become too awkward to navigate everyone else's assumptions.

Brendan rotated until he'd taken in the whole room. He stopped when he was facing her again.

"Kate," he said, his face serious, his eyes sad.

She felt her heart skip a beat. Even in this afterglow her anxiety couldn't take a break from spinning worst-case scenarios. "Yeah?"

"Where are your medals?"

Of all the things she'd thought he might say, she hadn't expected that. "What?"

"Your medals. They weren't downstairs, so I assumed you had them up here. But...nothing." He looked around at her walls. "Not even the one from Harbin."

All of her medals from the last twenty years of her life were in the bottom drawer of her dresser. The one from Harbin was on top, carefully nestled in its box. Katie hadn't been able to look at it since she'd put it there.

"Why do you care?" Katie couldn't help how sharp her voice went.

"You spent twenty years of your life working for that gold. It cost us everything. You can't tell me it doesn't mean anything to you now."

Katie looked up at Brendan from her seat on the bed. He was still standing in the middle of her room, his hands in his pockets, his face lit by the soft glow of the lamp, his brow creased in concern.

"Maybe I didn't hide them away because they don't mean anything," Katie said. "Maybe I hid them away because they mean too much."

She hoped Brendan would understand. She hoped, after all the fights and arguments and conversations, that she wouldn't need to use words to explain this to him: that she hadn't been able to plan for a life after skating because she couldn't bear a life without skating. That, if she couldn't compete and couldn't be on the ice with Brendan, she couldn't bear the reminders. Not of her success, not of who she had been, and most importantly, not of who she could never be again.

Brendan's face melted from concern into tenderness. "Oh, Kate," he said. He sat down on the edge of her bed and wrapped an arm around her shoulders.

Once more that night, she turned her face into his chest and cried.

✦

Katie woke at three-forty-five, like she had every day she'd been back at the farm. But instead of being alone in her bed, Brendan was next to her, his arm thrown over his head and his face gentle in sleep. Katie could hear the sound of water from a bathroom somewhere else in the house, but she didn't have to go anywhere. And she didn't want to.

She rolled closer to Brendan, draped her arm across his bare chest, threw a naked leg over his, and closed her eyes again.

Next time she woke, the sky was barely light. But instead of Brendan's body wrapped around hers, the other half of the mattress was empty. From her closet came the sound of rummaging.

"What in God's name are you doing?" Katie asked groggily. She was usually a morning person, but not today. She wanted to keep sleeping with Brendan beside her.

Brendan pushed her closet door open further so she could see him. He was crouched on the floor and held his phone, the flashlight turned on, in his teeth. To her vague disappointment he'd put on his jeans from last night, though his chest was still bare. At least his ass looked great in those pants.

What the hell was he doing? *If he's looking for my medals, I'm going to kill him.*

Katie heaved a sigh of profound aggrievement and turned on the lamp on her bedside table.

Brendan took his phone out of his mouth and switched the flashlight off. "Where are your skates?" he asked.

"What the hell?" *Good. Not my medals. Still inexplicable, though.*

"Your skates, Kate."

"Why do you want to know?"

"Because there are two ways this can go from here. Either you can trust me on and off the ice and we can make this work for more than a night, or you can't and we can't. Until we figure out which one it is, well…stuff could get messy."

Katie started to protest, but he held up a hand.

"Messy got us here, it's okay," he said with a smile she couldn't help returning. "But what I would like more is for us to figure out how to make our lives work together, while having as few unnecessary fights as possible."

Katie stared at him. "What about my knee?"

"Your knee is a medical condition you can treat. Whatever happens with it happens; I love you for a lot more than your knees. Most importantly, it's not an omen or a sign. It's just something for us to work around." He looked at her expectantly.

Skating with Brendan again was everything she wanted but didn't know if she could have. What if, after the wonder and magic of last night, they fell apart again? But he was right. They needed to find out eventually. In the meantime, the uncertainty had the capacity to tear them apart.

Feeling brave, Katie sat up and threw the covers back. "Okay. My skates are in my truck."

◆

Katie drove. Brendan sat next to her, both of them wrapped in friendly, barely-conscious silence.

Eventually, Brendan spoke. "You walked away from skating three months ago. Why are your skates in your truck?"

He'd found them, finally, after Katie had followed him outside and given him very specific directions: Safe in a case that would protect them from whatever elements they'd encounter in her truck, wedged behind the seat where neither he nor anyone in the family would notice.

"Maybe they're like the condoms," she said. "I just didn't have the opportunity."

Brendan shook his head. "I don't think so."

"Why'd you bring your skates?" she challenged.

"Hope or habit," he said. "Who knows."

Katie sighed and gripped the steering wheel more tightly. His honesty bought her own. "Whenever I go into Minneapolis for therapy? I've been going to the rink after."

"I knew you missed it."

"You don't need to sound so smug about it," Katie retorted. He wasn't wrong, though.

"I'm not being smug."

"What are you, then?" Katie glanced sideways at him.

Brendan seemed to think about that. "Relieved," he finally said.

"Why?"

"It's a selfish reason."

"I'm okay with those. Selfish is how we won.' For the first time in so long thinking about the past-tense nature of that accomplishment didn't hurt.

"It's also not complicated." Brendan traced his fingertips across her knuckles on the steering wheel. "I love the work I'm doing now. But I don't want to skate without you."

✦

During her stolen sessions on the ice over the last few months, Katie hadn't bothered with elaborate warm-ups. She wasn't skating hard enough to need them, after all. But today Brendan insisted they go through their usual routine, adjusted for what her knee would tolerate. Katie teased him for using his coach voice on her, which made Brendan look so sweetly pleased with himself she couldn't help squeezing his hand in hers.

The ritual of the routine was good. Being here was what mattered as she helped Brendan with his stretches and let him help her in return. Still, she was nervous as Brendan offered her a hand after she tied her skates. Last night they had slept together, and now they were going to skate, sore muscles and all. The last time they had so much as kissed, skating – and an entire tour – had gone miserably.

Brendan looked so hopeful as he held her hand. Katie felt as terrified as she ever had before a competition.

"Hey." Brendan wrapped his arms around her waist from behind as soon as they stepped out onto the ice. Together they glided around the rink along with everyone else. He tucked his chin into her shoulder. "You're nervous."

"Of course I'm nervous. Nervous is what I do."

"Okay. Why? Because you think we're about to fall on our asses?"

"It's happened before."

"A lot of things have happened before. Do you trust me?"

Katie wasn't sure of the universe. She wasn't sure of herself; her anxiety muddled so many things. But Brendan had always held every part of her. Last night hadn't changed that. It had just reminded her. She nodded.

Brendan squeezed his arms more tightly around her waist. "Then trust me."

She knew she had missed him beside her these last months. But now, with him actually here where he belonged, she was able to acknowledge how much she'd missed him, how very wrong his absence had felt, and how incomplete she had been without him.

Brendan spun her around in his arms so she was facing him. "Footwork first?" he asked.

"Sure."

There would have been a point, probably not too long ago, when Katie would have been angry at him for wanting to start out with something that didn't have the flash, drama, and risk of jumps. Her anxiety – and her ambition – would have thought he was doubting her. But time and her sessions on the ice by herself, not to mention therapy, had given her both distance and perspective. Brendan wasn't doubting her; he was making a reasonable choice. One he'd make for anyone. Katie had trusted him with everything else; finally, she was learning to trust him with this, too.

No one paid much attention to them as they glided around the rink wrapped up in each other. But as they started working through the footwork sequence from Harbin, heads turned as other skaters on the rink, and people sitting around the edge with cups of coffee, noticed them. The Olympics had been months ago, but this was their hometown, their real hometown, and people knew them. If not immediately by their faces, then definitely by their skating. Coming to this rink by herself and keeping things relatively simple, Katie had mostly avoided such scrutiny herself. Or so she had assumed. She hadn't looked on social media for mentions of herself in months.

"I think everybody's watching," Katie said to Brendan as he steered her through a series of turns.

"Oh?" Brendan looked around the rink for the briefest of moments before turning his eyes back to her. "I hadn't noticed. I was too busy looking at you."

Katie punched him in the shoulder, lightly. "Sap."

"Guilty. Pretty sure I've earned it, though. Does it bother you?"

Katie shook her head. "Makes me want to show off." She had always skated for him, just as he had always skated for her.

Brendan grinned at her.

Katie smiled back, unable to deny her happiness.

"Well then," he said. "Let's kick it up a notch."

They still kept things relatively easy. Pair spins without too many changes of edge or position. Some single jumps to check their synchronization – which was, as Katie had hoped, still perfect.

"Let's do a lift," she said after they landed their third single axel. They'd been careful not to tax her knee, and it was holding up so far.

"You sure?" Brendan asked.

Katie glared at him. If she was going to trust him, he needed to trust her too.

"Hey, no, I didn't mean it like that," Brendan held up his hands. "I just mean there are a lot of people here and we take up space with those."

Katie nodded. "We can make it work. We don't have to cover a lot of ice or do anything fancy, but if we're making sure we can do this, I want to make sure we can do all of this."

"Fair enough. Which one are we doing?"

Katie loved lifts. The fact that they had to work harder at them than other pairs thanks to their lack of height differential just made them that much more satisfying and fun. So far above the ice, Brendan's hands strong on her waist, Katie felt like she was flying.

Not once was she afraid Brendan would let her fall. And he didn't.

He finally set her back down, her feet landing gently on the ice. Katie collapsed with relief and happiness into Brendan's arms and let him lead them in a gentle turn around the rink. The moment felt, in so many ways, like the one last night after they'd both come and had stood shivering together in the Wisconsin night.

That skate had been lovely. Exquisite, even. There were so many things she couldn't attempt right now. But for the first time, she didn't care. She was with Brendan, and they could still skate. She'd never win another gold medal, and maybe that was okay.

With a nudge and a word, Brendan guided them into another spin. They came out of it laughing, grinning at each other like fools.

"Okay," Brendan murmured in her ear as they slowed their momentum. "So, we're good. Do you want to get married?"

Katie didn't come to a screeching halt only because Brendan's hand was there on her back, guiding her gently into another lap around the rink. "You can't ask me that like this!"

"No one heard me; it's cool," Brendan said as they kept skating. "No pressure, either. I like you plenty either way. Just thought I should ask. We've been doing this a long time."

Twenty years. One night. There was a huge difference between the two. Or none at all.

"I can't believe you're saying this." Katie ducked out of Brendan's grasp. She needed space to think.

"Wait," Brendan trailed behind her, then circled in front. "Which part?"

Katie gestured at the rink around them. "We're in

public. Don't whisper at me like we're not."

She took off around the oval. Her heart was racing. She hoped Brendan figured out what she needed him to do before she had to really and truly yell.

As she completed the loop Brendan cut in front of her casually, gliding smoothly backwards as he kept pace with her. "Tell me if I'm getting this wrong, but do you *want* people to hear me ask you?"

Finally, he understands. Katie felt a rush of triumph. "If you want the farmgirl who won an Olympic medal that one time to be absolutely, positively sure you really want her for the rest of your life then yes, people need to hear you."

"Okay, I can do that," he said far too loudly, his face bright with delight.

He was, however, still blade to ice and Katie wasn't here for that at all.

"This is the only time," Katie said, "that I ever want to see your knees on the ice."

Brendan stared at her, his brow creased. Katie knew what that expression meant, though they'd never been in a situation like this before. He was trying to figure out if she was about to say yes or about to set him up for a massive humiliation. *I know I'm difficult,* she thought, *but I would never make you do that and then say no. Trust me,* she willed, *trust me like I'm trusting you.*

She would always be sharp, she would always come from a farm, and, with any luck, she'd always live on one. Brendan had to know that any yes from her was fierce and any partnership between them would always take the form of beauty born out of contentiousness.

Brendan shrugged, as easy as ever. "Okay," he said and grabbed her hands.

He skated backwards and pulled her into the center of the rink where it was reasonably clear of other skaters. The few people who hadn't already been watching them certainly were now.

Brendan dropped to his knees with as much grace as skates allowed. A young boy skating past gasped loudly. He would crash into someone if he didn't keep his eyes on his own skate, Katie thought. She knew, because she'd made the same mistake often enough as a girl. Proposals on the ice were kind of a thing. She tried to ignore the giggles behind her, and, perhaps most bizarrely, the sight of people retrieving phones from their pockets to record the inconceivable thing that was about to happen.

"Kaitlyn. Katie. Kate."

Oh God. Brendan had started talking and, Katie quickly realized, wasn't going to be able to stop. How many iterations of her name was he going to use? This might be mortifying. But it might be perfect.

"Light of my life and bane of my existence. I love you. I love your cows. I love skating with you. I love getting up at three in the damn morning with you, whether that's for the cows or the skating or wherever our ambition takes us next." Brendan gripped her hands more tightly, his voice clear and earnest and so, so sure. "I want to keep doing whatever it is we do, with you, for the rest of our lives…although with slightly less murkiness than in the past, to be clear. So. Will you marry me?"

Katie relished the moment – Brendan's babbling, the people watching them, the vague soreness in her body lingering from the night before. So much of her life had been a success because people had liked watching her and Brendan together. To be able to bask in that attention now, when it was about all of what they were, not just the skating…. Katie felt whole for the first time in her life.

She pulled one of her hands out of his grip and covered her mouth in one last self-indulgent moment of disbelief. *This is real. Trust him. Like you always have,* she told herself.

She held her hand out to him again. He caught it and pressed a kiss to her knuckles. They were so in public, so exposed, but his gaze was utterly fixed on her.

"Yes," she said. "Of course. Now stand up because I am not getting down on that ice with you."

Brendan laughed as he climbed to his feet and wrapped his arms around her. The rink applauded, but once again, Katie was safe from the lights and the world, her face hidden in Brendan's chest.

✦

They were giddy, if practical, on the drive back to the farm.

No, Brendan could not take her to go get a ring right now, because she wasn't sure how she felt about the expense or the symbol. Yes, they should really stop somewhere and get some food. And, most importantly of all, they should get back quickly, if they wanted to be the ones to deliver their own news. Otherwise, someone at the rink would tell a friend who would tell a friend who would tell the internet and then who knew who would get to her and Brendan's families with the news.

"Do you want to call your parents?" she eventually asked. They hadn't spoken much about them since that awkward dinner conversation on Brendan's first day here. She wondered if he had ever told them he was in the area.

"Let's deal with your family and have all our ducks in a row first, if that's okay." Brendan's voice was hesitant.

Katie didn't necessarily want the answer to her question, but she brought herself to ask anyway. "They're not going to be happy, are they?" She drummed her fingers on the steering wheel.

"They're not going to know what to make of it, that's for sure. And that's fine," he hurried to add. "That's not our problem. But if we know the answer to anything they're going to ask first –"

"You mean other than 'are you sure?'" Katie said darkly.

"Well, I am sure, but yes. It'll just be easier."

"You know, I want to be furious. Or worried. But –"

"But?" Brendan teased.

"I won you a gold medal. If I'm not good enough for them, even I can tell I'm not the problem here."

To her infinite relief, Brendan laughed.

"All right, then. What do we have to figure out?" Katie asked.

The short answer was everything. Timing. Logistics. Where to live. Skating. Her health. If she hadn't been driving and if Brendan hadn't had halfway sensible – and generous – answers to most of it, she might have panicked. Instead, she was relieved that someone seemed to know how to make the chaos of her life over the last three months into some sort of pattern. But that was what Brendan did now. Choreography was a way of making people's talents and skills come together into a coherent story.

They practiced talking through their plan as they drove. They'd done that a hundred times before for wildly different things: Travel and training plans, a new program, a high profile interview or public appearance. Katie didn't want to get flustered under pressure, especially if family decided to balk in the face of big plans or big asks.

Not only did they want to have the wedding on the farm – and soon – they wanted to live there together for at least a few months afterwards. Long enough, anyway, for Brendan to sell his apartment in Denver and Katie to have and recover from surgery. After that, they could get a place and some land. Eventually they could do a comeback tour and whatever else was viable considering Katie's flight from New York. Then they could do whatever they wanted to. Brendan could help Katie set up a farm. Katie could help Brendan coach. The plan made more and more sense each time they went through it.

"There has to be a flaw in this. It seems too easy," Katie finally said when they were ten minutes out from the farm.

Brendan shrugged in that easy way she found infuriating. "I'll remind you that you said that when you wake up from surgery, and I'm freaking out about real estate, and you still haven't answered any of your business emails."

"Great. Can't wait. Marriage is going to be awesome." Despite her dry tone, she did mean it. But Brendan also wasn't wrong. The rest of this year was going to be hard.

✦

The farm, when they got there, was still a working farm. Which meant everyone was busy, difficult to find, and not interested in being in the same place at the same time. Katie dragged Brendan from house to barn and across the grazing area twice before she was able to extract promises from everyone to meet them in the kitchen. In the process, her mom handed them a crate of vegetables from the garden to bring back to the house and Jesse gave them instructions to work on packing the online orders for jams. After that, the only thing left to do was wait. At least they had work to do.

"You should let me get you a ring," Brendan said as they sat at the kitchen table assembling the jam orders.

Katie was scooping eco-friendly packing peanuts into cardboard boxes and pushing them across to Brendan, to nestle in the jars. She looked at him in exasperation and vague disbelief. "Are we really going to start fighting about that now?"

"Is it something worth fighting about, to you?"

"Clearly, yes, because I just said that."

"Okay." Brendan set down the printed list of orders they were working from and turned to face her fully. "Tell me what's going on in your head so I can go from there."

Katie took a breath. She had explained some of this in the truck, but apparently more depth was needed. "Money is a finite and valuable resource and can be used for more practical things. Engagement rings are kind of an archaic symbol of ownership. And I couldn't wear anything fancy on the farm anyway."

"Wouldn't have to be fancy. Or expensive. Or mean anything terrible." Brendan shrugged.

"I don't know," Katie said. She was intrigued enough by Brendan's interest in the subject to continue the conversation despite her discomfort. "I know girls get taught to grow up dreaming of the diamond ring and the white dress and all that. My dreams were all about skating dresses and gold medals."

"And you have those now."

"Yes. Your point?"

"Maybe I've spent my life dreaming about giving a girl a ring," Brendan said.

Katie looked sideways at him. "A girl, or me?"

"You. You fool."

"You never said before."

"I can't imagine why not."

"A wedding ring wouldn't count?" she asked.

"Katie," Brendan sounded exasperated now too. "I'm agreeing to live with you, in your world, with your cows, who I did say I loved earlier – and I do! – but are, to be fair, still gross and weird. Let me get you a damn engagement ring."

Katie stared at him in something like awe. He didn't often push back so hard against her – at least, without it turning into a shouting match. This was interesting. And felt unexpectedly very, very good.

Before she could say anything else, though, Rob knocked on the frame of the open door. "Hey kiddo. You wanted to talk?"

"Yeah, come in."

Rob crossed the room to the table and stood across from them, his hands wrapped around the back of a chair.

"What's going on?"

"Nothing bad. I promise," Katie said.

"Okay...."

Brendan opened his mouth, but before he could speak, Katie nudged his foot with hers under the table. "I only want to do this once," she reminded him.

"Uh, I think Katie wants to wait for everyone else to show up?" Brendan said to Rob. "So you can just hang out? If that's cool?"

Katie tried not to laugh at the possibility Brendan's voice had turned into a permanent nervous question.

"Okay," Rob said again, looking between her and Brendan. He sounded suspicious. In his place, Katie would probably have been suspicious too. Impromptu all-hands family meetings were a rarity. And, despite her recent assurances, usually involved bad news.

They were saved by having to stall further by her mom walking in. Jesse trailed behind her distractedly, typing something into his phone.

"What's going on?" Jesse asked "I only have a few minutes, I have to call the vet before they close for the day."

Katie looked at Brendan. He looked terrified, but she didn't know if that was of her family or of her if he handled this wrong. In any case, he nodded encouragingly, as if she were scared too.

Maybe she was. Now that they came to it, she had never expected to be making an announcement like this. Her family didn't do this sort of thing. Her mother was single. Rob and Jesse had gone to the courthouse in nice suits when marriage equality came in. But there had been no engagement, only the happy formalization of a relationship that had been strong and committed for years.

Brendan, as if reading her thoughts again, smiled at her and reached across the table to cover her hand with his. Maybe she hadn't ever planned on marrying, but in the rare moments she'd let herself think about the future, she had seen Brendan right by her side, always.

She flipped her hand under Brendan's and laced their fingers together. Brendan still looked nervous, but his eyes were alight with excitement. Katie turned to her family.

"We're getting married," she said.

"Yup, we know," her mom said.

Jesse and Rob exchanged smiles.

Katie felt herself deflate a little. After all the planning they'd done for this conversation…. "You know like you assumed we'd always get it together eventually or you know like –"

Her mom grinned. "Like someone filmed you at the rink and put the video on the internet, where one of your skating buddies saw it and shared it on Facebook."

"You never go on Facebook." Katie was definitely confused.

"I do when three of the neighbors saw the video and called me to offer their best wishes," Samantha said

Katie was torn between horror and a wild desire to laugh. This was too awful. And too perfect. "You could have told me you knew!"

Jesse and Rob were laughing outright now.

"And ruin your announcement? When you two snuck back here and tried so hard to round us all up? Not a chance," her mom said.

"We didn't *sneak*." Katie protested.

"By the way, Brendan," Rob said.

"Mm?" Brendan finally turned from Katie to look at him.

"That was a good speech you gave."

"Oh my God." Brendan didn't let go of Katie's hand, but he did bury his face in his arm on the table. The tips of his ears were red. Katie ruffled his hair with her free hand.

"Don't be embarrassed now!" Jesse said, circling around Brendan's chair to clap him on the shoulder. "Your fans are incredibly excited. Also very sad you'll never propose to any of them that way."

"I told you people came to see you skate," Katie said to the top of Brendan's head. His face was still hidden in the crook of his elbow. "And now we can do our whole comeback tour without the audience wanting you to propose to me right there on the ice."

For her own part, Katie wasn't embarrassed in the least. Maybe having her family be second-hand witnesses to one of the most romantic moments of her life hadn't been the plan, but now the whole world knew how Brendan felt about her. And Brendan – blushing aside – wasn't running away from that fact.

"Okay, well…do any of you have any feelings about this other than an utter lack of surprise?" Katie said. "Because we're about to ask you a ton of favors and –"

Brendan lifted his head from his arm. "Would anyone mind if I moved into Katie's room?"

Katie looked at him sharply. *Timing, Reid. What are you doing?*

"Are you including me among the people who might mind?" she asked. His question was hardly the most pressing one on the table. Although possibly the most immediately practical one.

"I thought we talked about this," Brendan said, half chastened, half made of stubborn determination.

"We did, but couldn't you have worked up to that?" Katie hissed.

"Maybe, but the look on your face."

"I hate you."

Brendan squeezed her fingers tightly, his eyes starry as he looked at her. "I know you don't."

Rob cleared his throat. Katie tore her eyes away from her fiancé to look at the rest of her family.

"Yes?" she squeaked.

"We're very happy for you," her mother said. "Now what do you need us to do?"

20

The Rest of the Summer

Denver, CO and Star Prairie, WI

Brendan spent the rest of the summer in constant transit between Denver and Wisconsin. He had to finish his training obligations to his skaters and help find someone who could take over his role on their coaching team. He also had to deal with a tearful Miguel and a devastated Shelby who were crushed that he was leaving, this time for good.

"I'll still be around," Brendan said, hugging them both tightly. "I'll see you at competitions. And you know you can always call me."

He hoped they would. He was fiercely proud of them and deeply invested in their future. Moving to build a life with Katie was the right choice, but one that came with costs.

There were also phone calls to be made and meetings to be had and paperwork to be signed to get set up as a coach in Minneapolis. He would be an assistant coach this time, but Brendan knew the day wasn't too far away when he would have skaters of his own. Katie had never been interested in having children, and that was fine by him; as long as he could teach and mentor people who needed and wanted it, Brendan was happy.

He also had to pack up his apartment and get it ready to put on the market. One week late in the summer, Katie flew out with him to deal with her own place and the car she'd left sitting in its parking spot since the winter. After one last night in the city that had seen so much of their struggles and triumphs, they drove back through Omaha together and stayed at their old hotel. Brendan was thrilled to replace his memories of their breakup there with newer, happier ones: Katie playing with his fingers as he got them checked in; Katie perched on the windowsill of their room, stretching her legs and looking out at the city with the lights playing across her face; Katie spread out on the sheets, sweaty and panting and perfect while he went down on her again and again; Katie curled up in his arms, both of them naked while they talked long into the night.

"Are you angry?" Katie asked at one point when Brendan was sure she'd been asleep. He'd been lying there, his head close to hers on their shared pillow, watching the gentle rise and fall of her chest as she breathed, relaxed and at ease.

Brendan traced a line with his fingertips across her collarbone and grinned to himself when a line of goosebumps broke out across her skin. "What could I possibly have to be angry about?"

"This is so wonderful. If I hadn't...." she left the thought unspoken, but Brendan knew what she meant. "We could have had years like this."

"We get years like this," Brendan said gently but very seriously.

He pressed his mouth to the soft skin of her shoulder and wished he could burn his love and surety there, like a brand, so Katie would always know she had it. She wore the ring she had finally let him give her; Brendan could see it now on her finger, gleaming faintly in the dark room. But he never felt like it was enough. Katie held his body, his heart, and his entire soul; a ring couldn't begin to communicate that.

"But when we were competing…." Katie said.

"We were competing. Those years were perfect because I got to spend them with you in the way we were meant to be at the time. I wouldn't change anything about them for the world."

Katie hummed thoughtfully. "Winning was a nice perk, I suppose."

"Yeah, I didn't mind the winning."

"I can't believe," Katie said, rolling onto her side and tucking her head into what seemed to have become her favorite place, his chest, "We actually get to have it all."

✦

The wedding was at Katie's family's farm – that had been one of the biggest favors they'd asked of her mother and uncles. Katie's neighbors were all there along with most of their skating friends. Brendan's family attended, but were clearly somewhat taken aback by the rambunctious, celebratory mood. They'd always looked down on Katie and her connections as provincial and hick, and Brendan was angry about that but he was also vastly amused to see his parents take in the sight of world-class skaters, male and female alike, dressed impeccably, their hair exquisitely done, traipsing through knee-high grass to get artsy photos of themselves for social media.

Dr. Meyer officiated the wedding with the same world-weary affection that had marked all her interactions with them. Natalya did double duty and served as an attendant to both him and Katie because Katie ruled, rightly, that none of Brendan's friends were quite up to the task.

Katie wore a gauzy sundress that was a riot of whites and yellows and oranges, with antique lace trim that fluttered in the breeze while Dr. Meyer read the vows for them to echo back to each other. Brendan would always remember this moment: The late summer sun dipping towards the horizon, making Katie's hair glow golden in its rays; the fields behind her green and amber in the mellow evening light; Katie's brown eyes fixed on Brendan's, her trembling hands clutched in his, as they formalized the promise that had always been there between them. *We're okay. We're together. We're one.*

Katie had wanted the reception to be potluck, but Brendan's parents had insisted on paying for a caterer. During the planning that had threatened to reopen the aggressively unspoken tensions between the two families. But now that the day was here, the joy of celebrating a marriage and the massive convenience of having someone else on hand to clean up after the guests had neutralized any simmering tensions. By the time the cake was cut, Brendan's mother was happily drinking punch with Samantha on the porch.

After everything they had been through together, Brendan found little more satisfying than he and Katie smashing cake into each other's faces.

The eating and drinking and dancing lasted 'til well after dark. The fireflies came out and the night got cool; Brendan draped his suit jacket, that he hadn't even worn for the ceremony, over Katie's shoulders as Lena and David proved themselves the undisputed champions of the dance floor. Natalya charmed Katie's neighbors, and if Brendan wasn't much mistaken, Justin was hitting it off *very* well with one of his cousins. No one punched anyone, and Katie didn't bother to throw her bouquet. She did finally put on boots, though, and led an impromptu tour of the farm so people could visit the cows, Brendan's jacket still wrapped around her.

The party was still going when Katie slipped her hand into Brendan's and led him into the house and upstairs. After the noise and joy of the day, Katie's dark and quiet room felt like the perfect haven. He was tired, and every muscle hurt. Katie looked as worn out as he felt. Tomorrow, they would celebrate more fully, in private and with just the two of them. For tonight, Brendan was happy to unfasten Katie's dress for her, pulling the zipper down to reveal her creamy skin, the dimpled knobs of her spine, and the cut muscle of her back and hips. She stepped out of the dress and left it puddled there on the floor while she undid the buttons on Brendan's shirt and helped him with his pants. They went to bed, naked limbs intertwined, too tired to do anything else and too happy to care.

✦

The next day, they made it up to the cabin in the absolute middle of nowhere on the Minnesota side of the border as the sun was beginning to set. Brendan had wanted to get on the road earlier, but Katie's family was having feelings at her and his parents wanted to take them to lunch in the city. By the time those obligations were done, they were both restless, weary, and more than ready not to make conversation in the car.

"I'm sorry this is nothing fancy," he said when they finally climbed out of his car. Katie's truck, though it would always hold a very special place in his memory, was needed for the week at the farm.

"Are you kidding me?" Katie stretched her arms above her head, her shirt riding up and showing a tantalizing sliver of skin above the waist of her jeans. Brendan was definitely ready to make good on the honeymooning they'd been too tired to start last night. "There are no other people and no work to do. I'm sure more than a week of this would make me crazy, but right now it really is perfect."

"I still want to do something fancy once –" Brendan started.

"– we've dealt with everything we're not talking about for the next week, yes."

Brendan couldn't blame her from wanting a break from everything from wedding planning to surgery scheduling. Now he just had to keep to his part of the bargain and not bring any of it up. Katie was not always the best influence in the ways she often chose to live in the moment, but these moments he didn't want to miss.

"Come on," he said. "Let's get everything inside."

No matter how chivalrous Brendan wanted to be, Katie wasn't having it. She grabbed her own luggage and the groceries they'd picked up on the way. Brendan wanted to protest, but knew better. *She let you buy her an engagement ring,* he thought, *let her carry the damn bags.*

He was relieved, however, when she dropped the groceries on the kitchen counter and hopped up beside them. "I love your rustic cabin brilliance," she said with a grin, "but I am not doing shit in this kitchen. The unpacking is all you."

Brendan laughed. "Thank you for being exactly the sort of wife I expected you to be."

"Were you hoping for me to change?"

He shook his head and stepped between her legs. He kissed her, her lips sweet and soft against his own. He was still stunned, often, that they could do this now. That he could look at Katie, playful and happy and smiling at him – and want to kiss her – and then actually do it.

"No," he said, answering her question. Katie took his hand and twined their fingers together, smiling as she brushed her thumb over the new ring on his left hand. "No," he said again. "I didn't expect or want you to change. Honestly, I know everyone talks about marriage being this big deal that turns everything upside down, but I don't feel like that at all. You, me, us – it's all what it always was."

And isn't that the best thing in the world?

"Is it bad that I don't feel like that?" Katie asked.

"No…but you should tell me more about that." Brendan was still curious about Katie's thoughts on marriage. Especially their own. Although hell, he was always going to be curious about Katie's thoughts on everything.

"I haven't changed, but everything around me has," Katie said pensively. "That's been a long time coming, and I'm so glad of it."

Brendan tilted his head curiously. "Okay, now you definitely need to tell me more."

Katie looked past Brendan's shoulder, gathering her thoughts. "I spent twenty years of my life skating with you and not thinking about the fact that someday that life we had would end. But then it did. And I had my breakdown, which, yeah, you know, 'cause you were there for that. But…against all odds, I got to keep you? We still have a life together. It's already really different than what it once was, so I feel different about that." She met Brendan's eyes again. "But I'm happy, because I get to keep you. To be clear."

"At this point, I wasn't really worried." Brendan kissed her again, on the side of her mouth, because why not? "Although, I know you'll miss competing. And I know I can't make up for that…."

She shushed him and put her fingers to his lips. "No talking. Not about that. You promised. Also, I have spent a lot of time in therapy working on seeing the world as a place where there are still opportunities and challenges open to me. And I fully intend on taking this week to explore some of those."

As she brushed her thumb across his lower lip, Brendan was as transfixed by her words as her touch. Katie was so good at taking his breath away.

"Why do I get the sense you're about to be full of surprises?" he asked.

"Because I am," she said, sliding off the counter and into his arms before moving past him. "Come on," she said. "Bed."

◆

From the moment they'd finally gotten together, they hadn't been able to keep their hands off each other. But time, as always, had been against them. Brendan had spent so many days in Denver wrapping up his life there. When he was in Wisconsin he stayed in Katie's room, but they both kept farm hours and Katie's family was always nearby. In the few months since they'd finally gotten their act together they had never had the luxury of privacy or the time to lose whole days in bed. While they managed to have as much sex as they could, Brendan wanted more.

For eight years their affair that had started in Annecy had burned in Brendan's memory as some of the best weeks in his life. More relationships than he cared to count had crumbled because nothing could measure up to what it had been like to be with Katie. And while he would always treasure those days with her, what they had now was better. So much better.

They were eight years older, a little bit wiser, and knew so much more. About themselves, about who they were, about what they saw in each other, and about what they wanted, in bed and out of it. They'd grown up together, and they got to spend the rest of their lives together. Nothing could have felt more natural. *Finally*, they had time away from the rest of the world to learn together and play together with no obligations to skating or cows or anyone or anything except each other.

Brendan couldn't wait.

Katie led him up the creaky stairs to the loft bedroom with high, sloped ceilings; huge windows looked out into nothing but trees. Through the shimmering late-summer leaves Brendan could see the blue glint of the river. Later, he wanted to investigate that. But right now, he wanted nothing more than the woman in front of him.

There was no tease as she began to pop open the buttons of her shirt, only her steady gaze and methodical rhythm, like a skating program she had learned in secret and that she would have to save him from fumbling his way through.

One of the reasons so much sex happened at the Olympics was that everyone there was deeply aware of what their bodies could do and profoundly appreciative of similar achievements in others. Almost a year had passed since Katie was skating seriously, but between two decades of training and her work on the farm, she was in remarkable shape. She was all angles and sculpted planes, every bit of her body evidence of the years of her life spent perfecting her abilities.

Brendan stumbled slightly as he sat down on the edge of the bed.

"This is going to be so much easier," she said as her shirt fell open, revealing the smooth lines of her breasts and stomach. She wasn't wearing a bra. Brendan swallowed heavily. Katie dropped her hands to her jeans and undid the button there. "If you'd just get undressed now."

Brendan laughed. "What? No warm up? No foreplay?"

Katie stared back at him as she stepped out of her jeans. "Nope," she said with a laugh. "I spent the entire drive up here thinking about riding this ride."

✦

She hadn't been kidding.

In less time than he had thought possible, Brendan was naked and on his back in the king-size bed, desperately trying to thrust up into Katie's wet heat. Condoms had been all well and fine between them, but right now he was deeply grateful for negative test results and IUDs. But every time he tried to grab Katie's thighs or snake an arm around her waist for purchase, she pushed his hands away.

"Remember how I let you buy me an engagement ring?" she asked, digging her hands into his shoulders. Her fingertips pinched his skin; he hoped she was going to leave marks.

Brendan could barely remember his own name but made a vague noise of assent anyway. He had no idea how Katie could make words.

"Then let me do this," she breathed. "Let me have some control." She leaned down to press an open-mouthed kiss to his clavicle, soothing the scratches her fingers had left. The new angle squeezed the velvet heat of her more tightly around him, and Brendan felt himself get even harder, if that was possible.

Katie leaned lower, her spine curving gracefully as her breasts pressed against his chest. Her nipples were hard and tight with arousal but then, so were his. Brendan touched her all the time, but he'd never been so grateful for her skin against his.

Katie made a sound that was half-desperation, half-contentment. "Let me take care of you. I want you to get lost in this." She circled her hips and dug her fingers into his hair.

For the entirety of their lives Brendan had been the one who had led and directed their movements on the ice. He struggled to let go and let Katie use his body as she wanted. He knew how to lift his hips, where to touch her clit, how to press the very tips of his fingers along the pale column of her throat to make her eyes go dark and her voice stutter with pleasure. He wanted to do all those things now. They'd both waited so long, and he wanted so badly to make her feel good.

"Close your eyes," Katie ordered with a sharp tug to his hair.

Brendan obeyed.

"Good," she hummed. "Good. Now stop thinking and just feel."

Brendan forced his hands to lie still at his side, clutching the cool cotton of the duvet so he wouldn't grab at Katie's waist again. He made himself focus on the sound of his breath, and then on hers. Without effort their breathing synced. As it always had on the ice, right before a skate.

Brendan gave himself over to Katie the way he always given himself over to skating.

Suddenly, everything was perfect. Exquisite. Katie's body against his, around his, moving and using him exactly as she wanted to was a revelation. It was if the shared quest that had initially brought them together had given way to the ability to live inside their victory at it forever, happy and delirious.

✦

Brendan stroked Katie's hair absently as she lay with her head on his chest, both of them slowly catching their breath. He couldn't see her face, but he didn't need to. He wasn't inside her anymore, but the barrier between them, if it had ever existed, felt thin.

"Was that all right?" she asked.

The question was absurd on the face of it, but Brendan understood why she had asked. "Of course," he said. "More than. Wonderful."

"I just thought –"

"No," he said. "Shhhhhh. Let me tell you about it."

Katie laughed and snuggled closer. "I was there," she pointed out.

"You were. You always are. But...." He trailed off, searching for words. "You showed me something. About trusting you. About learning all sorts of new ways I can be. I mean, you've always done that. But this was, shall we say, a uniquely effective lesson?"

"Excellent. I hope you'll want lots of repeats."

"I already do." He couldn't wait to keep learning more ways to love each other for the rest of their lives.

✦

After they returned to the world from their honeymoon, the next few months were exactly as challenging as Brendan had suspected. And feared. He was travelling back and forth between Denver more than he wanted, the slide into colder weather on the farm was grueling, and a Katie approaching surgery was a Katie in the very worst of her anxiety. But they were a united front and did what was necessary. That there was never any shortage of work to bury themselves in, was largely a blessing.

Katie was, predictably, a terrible, stubborn patient who wanted to do too much too soon from the moment she woke up from the anesthesia. Brendan was glad he'd talked her into deciding not to even think about looking for their own place until she was comfortably back on both feet. He loved her, but having her mother and her uncles at hand to help her – and keep her distracted from her pain and frustration – was better for everyone.

But as long as her recovery felt to Katie, and everyone around her, it was not actually eternal.

"You know what we were doing this time last year?" Katie asked as Brendan sat next to her on the bench, lacing up his skates. She looked down at her feet, her laces draped loosely across her knuckles.

"What's that?" Brendan knew, but he also knew Katie needed to say it.

"We were getting ready for Harbin. And now I don't even know if I can skate anymore."

"Well," said Brendan. "I guess there's only one way to

find out."

Despite her nerves, Katie's eye were bright with tears of what Brendan knew was happiness when she stepped out onto the ice for the first time in months, his hands wrapped tightly around hers.

An entire week of skating practice – with no elements, just re-learning how to skate so she didn't hurt herself all over again – passed before Katie's tears of joy turned to ones of frustration. More months of hard work on and off the ice went by before tears of any sort gave way to them yelling at each other about jumps and choreography. Which was how Brendan knew everything was going to be okay and that it was time to move on to the next phase of the plan.

Brendan set up a shared business email for the both of them. That way Katie didn't have to look at anything she didn't want to, but things could get done or at least politely declined. Going through the endless emails she had ignored in the period in which they hadn't been talking was less fun. Eventually, they agreed that Brendan should delete all the ones from him and make a list of everyone else she owed apologies to. Katie tried to have a sense of humor about it, adding email therapy to physical therapy and mental health therapy, but Brendan knew the situation made her ashamed and unhappy.

Their real estate concerns were more complex. Selling an apartment was hard. Finding land and a house to buy to start a farm – but not right now – was possibly harder. And while Katie's family was more than happy to provide advice and guidance, Brendan's parents were far from thrilled he was trading his Denver apartment for some Wisconsin farmland. But he and Katie needed their own space and a framework around which to plan the rest of their lives.

The rest of their lives...that phrase, truthfully, still made Brendan swoon. Unfortunately, there were still moments when it made Katie tense. But if they approached life the way they did a skating program, focusing only on what was right in front of them before going on to the next element, then she was okay, then she was happy.

The high-stress filter of competition had for so long allowed them both to ignore whatever they didn't want to deal with, in themselves and each other. They both had to learn to appreciate Katie's brain without that filter. Much like learning to appreciate the farm and the cows, that was a work in progress for Brendan, but it was work he was happy to do.

Eventually they bought a house with a somewhat run-down dairy from one of Katie's family's connections. They didn't have any animals yet, but that was fine; the buildings needed some repairs and the equipment needed modernizing. The work would keep Katie as busy as she wanted to be as they got the rest of their lives in order.

By the time Katie was rebuilding her stamina and starting to do jumps again, it was time to go to New York. He would have been lying if he had said he wasn't nervous about it. Katie hated New York, and after what had happened there, so did he.

Brendan got them a room at a B&B in Brooklyn. He hadn't known such things existed and until they actually got there, he wasn't convinced he hadn't created some new disaster. Katie was wary, confused, and then delighted, all of which was more than he could have asked for. They went over their schedule for the three days of their trip, got some wildly indulgent double cheese pizza from a place down the street, and spent the rest of the day making out and watching bad reality TV, both of which were much, much better activities when they weren't being done on a tour bus.

The meetings were exactly as awkward as Brendan had feared they might be, but they were also as successful as he had hoped. Katie brought her game face like Brendan hadn't seen since they were competing. When she was asked to dye her hair again, because that was her brand, she smiled and said no. In the end they signed a book deal that would be announced while they were still in the city and a tour that would, Katie's health willing, be announced when the book came out.

As they walked out of the midtown office building, Brendan let Katie take his arm and wrap it around her waist.

"Put your hands on me," she said. "Hold me up.'

Her words echoed what she had said when her knee had finally given out at the end of the tour, here in this same city. But this time, thankfully, they were about something entirely different.

He squeezed her waist. "Always. Now. Are you happy?"

She grinned at him. "Incredibly."

At their media appearances the next day, eighty percent of the questions were about their wedding or Katie's hair, and somehow, they didn't mind at all.

When they got home to Wisconsin, Brendan watched as Katie started two new countdown calendars on their whiteboard – one for the estimated start of their tour, labelled *skating* and one for the estimated end of their tour, labelled *cows*. He'd never accuse Katie of not having a plan again.

21

One Year Later

Denver, CO

Katie paced in the dark tunnel wringing her hands together. Out in the arena, a video montage of her and Brendan's best moments on the ice was playing to a ridiculously sentimental song she was fairly sure had been used at his high school graduation. *Why did I agree to this?*

Brendan stood at the very edge where the flooring ended and the ice began, peering out at the arena. "They were right. It's a sold out show."

"You're not helping!"

Brendan looked back over his shoulder at her. Despite the urgings of the tour management, they'd insisted on keeping their usual costume style: Simple. Understated. Brendan wore black pants and a grey collared shirt open at the throat. The part of Katie's brain that wasn't flirting with a panic attack wanted to devour him.

"You okay?" he asked.

"I am freaking out." Katie tried to make her hands stop shaking, but her body wasn't listening to her. This was their first tour stop. In Denver, one of the two places that would always mean the most to them. They'd spent over a year putting this venture together. Not just on the ice, but with management, public relations people, a relentless advertising campaign, and more social media than Katie ever wanted to do again. Sponsors had sunk ridiculous amounts money into the tour. Thousands of people across the country had bought tickets in the hope that Nowacki and Reid, one-time Olympic gold medalists, could bring some small part of their magic to their home cities. If her knee suddenly gave out again, if they made any one of a million small mistakes, if their programs weren't what the audience wanted to see....

There are so many people to let down.

"Hey." Brendan's face softened, and he took the few steps necessary to come stand in front of her. He pulled her in for a hug, one arm strong around her waist, his other hand cradling the back of her neck. "Breathe with me."

Katie closed her eyes and clung to Brendan. His body was warm in the chill of the arena, and as she matched her breathing to his, she felt some of her anxiety drain away. Not all of it, but enough.

Brendan pressed a kiss to the side of her head. "I think our cue is coming up."

Katie nodded, but didn't otherwise move. She'd waited so long for this moment. She wanted everything to be perfect. She needed to accept her fear that it wouldn't be as just one more part of the experience.

"Okay." She took one last deep breath. Brendan let his arms drop from around her, and she stepped back. "Let's do this."

✦

The crowd roared as they glided out onto the ice, hand in hand. Katie didn't have to remind herself to smile; a grin broke out on her face as soon as the spotlight found them.

She tipped her head up and waved at the audience, trying to project her gratitude and excitement to the most distant parts of the arena. She was still nervous; she would probably always be nervous in these moments, but she was learning to let it be fuel for the performance.

"With me?" Brendan whispered to her as he twirled her around to face the other side of the arena.

"Always," she replied. The words of the question and her response were perhaps beyond unnecessary at this point, but Katie had no intention of giving up on the ritual that had kept them together even when they had been falling apart.

Katie took her starting position. Behind her, Brendan rested his hands on the sharp curve of her hip, his fingers pressing into the spot where her thigh met her waist. As soon as the music began they skated apart, but they had discovered in rehearsals that Katie couldn't endure going into a performance without Brendan right there beside her.

This program, which Brendan had begun back in her family's farmhouse, started with a deceptive quiet and focused on the lyrical beauty of their skating. Katie had no trouble portraying the yearning the story demanded as the space between them grew. She and Brendan mirrored each other from afar, and just as when they skated close, they never broke eye contact, unless an element absolutely required it.

As they reached out for the other as they did simultaneous flying camels, Katie imagined the internet analysis of the program – surely it was about all the years they were apart. But anyone who assumed that would have been taking the easy, incomplete path. It was, instead, about the thread between them, that when it finally stretched too far didn't snap from strain so much as loudly demand that they come back together.

That moment of pulling back together was where the music changed into something full of force and drama and relentlessness, where Katie and Brendan were finally able to unleash what their skating had always been known for.

Brendan's hand caught hers just as they seemed about to pass each other. The mirror of the choreography broke as they shifted to skating side-by-side and hand-in-hand. Katie could feel the whole arena lean forward on the edge of their chairs as Brendan pulled her into a death spiral so low and well-executed that when she came up from it there were ice shavings in her hair.

As they exited the move, just before they had to drop each other's hands, Brendan leaned towards her and brushed his mouth against hers. That wasn't in the choreography, and the audience roared their approval. *Voyeurs*, Katie thought. Not that she minded in the least. She and Brendan were nothing if not exhibitionists.

Brendan grinned at her as they skated apart, leaving the smallest possible amount of space between them that would still allow them room to jump. With his smile bright and his eyes locked on hers, Katie went into their side-by-side toe loops without any fear at all.

They landed them perfectly, the crowd roared, and nothing hurt. Katie balled her hands into fists, feeling so fiercely victorious. There were no medals left to win, but right here, right now, she didn't remotely care. This was what they were meant to do.

22

The First Skate of the Rest of Their Lives

Denver, CO

Brendan was absurdly proud of this program. It wasn't the only one he'd crafted for this tour, though he'd had help and input from their own former choreographer and the choreographer from their past tours for some of the numbers. But it was the first one he'd dreamed of doing back when he'd first let himself imagine the possibility of skating with Katie again. It was his gift to her. More than the engagement ring she wasn't wearing tonight because she hated wearing sparkly jewelry when she skated; more than all the time and energy he still gave the farm and the cows whenever they stayed with her family. They'd spent their competitive lives playing characters from other people's stories. Now, the only roles they had to play were those of themselves. There was no drama, no filter, no bullshit, no narrative to hide in or behind. Just them. Together. Always.

Without the strict requirements of competitive pair skating, they could have more fun with the lifts. Yes, hoisting Katie above his head while he covered the entire length of the rink and she moved from a curve to a split to a full Biellmann position was impressive and a skill he was glad to show off. But Katie jumping into his arms while he spun lazily across the ice, her legs wrapped around his waist, her head tucked into his shoulder was a self-indulgent sweetness the audience loved.

But as lovely as quiet moments with Katie were, both on and off the ice, they weren't here *just* to enjoy touching each other. They were here to push each other, to keep learning, to keep improving, to keep trusting each other. As they reached the corner of the rink, Katie slid back to the ice, her head ducked but her eyes fastened on Brendan's face. They circled each other, the desire between them sparking and as palpable as ever. Brendan took her by the waist, spun her so that her back was pressed against his chest and counted the beats while they both skated backwards, picking up speed.

At precisely the right moment Brendan tightened his hands around Katie's waist and felt her body tense as she prepared for the jump. He lifted her and threw her, every muscle in his body straining and satisfied at the work. Katie spun through the air and landed perfectly, arms raised above her head in victory, while the crowd went wild.

In seconds, Brendan had closed the distance to get to her so that they could fold into each other for the last pair spin, their bodies twining against each other. The speed and force of the spin and its position changes meant it was impossible for them to focus on each other in any way that made sense to anyone else. But, more than any other element, this was the one that required them each to be part of a greater whole. Which they were and which they had always been.

They pulled out of the spin and hit their final marks. The music ended, and Brendan looked over Katie. As the audience went to its feet, she was the only thing he cared about. He watched as she broke the pose and put her hands to her face in shock. This was, he hoped and suspected, the moment he'd been trying to give her his entire life.

"I'm so proud of you," he said as he scooped her up in his arms and twirled her around the ice.

For a moment, he thought she was going to protest, but he felt her straighten in his arms. He watched as she looked out at the crowd, full of wonder and pride. Reluctantly, he set her down. They needed to do their bows, but more than that Brendan wanted to get her alone. There was a celebration to be had here, with the audience, but they also needed a moment alone while the other skaters who had joined them in this venture took the ice.

Brendan led Katie through their bows, sure he was waving and blowing kisses to the audience as much as she was by the end. Finally, when the lights dimmed and it was time to skate away, Katie stopped him with a squeeze to his hand.

"What?" he asked, puzzled in the dark and worried something was somehow wrong.

Katie smiled at him. "With me?" she whispered.

"Always," he said. He'd always be happy to follow Katie wherever she led.

More by These Authors

Visit www.Avian30.com to join Erin and Racheline's mailing list and get information about new releases.

A Queen from the North

Library Journal's Best Indie Ebook 2017

Lady Amelia Brockett, known to her family as Meels, is having the Worst. Christmas. Ever. Dumped by her boyfriend and rejected from graduate school, her parents deem her the failure of the family.

But when her older brother tries to cheer her with a trip to the races, a chance meeting with Arthur, the widowed, playboy Prince of Wales, offers Amelia the opportunity to change her life – and Britain's fortunes – forever.

The Art of Three

24-year-old Jamie Conway has just moved to London, is starring in his first feature film, and hasn't yet figured out how to navigate fame, adulthood, or being bisexual in public.

When Jamie hooks up with his much older polyamorous costar Callum Griffith-Davies, he sets off a chain of delightful complications, including an unexpected affair with Callum's no-nonsense wife, Nerea.

This Rainbow Awards-winning romance features three countries, two men, one woman, and absolutely no love triangles in a lush coming-of-age story sure to enthrall fans of *Call Me By Your Name.*

The Love in Los Angeles Series

Starling, Book 1
Doves, Book 2
Phoenix, Book 3
More coming soon!

Love in Los Angeles is a queer romance series, with elements of magical realism, set in and around the TV and movie industry.

When J. Alex Cook, a production assistant on The Fourth Estate (one of network TV's hottest shows), is accidentally catapulted to stardom, he finds himself struggling to navigate both fame and a relationship with Paul, one of *Fourth*'s key writers. Love in Los Angeles is the story of Paul and Alex – and of their friends and family – as they navigate love, and life, both in and beyond Los Angeles.

The Love's Labours Series

Midsummer, Book 1
Twelfth Night, Book 2
More coming soon!

42-year-old John Lyonel has never been attracted to men before, but falling for 25-year-old Michael Hilliard is actually the least screwed up thing that's happened to him in years. Even if sometimes he thinks Michael's a changeling.